Disney and the Wonder Within

BOOK ONE:
EARS OF VIRTUE

Charles E. Zitta

Editor: Bob McLain
Layout: Artisanal Text
Cover Illustration: Jamie Hood

ISBN 978-1-68390-089-4
Printed in the United States of America

Theme Park Press | www.ThemeParkPress.com
Address queries to bob@themeparkpress.com

EARS OF VIRTUE

Chapter One

Somewhere, in the not-so-distant past...

It was a cool fall evening, the clicking sound of two pairs of shoes echoed through the dimly lit streets. One pair, chasing the other. In the lead was Ben. A curly, red headed young man with a portly build. He was dressed in old, weathered clothes, with a scraggly fall jacket and scuffed brown shoes. Running as fast as his legs could carry him, Ben made his way through the dark, moonlit streets of a sleepy little town he thought was safe just moments ago. Chasing Ben was someone, or better yet, something he thought would never find him. Something rotten; something villainous. An evil man, who desperately wanted the box Ben was carrying under his arm.

With each stride, Ben's warm breath burst through the cool, fall air like a trail of white smoke from a steam locomotive. The chase continued through the center of town, past the bakery, clock shop, post office, and down to the end of the street, into the local park. It was a park with lots of trees, bushes, benches, and statues—a good place for Ben to find a hiding spot. He looked left, then right, then left again, scanning the park for the perfect place to hide. Beyond the small hill, and past the two maple trees, was a large cluster of bushes. Ben hurried over the hill, past the maples, and stumbled awkwardly forward—tripping over his own two feet and into the shrubs, with his hands extended outward in order to protect his face from getting scratched up by the gnarled branches. Click-click, crack, thump. Ben's body came to an abrupt halt as it met the firm, cold ground. At last, if only for a moment, he had a chance to catch his breath, with small twigs and leaves from the shrubbery entwined throughout his curly, red hair.

Ben spotted his pursuer coming around the brick pillars near the park entrance, just as he was getting to his feet. He put his hands on his knees, still trying to catch his breath, wondering how did they find me? Did the red hair give me away? Who could have told them where I was hiding? Were there spies in the town? Why is this happening to me? These, and many more thoughts, continued to race through his mind, over and over again. He broke out of the bushes and pressed on through the park, staying merely seconds ahead of the vicious man who was closely following him through the night shadows—no more than a stone's throw away. "Must keep going," Ben mumbled to himself, his body tiring more and more with each stride. His legs, now at the end of their usefulness, could carry him no farther. Ben stopped in the middle of the dimly lit road, near the corner of the candy store and clock shop. He gazed back into the shadows, out of breath, with fear in his heart.

"I can hear you breathing, Ben," said the evil man, with a low, gravelly voice, from just beyond the light of the moonlit street. "I'll take the box now, please, if you would be so kind as to...hand it over." The very sound of his slow, deliberate voice sent chills through Ben's tired body.

"And why do you think I would ever do that?" asked Ben, his lips quivering, hands and body shaking from the cool night air.

"Well, Ben, because quite honestly, it's the only choice you have. You have nowhere left to go."

"There's always more than one choice in a situation like this," Ben replied.

"Well, maybe you're right. Perhaps you do have choices, as in, you could choose to quietly hand over the box resting securely under your arm. Or, you could refuse to do so and suffer the consequences of your poor decision." A pale, thin hand with dirt-filled fingernails slowly appeared from beyond the night shadows—open and ready to receive the box Ben held so dearly in his possession.

Ben acknowledged the greedy hand, slowly gazed downward at the box, returned back to the out-reached hand, then directed his eyes upward toward the darkness, beyond the ghastly hand. Yearning to see the face behind the voice.

"Well, sir, Ben said in a confident tone of voice, you have overlooked a third, and probably the most important, choice that stands before us."

The air became quiet and still. Only the chirping of crickets and the hoot of an owl from the nearby woods could be heard. Then...dead silence.

"And what would that be, Ben?" The gravelly and impatient voice beyond the shadows asked, as an evil face slowly emerged from the darkness, beyond the moonlight. It was that of a middle-aged, poorly groomed man. His skin was pale, with a sickly blue cast, and carved in detail with deep, cavernous wrinkles that ran around his eyes, drooling mouth, and forehead—no doubt from years of frowning due to anger and frustration. Layered on top of the wrinkles were smudges and smears of dirt and filth. It was hard to tell one from the other. The whites of his eyes glowed brightly in contrast to his filthy face. As Ben looked closer, he noticed the man's eyes were two different colors. The left was brown and the right blue. Both were filled with the look of a crazed soul that had nothing to lose, except possibly the old wrinkled newsboy hat that sat atop his head. From underneath the hat grew frizzled strands of dark, tangled hair that appeared to have not been washed for quite some time. And as he spit and spat out his words with a sinister smile, his stained, yellow teeth shown from behind a set of crusty, chapped lips.

As the diabolical man's outreached hand edged closer, Ben began to slowly move backwards, away from a fate he did not care to know. The man continued to move closer, his upper body now visible. Ben took another step back. Then, a second later, a pair of skinny legs in old pants appeared. Ben took yet another step back, carefully making sure not to trip on any unforeseen objects. He could now see the man's entire body—highlighted by the pale light of the moon. His frame was tall and stick-like, with a pot belly, overgrown feet, and an old brown suit that matched the tattered hat. The stranger's body was a perfect match to his hideous face. But who was he and why did he want the box so badly? And how does he know my name? Ben thought to himself.

"Hey there, Ben."

The two men immediately turned their attention to the woods, both staring as hard as they possibly could, trying to make out exactly where and who the voice was coming from. It appeared to be coming from high up the trees.

It only took Ben and his enemy a brief moment to realize the voice coming from the woods could not possibly be human, as no person would be crazy enough to climb high up in a tree during the middle of the night.

Before the two could think any further, from out of the woods, atop the tallest tree, a brilliantly feathered white owl came swooping down, emerging from beyond the shadow. Highlighted by the moonlight, and effortlessly gliding through the air in miraculous fashion, the unexpected visitor came to rest atop a nearby lamp post, exposing his identity to the astonishment of Ben and his adversary. Both stood frozen like statues, wide-eyed and slack jawed. The talking white owl had indeed caught them off guard.

"Well, aren't you going to say something to me, Ben?" The owl asked.

The two men continued to stare. Still motionless. Still speechless.

The owl spoke again. "You do remember who I am, don't you?"

At that moment, the owl's spoken words ignited Ben's thoughts, as a tidal wave of memories roared through his mind. "That's it!" he said with excitement in his voice. "Alexios, is...is that you? How...how is that possible? You're...you're an animated character. Well, an animated character that never made it past the concept phase. And you're talking to me? Here? Now? I...I don't understand?"

Alexios was an older owl who, in his prime, was quite a specimen to behold. With white and silvery gray feathers, worn talons, and tired yellow eyes, he no longer carried the air of intimidation that once surrounded his presence, especially now that he also wore a pair of black-rimmed glasses to aid his vision. And though the owl had grown older, he had become much wiser, more cunning, and was still very capable of carrying out his duties. After all, he was Alexios, defender of the Kingdom Crystals.

"Well, of course I'm talking to you, Ben. I've been a part of your life for quite some time. Why, let me think. If my memory serves me right, I believe we first crossed paths when my sketch lines were being created at Disney Studios. You were just a young lad, sweeping floors in the animation building on weekday evenings after school. On one particular evening, you were cleaning the floor in one of the animator's offices, and there I was, sitting on the drawing board, sketched lines and all. Why, you practically drooled all over me, you did."

Ben scratched his head as he frowned in confusion.

"C'mon lad, surely you remember that night?"

Ben continued to scratch his head, perplexed and still trying to figure out how an animated character could be speaking to him. Here. Now. In fact, he'd become so sidetracked with his thoughts that he had completely forgotten about the villainous man, whose shifty hands were getting closer and closer to snatch away the box that rested securely under Ben's left arm.

"Uh...well. Oh, wait. Now I remember. I was cleaning Mr. Johnson's office and I noticed the sketches of you, scattered all over his desk. I think he was working on facial expression and body movement studies of your character."

"Exactly, my young squire."

"There was one sketch in particular that caught my attention. You were winking. At what, I'm not exactly sure."

"Yes, that's right. I was winking at you, Ben."

"You were?"

"Yes. Is there anything else you can remember from that sketch?"

"Uh...I don't think..."

"Well, let me refresh your memory, young lad."

Frustrated, Ben jumped in to cut off the lecturing owl. "Why do you keep referring to me as young?" Ben was getting a little annoyed with the owl's patronizing references. "I'm a grown man, I am. A young man. But a man none the less."

"Well, lad. Compared to me, you are young. Very young. Why, I'm more than twice your age, and twice as wise, too." The angered owl's eyes became extremely large, and his chest puffed out as he gave Ben a scolding look—similar to what a teacher would give a student for misbehaving.

Ben felt an overwhelming sense of embarrassment suddenly come over him. His face, flushed of any color. "Oh...yeah... right. I forgot. I'm quite...I'm quite sorry for interrupting. Please continue. Yes, please continue."

Urrrrrr-urrrrr-urrrrr-m-ahemm. Alexios cleared his throat. "Well, then. Now. Where was I? Oh, yes. As I was saying, Ben, not only was I winking at you, I was also pointing to the old red box that was sitting on the shelf behind you.

The villainous man they'd forgotten about now stood right next to Ben, his shifty hands, rolling over and over one another, with nervous excitement, his patience becoming increasingly worn by the second.

Ben was ecstatic. "That's right, Alexios. Mr. Johnson told me about..."

"ENOUGH of this nonsense." The evil man had reached the limit of his patience. His body began to bounce up and down off the ground in shivering convulsions, as if he had been electrocuted. His face turned bright red, his eyes ready to explode out of his head. If he were a cartoon, there would have been steam blowing out of his ears.

The sudden outburst startled Ben, which caused his arm to jerk and allowed the box to break free of his control. As the box spun through the air, a mad scramble of flailing bodily limbs, hands in faces, fingers in ears, and squashed toes ensued. Both men were caught in an unrehearsed, awkwardly funny battle for possession of the mysterious red box.

"Give it to me, Ben."

"Never. It doesn't belong to you."

"Yes, it does. Give it to me now."

"No, it doesn't."

As the battle continued, the box gained altitude, spinning end-over-end between the two crazed men, like a jump ball in a basketball game. Simultaneously, Ben and his adversary leaped into the air to gain control of the box as it continued to spin in suspended animation.

All the while, Alexios was eagerly watching, eyes bulging, wings flapping, pacing back and forth on top of the lamp post, as he tried to figure out what to do. His patience could not take any more of this foolishness. But what was the solution? The great white owl leaped from the post, his wings flapping hard, as he dropped toward the ground, gaining speed as he began to soar high up into the air and disappearing into the silvery blue shadows of the night sky.

Ben and his rival were so wrapped up with their obsession for the box that neither noticed Alexios had flown off into the night air.

And then, clunk. The two men met head-to-head. Their arms and legs became limp as each fell back toward the ground in opposite directions. The box began its rapid descent from above the two fallen bodies, which were both moving slowly in an effort to recover from the collision.

Swoooooosh! Alexios swept in from the sky above like a blurred streak of silver and white, grabbing the box by its twine ribbon. His talons held on tightly as he climbed higher and higher, carrying the box to a nearby tree at the edge of the forest, and far out of reach of the aggravated man with yellow teeth who had come so close to obtaining the mysterious object.

"Hurry Ben, we have little time to waste!" Alexios called out.

The sound of Alexios' voice helped Ben regain his orientation. He took a quick glance at his disoriented nemesis, who was still on the ground shaking and rubbing his head from the collision. "I'm coming!" Ben shouted back, as he quickly jumped to his feet and took off running rapidly toward the woods. The young man never looked back, fearing that he might see his enemy chasing closely behind. This fear fueled Ben's energy,as he ran faster and faster, until he was no more than a faint wisp of shadow, melting into the dark silhouette of the woods.

"I'll get you for this, Ben!" Shouted the angered man whose head continued to spin as he sat in disgust, realizing there was no chance to catch the little red-headed fellow now. And more importantly, no chance to get his hands on the red box he had come for. The Dark Thorns would not be happy to hear the news.

Beep-beep-beep-beep-beep-beep-beep-beep. THWAT. The snooze button on the clock was swatted by a very tired, young hand.

"Charlie. Time to get up. C'mon. Up and at 'em. You gotta get going, or you'll be late."

Charlie, about as fast as a frozen snail, rolled over, scratched his head, and yawned. Then he sat up with a look of confusion in his eyes. He wasn't exactly sure if the screaming he had just heard was from the angry man in his dream, or from the shrieking sound of his mother's voice, resonating through the dimly lit hallway beyond the crack of his bedroom door. Either way, his brain was still only partially awake, thanks to a restless night of sleep—obviously due to the three large holiday chocolates he had eaten the night before. As his mother once told him, loading up on sugar before bedtime can bring on crazy dreams and prevent someone from sleeping well. Regardless, she continued to shout from the bottom of the stairway, trying to get her boys moving for another wonderful and glorious day of school.

Chapter Two

It was just another routine day of school for Charlie, but there were two things that made this day particularly easier than most. First, it was Friday. Fridays were always the easiest day of the week for Charlie to get up for, because once the school day was over and the final bell rang, that meant the weekend had begun. It was quite obvious that Charlie, like any other ordinary kid, truly did enjoy Fridays.

Second, it was also the last day of school before the holiday break, a two-week vacation. And unlike most ordinary weeks of school, this week had been filled with the likes of gift exchanges, holiday shows, letters to Santa, caroling classes wandering the halls, Christmas cookies, candy, punch, and so many more fun, out-of-the-ordinary, holiday activities. As Mr. and Mrs. Zastawits always told Charlie during this time of the school year, it was like they were already on vacation.

Needless to say, the entire Zastawits household was in jolly spirits on this very special Friday morning. Even Mrs. Zastawits, who just moments ago had been on her usual morning rant to get the boys moving, was now in the kitchen humming Christmas carols as she prepared the boys' lunches for school. Meanwhile, Mr. Zastawits, humming along as well, was busy making breakfast. And today's breakfast featured one of the boys' favorite weekday morning meals: booger toast, better known as cinnamon toast, with an extra sugar kick, plus two large glasses of milk. The cinnamon toast with extra sugar kept the boys happy, while the two large glasses of milk, loaded with vitamins, kept Mom in good spirits. Mr. Zastawits always knew how to keep everyone happy.

"There's my Charlie warlie, good morning, sweetie," said Mrs. Zastawits, in a high-pitched voice. Charlie was always the first of the two boys down for breakfast. Mr. Zastawits thought it was because of the breakfasts he prepared each weekday morning, but in reality, Charlie wanted to make sure he took the first shower, assuring himself plenty of hot water.

He acknowledged his mother's cheery, morning greeting with a soft "Good morning" and a yawn.

Mr. Zastawits chimed in next. "Hey Charlie, look what I made for breakfast, buddy, one of your favorites. And a big glass of milk to wash it down with."

"Thanks, Dad," Charlie replied.

"So, what do you get to do in school for your last day before the big vacation?" asked Mrs. Zastawits, as she was finishing up making the boys' lunches—which she saw as an opportunity to make sure they were getting the daily nutrition their growing bodies needed. As she knew, some day her boys would be making their own decisions on what to eat for lunch at school. She dreaded that day.

"I think we get to finish making Christmas presents for you guys, have a party in our room, and watch holiday movies after lunch," replied Charlie.

Mrs. Zastawits pretended she didn't know exactly what Charlie meant for a second, and asked, "So, what do you mean by you guys?" She was playing a game with Charlie, which many parents liked to do: get their child to explain things with more detail without being so obvious about it. Charlie was in the 5th grade, and it wouldn't be long before he was in middle school, where the teachers expected a little more from their students. And Charlie's mom new this.

"The parents," said Charlie, as he rolled his eyes.

"Oh, I see. So, what kind of present are you making for your father and I?"

"I can't tell you, Mom. It's a secret."

Mrs. Zastawits played along. "Aw, that makes me so sad," she said with pouty lips.

"Yeah, I guess we'll just have to wait, honey," added Mr. Zastawits, in his best sad voice, followed by a deep sigh.

Charlie just continued to eat his toast as if he heard nothing. Playing it cool.

Moments later, as Charlie was finishing up with his breakfast, Michael, the younger of the two boys, came zipping down the stairs and into the kitchen. Jumping up onto the stool next to Charlie, Michael eagerly awaited his booger toast from Dad. He had overheard his father telling Charlie what was for breakfast just a moment ago, and unlike his older brother, Michael was an early riser. He practically jumped out of bed and ran through the shower every morning before school, eagerly anticipating what daily challenges lay ahead.

Almost simultaneously, Mrs. Zastawits came back into the kitchen from getting her jacket. "Good morning, pumpkin. How about a kiss for Mommy?" Michael was the baby of the family, especially when Mrs. Zastawits was around.

Mr. Zastawits shook his head, feeling embarrassed for his younger son, as he continued to prepare Michael's toast and pour him a glass of milk. He knew what was coming next. He'd witnessed it many times before. In fact, it had practically become a Zastawits weekday morning tradition. Here it comes, Mr. Zastawits thought to himself, as he laid the plate of booger toast down in front of his already embarrassed son.

Mrs. Zastawits moved in to smooch her younger son on the cheek and give him a big, morning hug.

"Mom. Mommy, please stop. Ma!" Michael pleaded as he tried to avoid the dreaded morning smooch.

But it was too late. His mother had achieved her goal, once again. "Aha. Mommy wins." Without hesitation, she turned and gave Charlie a quick peck on the cheek, then made her way around the counter to give her husband a goodbye smooch as well. "Have a good day, everybody," she said, as she made her way out the door to her car. Mrs. Zastawits was a home health-care professional who worked primarily with the elderly, and they were always up early. So it was customary for her to be the first one out the door every morning. She truly enjoyed helping other people—and it showed each and every work day, as she headed out the door with enthusiastic flare.

"You too, honey," replied Mr. Zastawits.

"Bye, boys," she said. This was a cue for the boys to reply to their mother.

"Bye," they said in synchronized, sarcastic tones.

On that note, Charlie chugged down the rest of his milk and headed upstairs to brush his teeth, with his brother following closely behind. Mr. Zastawits cleaned up after the boys, then finished his breakfast before heading upstairs to brush his teeth as well.

The drop-off line at school was very long, packed with cars of happy children dressed in warm, fluffy jackets, stocking caps, and winter boots, their parents singing along to the Christmas music on their car stereos as they watched the wipers brush away the gentle, falling snow flakes that came to rest on their front windshields. It was clear to see everyone was eager for the holidays to begin. The drop-off line moved like a well-oiled machine; in sets of three, the vehicles pulled up to the unload area, doors opened, children kissed their parents goodbye and jumped out, then Principal White and her office staff would safely escort the children from the parents' cars to the front doors of the school. From there, the children were greeted by smiling teachers in the hallways, assuring that all the boys and girls found their way to their lockers to shed jackets, hats and boots, put on their indoor shoes, and head into the classrooms.

After just a short wait, it was the Zastawits turn to pull up and unload. Mr. Zastawits pulled to the curb and hit the side door opener.

"Well, here we are, boys; I'll see you guys later, OK?"

The boys acknowledged their father as they worked to undo their seat belts, grab their backpacks, and exit the minivan.

"Good morning, Zastawits boys," said a very happy Miss Farren, as she helped the boys navigate the first few steps from vehicle to curb, assuring no one tripped and fell. "Hi, Mr. Zastawits. How are you doing this morning?"

"I'm doing well, and you?"

"Just fine, thank you," she replied.

"OK, boys, see you later. Have a good day."

This was the speech Mr. Zastawits delivered to the boys, often more than once, every day as he let them out of the van. It was standard school day drop-off procedure.

"Good morning, boys," said Mrs. White, smiling as always. She was a terrific principal, a favorite of the Zastawits family.

The boys quickly acknowledged Mrs. White as they continued on into the school. Mr. Zastawits waved goodbye to the school staff as he hit the auto-close button for the door and slowly pulled away, humming one of his favorite Christmas tunes.

The school hallway was swarming with children. Boots were clunking, back packs thunking, and lockers clicking and clanking. Charlie had systematically made his way into the classroom and placed a little gift next to the others that had already been piled up on the teacher's desk. Then he organized his own desk so he would be ready when class began. He always liked to be prepared. A few other students had done the same, and were patiently waiting at their desks as well.

As the clock neared the school's starting time of eight fifteen, all the other kids in the hallway began to filter inside. Most of them were the extremely social type who always wanted to be in the middle of every conversation, with every person in the room. Not that Charlie minded. It was just not the type of person he was. Charlie was more low-key, more soft-spoken. And even though he got along with most everybody, he preferred to hang around just a few close friends.

One of those friends, Johnny Bibbs, came trotting into the classroom, chatting away with a couple other boys from their fifth grade class. Johnny was a large-proportioned boy with sloppy hair, blushed cheeks, floppy clothes, and untied shoes. But nobody ever noticed what he looked like, as his personality more than made up for it. He spotted Charlie right away, immediately broke off the conversation with the other two boys, then headed straight to his buddy's desk.

"Hey, Charlie Z. Looks like you're ready for class; as usual."

Around school and his friends, Charlie was not just "Charlie," but "Charlie Z." All the kids and teachers liked the way it sounded, as well as Charlie himself. Best of all, it was his good friend Johnny that had given him his nickname near the beginning of the school year. It was Charlie's first year at Washington Elementary School, and he was one of the new kids when the school year began. So, it was only a matter of time before someone came along and gave him a nickname. A common practice for kids at their school.

Shaking his head, Charlie looked up at his friend and replied in a sarcastic tone. "Well, of course I'm ready, Johnny, class is almost about to start. Have you even looked at the clock?" Even though Charlie may have been on the quiet side, he did not lack confidence. In fact, he was very comfortable with who he was and how he handled things. So, if someone gave him a jab, he was always ready to return the favor.

Johnny just laughed at Charlie's response, then quickly moved on to his next topic. "So, uh, what did ya get me for Christmas? Anything good? You did bring a present to exchange with me, right?"

Charlie and Johnny had drawn each other for the holiday gift exchange. They couldn't have been more thrilled. Imagine, drawing your best friend for a gift exchange. The two boys were filled with anticipation, wondering what each had gotten for the other.

"Yeah, I think I brought something for you, but I'm not sure. I may have left it on the kitchen counter at home, or in my dad's van. I don't know. Wait a minute. Yep, that's it. I think it's in my dad's van."

"Really, Charlie? How could you leave it in Mr. Z's van?" Johnny was referring to Charlie's father. The nickname Johnny had given Charlie had become so well accepted that the entire Zastawits family was now tagged with the "Z" brand. It all started last summer when the Zastawits family moved into a new house, not too far from their old house, just before school started. And because the houses were not far from one another, Charlie and his parents assumed the boys would continue to go to the same school. Little did they realize, this small move would have a huge impact on all their lives, in a very good way. Charlie met his new best friend, as did Michael. Both boys started the school year with teachers they enjoyed, thoroughly. And their new principal, Mrs. White, was the best principal in the entire district. She ran the school with a firm, but gentle hand, and a warm, kind smile on her face. She was always the first one in, and the last to leave, each and every school day. She really did care about the children and their futures, and it showed. As a result, Mr. and Mrs. Zastawits were happy with the school change. In fact, they were so happy, they volunteered their time, if possible, in quite a vast array of school activities, making them very popular amongst the children, other parents, and school staff. Because of this, Charlie's nickname, "Charlie Z," had grown to also include the entire Zastawits family. So Michael had come to be known as Mikey Z, and their parents were often referred to as Mr. and Mrs. Z. It was just easier for everyone to remember, and catchy, too.

"I don't know, Johnny, it could have fallen out of my backpack when I was getting out of the van. I think it was in the top pouch and the gift was too big, so I couldn't zip up the pocket. But... I'm still not sure." Charlie was really having fun at Johnny's expense.

"Oh, sure, Charlie. Then what's that under your desk? All wrapped up in candy cane-striped paper with a green bow?"

"Where?"

"Right there, behind that big foot of yours." Charlie had been trying to block Johnny's vision with his feet.

"Oh, that. I guess that's your gift? Thanks for pointing it out for me," Charlie said, with a big smile.

"Whatever," Johnny replied as he scanned the room, pretending not to be interested in what Charlie had to say. Jokingly, of course. He was just trying to get back at his buddy.

"How about you? What'd you get me for a present? And where is it?"

"Um, it's in my desk. Been there for a few days. But, I have to tell ya, it's not anything Disney related." Johnny new that Charlie was a huge Disney fan. Disney movies, Disney parks, Disney books, almost any type of Disney collectible; it didn't really matter, Charlie would be grateful for anything he received that was associated with Disney.

"Yeah, right, Johnny. What else could it possibly be? You know what I like. "

"No, really, it's not." It was Johnny's turn to have a little fun.

"Really? Well, I guess any gift from you would be special," Charlie said with a content smile.

Johnny smiled back, thinking to himself, boy, is he going to be surprised. Charlie's friend turned and walked up to his desk, slowly sat down, leaned back in his chair, and placed his hands behind his head, all the while sporting an uncontrollable grin. He had won. Oh, yes, he had won this round.

As the bell rang, all the kids still standing or wandering around the classroom darted to their desks and sat down. It was time for school to begin.

The school day was flying by for Charlie and Johnny. The morning had been filled with holiday activities, games, and treats. And lunch time had just ended, as the kids eagerly headed back to their rooms, giddy as could be. The time had come. It was time for the gift exchange. All the kids in Mrs. McFrey's fifth grade class, including Charlie and Johnny, quickly filtered back into their classroom, dodging, weaving, and diving, until all were back in their seats facing straight ahead, eyes wide open, fingers twitching, with the biggest smiles Mrs. McFrey had seen all year.

Mrs. McFrey addressed the class. "If everyone would please open your science books to page sixty seven, we will begin our next chapter, "The Anatomy of Elves."

Charlie immediately caught on to Mrs. McFrey's joke. Smiling, he looked over at Johnny, who turned around to acknowledge with a wink that he knew as well.

Mrs. McFrey's facial expression slowly changed from serious into a big smile as the class burst into laughter.

"Okay, class, now that you all know that I was kidding, please go ahead and exchange gifts with the person whose name you drew, then return to your seats, please. We will start with Tommy, then work our way to the back of his row. Then the same for rows two, three, and so forth. So Charlie, you will be the last one to open a gift."

For a 5th grader, Charlie was extremely patient. So, being the last one to open a gift did not bother him in the least bit. In fact, it gave him more time to wonder what his friend had gotten for him. He relished every minute, every gift that was opened, until his turn finally arrived. The gift Johnny had gotten for him was rather small and oddly shaped. One could easily tell it had been wrapped by someone with little or no experience. There was no way for Charlie to tell what could possibly be hidden underneath the blue and silver snow flake-patterned paper. This made it that much more exciting for Charlie. He couldn't take it any longer. His fingers tore through the wrapping paper with reckless abandonment one, two, three times, until Charlie had exposed enough of what laid within the crudely wrapped paper to pull it out. It...it was...it was a small envelope, with a balled-up piece of paper taped to one side and two empty macaroni-and-cheese boxes, in the shape of a "T," taped to the other side. Johnny had made extra-double sure there was no possible way his friend would ever be able to guess what he had gotten him for a gift. Charlie flashed his friend a look of bafflement as he removed the taped-on paper ball and macaroni boxes from the envelope. Johnny, wearing a smirk, giggled under his breath as he watched in amusement. Finally, after all this, Charlie's fingers made their way to the envelope, opened it up, and pulled out a gift card. It was a Disney gift card. Charlie's face instantly lit up like a candle. He immediately looked up at Johnny, with a spark in his eyes, to thank his best friend in the whole world.

Johnny, smiling back with raised brows, responded with, "Gotcha!" The two boys broke into laughter, as did the rest of the class, including Mrs. McFrey.

After cleaning up from the gift exchange, Mrs. McFrey's class spent the rest of the afternoon watching holiday movies and snacking on goodies. And before they knew it, the day had come to an end. Students filled the halls—once again—clunking, thunking, clicking and clacking, as they bundled up and made their way down the hallways to be greeted by parents who picked up their children, or to the big yellow buses that took them home. Either way, all the children were happy and in good spirits. Christmas vacation had begun.

Charlie and his brother, Michael, spent the next few days thinking, and the nights dreaming, about Christmas. In the mornings, they did house chores and played outside in the powdery Michigan snow with the other kids. In the afternoons, it was lunch and fun activities with dad. Mr. Z was a freelance graphic designer who worked out of the house; which meant he could work when he wanted, for as long as he wanted, as long as he kept his clients happy. So, while the boys were on vacation, he pulled double duty. Half the day working, the other half keeping the boys fed and entertained. Basically, Mr.

Z spent most of the holiday break acting like a big kid, which he thoroughly enjoyed. Most of his clients had all their projects wrapped up for the year, so as a father, he did everything he could to give his boys a memorable Christmas vacation. Snow forts, snow men, sled races, ice skating, matinee movies, lunches at the local shake and burger joints, and gift shopping for Mrs. Z and the grandparents. It was an endless line-up of fun winter activities.

While Dad and the boys had been quite busy with their holiday activities the past four days, Mr. Z always made sure they were home by late afternoon so he could prepare a nice dinner for the family, especially for his lovely wife, who had been working hard all day to help others get better. The dinner conversations within the Zastawits household were usually straightforward question-and-answer sessions between parents and children. However, this was a special time of year. It was the holiday season. A time to wonder, and a time to share. So, for the past week, the dinner conversations had been charged with wishful requests, cheery replies, and holiday dreams. The entire Zastawits family was overflowing with holiday spirit, and expectations had become almost unbearable.

And now, the time had come...this was it. The final dinner before Christmas Eve day. The last chance for Charlie and Michael to get in any final gift requests before the big night, which was now only twenty-four hours away. Mr. Z called the boys downstairs to set the table for dinner, while he finished preparing one of his specialties; oven-baked parmesan chicken with garlic mashed potatoes, and a side vegetable. The early evening winter sky glowed of soft oranges and purple-like reds. It would be dark shortly. Both children hurried through their chores of setting the table, and moved on to the family room so they could inspect the gifts that were under the tree. "There's one with my name," blurted Michael—hardly able to contain himself.

"Over there in the corner is another one with your name on it," Charlie told his brother.

"Oh, here's one for you, Charlie."

"Yeah, I see it," Charlie told his brother with little emotion. It wasn't because he lacked enthusiasm for Christmas, but because Charlie was two years older, so he was more experienced at controlling his emotions for such occasions.

As the boys continued to hunt for presents around the base of the Christmas tree, Cocoa and Skats, the family pets, came prowling into the room as only cats could. Cocoa was a short hair with black fur, short legs, olive green eyes, and a healthy appetite. He also enjoyed drinking the tree water during the holidays, much to the chagrin of Mr. and Mrs. Z. Skats was also a short hair, with a grey coat, a spot of white on his chest, and yellow eyes. He had a lean build and a floppy belly that swung from side to side whenever he walked quickly or ran. Through the years, the cats had paired up with the boys: Cocoa belonged to Michael, while Skats was Charlie's favorite. Cocoa, seeing Michael by the tree, used it as the perfect excuse to make his way toward the tree water. Sneaky, he was. Skats walked over and rubbed on Charlie's leg. That was cat talk for, "Please lay on the floor with me and pet my furry belly." Charlie accepted the invitation, lying down on his side as Skats curled up next to him, belly up and purring, ready for his friend to start petting him.

All along, Mr. Z had been working diligently in the kitchen, making sure all the items he was preparing for dinner would be finished cooking simultaneously, to ensure nothing would turn cold. Just as he was pulling the chicken from the oven, a flash of bright headlights moved across the living room where the boys were hanging out with the cats. This could only mean one thing.

"Okay, boys, Mom's home. It's time to get up and wash your hands for dinner. Then get your drinks ready."

"Coming!" they answered in unison.

As Charlie and Michael jumped to their feet, the cats scurried about, trying to avoid colliding with the boys' feet, who quickly headed for the kitchen sink to clean up. At the sink, the two battled for position, one nudging the other. Back and forth the battle continued, until Charlie, being two years older and much larger, won out. In frustration, Michael backed off until Charlie had finished. This had become the norm, though hard for the younger brother to accept. Michael saw himself as being the same age as Charlie, though when the two stood side by side, it was very evident that Charlie was the big brother.

Compared to his friends, Charlie was pretty average in height and weight; not the tallest, but by no means the shortest either. He had dark brown, wavy hair with hazel eyes and puffy cheeks. Your typical looking fifth grader. However, his younger brother, Michael, was only in third grade, and had not gone through a growth spurt in quite some time. His hair and facial features were similar to his older brother's, but that was all they shared from a genetic standpoint. Michael was much shorter and had a leaner build than Charlie. However, he was rather quick, more agile, a little feistier, and definitely craftier than his big brother, which came in handy for someone of his stature. And although the two had their differences at times, more often than not, they got along very well. Charlie was the ideal big brother and protector, who always kept an eye on Michael, making sure no harm ever came to him.

Just as the boys were getting their drinks for dinner, their mother entered through the mud room door. "Hello, everyone!" She said in her best jolly voice. "How are my three favorite boys doing tonight?"

"Oh, we're just happy to see you, sweetie. How was your day?" asked Mr. Z.

"It was a very good day, I must say. But it's even better, now that I'm home to share the holiday with my family," she said with a big wide smile.

Mr. Z gathered up the food and brought it to the table to complete the festive ensemble. The plates were set in an alternating pattern of red and white around the table; with a white prancing reindeer centered on the red plates and a red reindeer on the white plates. The same held true for the bowls. The silverware was detailed with holiday swirls, napkins were checkered in red and green, and the red placemats were patterned with subtle reindeer. The table cloth was also checkered with red and green, with fine gold overlapping lines. The Zastawits family truly enjoyed this time of year.

As everyone at the table worked their way through the delicious meal Mr. Z had prepared, conversations floated from parent to child, child to parent, and parent to parent. Mrs. Z asked Mr. Z if all the presents had been wrapped to take over to the grandparents for Christmas Eve. Mr. Z passed the same question on to the boys, who were responsible for wrapping their gifts to the Zastawits grandparents. Mrs. Z also asked Mr. Z whether or not they were to bring food over to the grandparents for dinner, upon which he replied, "The only thing they asked us to bring were our grandchildren," as he looked at the boys with a grin. This really got Charlie and Michael excited. They were practically incapable of sitting still in their chairs, being so wound up for the holidays to begin.

"Now you've done it," stated Mrs. Z, as she rolled her eyes at her husband in an exaggerated manner. "They'll never get to sleep now."

Mr. Z played along. "Gosh, honey, I was only trying to make the boys happy."

"Yeah, Mom," responded Michael.

"Well, I'm afraid we may just have to skip dessert tonight. The boys already have entirely too much energy as it is. If they have desert, all that sugar will surely keep them up all night. And if they're up all night tonight, they'll be too exhausted to go to Grandma and Grandpa's house tomorrow night."

Like soldiers coming to attention when a superior officer walks into the room, the boys immediately straightened up and sat perfectly still. Only their eyes moved, to look at one another and confirm each had responded appropriately.

Mr. Z acknowledged the boy's reactions. "Would you look at that, dear? I'd say the two of them must really want dessert. Or maybe they're just bored stiff?"

"No Dad, we really do want dessert," Charlie replied, with a face of desperation. Michael followed suit, with the same desperate look.

"Well, Dad, I guess you could give the boys each a very small piece of Dutch apple pie."

"We'd be OK with full pieces, Mom, really, it wouldn't keep us up. We promise. Please?" Charlie begged, giving his mother a dose of sad eyes.

"What do you think, Mother? They did make a promise," Mr. Z replied.

Both boys focused their pleading eyes on their mother.

"I guess it wouldn't hurt," she said as her eyes wandered upward.

"Yay—wahoo!" shouted the boys, as they sprang from the table to...

Mrs. Z cleared her throat. "Wait just a second there, young men. Before you both can have dessert, the table needs to be cleared."

"Aw, Mom," they responded.

"Your father worked very hard to prepare this meal. The least you can do to show your appreciation is to help clean up." There was a slight pause. "Otherwise, there won't be any desert."

The boys snapped to it—cleaning off the table in record time.

After everyone had enjoyed their dessert, Charlie and Michael spent the evening in front of the television watching Christmas movies, while their mother was busy in the kitchen making Christmas cookies. But Mr. Z had snuck off to the reading room, spending a great deal of time on the computer.

Why was Dad on the computer for so long? Charlie wondered. He didn't have any work to do. Why wasn't he in the family room with us, watching Christmas movies, like he usually does? Charlie got up and walked over to the reading room, which was mostly dark, except for the small desk lamp highlighting his father's thick black hair and middle-aged face.

"What are you doing, Dad?" Charlie asked as he leaned on the corner of the wall that divided the stairway in the foyer from the reading room, unable to see what was on the monitor from where he stood.

His father's attention was so wrapped by the computer, he did not even hear Charlie's question.

"Dad, what are you doing?"

Mr. Z jumped. Startled by Charlie's voice, he quickly turned his head. His reading glasses teetered on the edge of his nose as he regained his composure and looked at his son. "Oh, I'm, I'm just checking the weather for tomorrow and trying to find a recipe for something I want to cook up on Christmas Day. Nothing special."

"What are you gonna make?"

Mr. Z didn't expect Charlie to ask any further questions. "That's why I'm looking; I still haven't figured that out yet. "

"Oh...OK," Charlie replied suspiciously with a little chuckle. What was Dad up to? he asked himself. His insides filled with bubbly excitement as he walked back to the family room to rejoin his brother in front of the TV, his mind wondering.

Christmas Eve at the grandparents' house had come and gone. The soft glow of the morning sun slowly rose over the snow-covered landscape, which sparkled like diamonds in a mine. The air was crisp, cool, and very still. Not a car, truck, plane, or train could be heard. The only sound was that of a chirping cardinal, sitting on a branch of the small apple blossom tree just outside the reading room windows. In front of the windows sat a couch. And on top of the couch, all curled up in a ball, was Cocoa, sleeping in his favorite winter spot.

Daylight gradually made its way to the back of the house, piercing the window blinds in Michael's room. His eyes suddenly opened, his mind realizing what day it was. Christmas morning had come. With his face filled with excitement, Michael kicked the covers away, quickly jumped out of bed, and headed to wake Charlie. "Charlie...Charlie, wake up! It's Christmas morning!"

Charlie rolled over, groggy and confused. His hair pointed in every direction, like it had been spun with a mixer. He sat up and gazed at his brother with a blank stare, still trying to figure out what was going on.

"Charlie, c'mon, get up! Its Christmas! It's Christmas morning, Charlie! It's Christmas!" Michael kept repeating himself as he tugged on his brother's pajamas.

On about the third tug, it finally dawned on Charlie what was happening. The gears in his brain started to move. "Christmas? Morning? Oh, yeah. Yes! Christmas! It's Christmas morning!"

"Yeah Charlie, get up! Let's go! C'mon!"

Charlie, now very awake, rolled out of bed as if his pajamas were on fire, and the two boys quickly made their way downstairs to the family room, where they came to a sudden halt. Their mouths opened wide, and their eyes filled with wonder. There was something very special about Christmas morning. The tree emitted a soft golden glow, highlighting all the ornaments and tinsel on the tree, as well as the presents surrounding its base. On top of the tree sat a majestic Santa figure, who overlooked this lighted spectacle of holiday magic. The stockings, which had been empty the night before, were now lumpy and full, with small little gifts rising out of their tops. And the air was filled with cinnamon and pine. Only a few crumbs remained on the plate of cookies, and the milk glass was empty—which could only mean one thing. Santa had come.

As the boys navigated around the gifts under the tree, looking to see what belonged to whom and how many there were for each of them, their voices began to escalate to a level that eventually woke their parents. Mr. And Mrs. Z slowly rolled and looked at each other. Both smiled and quietly wished each other a Merry Christmas.

"I guess it's time to get up?" Mr. Z whispered, as he stumbled out of bed and into his comfy slippers.

His wife followed suit, and the two of them made their way downstairs to wish the boys a Merry Christmas. Mr. Z turned on the Christmas music, Mrs. Z made herself a cup of coffee and got the cinnamon rolls started in the kitchen. Then everyone gathered in the family room for a spectacle of gift giving, receiving, and opening. The sound of shredded paper, "thank you" and "you're welcome" filled the air repeatedly, as everyone made their way through the presents they were given. The discarded paper, ribbons, and boxes covered the entire living room floor, which the cats thoroughly enjoyed, until finally, the last gift was opened, a special gift to Mrs. Z from Mr. Z. This was a Zastawits tradition, carried out every year, when presents were opened on Christmas morning.

Charlie and Michael had each received wonderful gifts, and were busy playing with them on the floor of the living room, as the cats frolicked around the tree and gift wrappings scattered throughout the room. Their father began to clean up a little, while their mother went back into the kitchen to put the finishes touches on the cinnamon rolls—another Zastawits Christmas morning tradition.

"Okay, boys, you too Daddy, the rolls are ready."

It only took a second for the boys and their father to respond, making their way to the kitchen counter for fresh cinnamon rolls and ice cold milk. Charlie and his family made quick work of the hot, delicious rolls. Within 10 minutes, all evidence of rolls had been removed from the pan, except for a slight hint of icing. When it came to cinnamon roll consumption, the Zastawits family didn't mess around.

"Everyone make sure you wash your hands before leaving the kitchen," said Charlie's mother.

"Don't worry, we will, honey. You hear that boys?"

"Yes, Dad," Charlie answered.

Their father washed his hands and quickly disappeared, while the boys finished washing up. A few minutes later, after the kitchen had been cleaned, Charlie, Michael, and their mother gathered back in the living room to play a new card game Charlie had received in his stocking. It was a game he was very excited to play with his family. Eventually, Mr. Z returned from his mysterious disappearance and joined in as well.

"What were you doing, dear?" asked Mrs. Z of her husband.

"Oh, I was just checking on the weather. Making sure no bad storms were coming today."

"But we always stay home on Christmas Day, so why would it matter what the weather is like?" Mrs. Z asked, as the boys looked at their father with questioning eyes.

"Well uh, I uh...want to make sure...just in case. You never know. The power could get knocked out, or something like that."

"Since when have you ever been worried about the power getting knocked out on Christmas Day?" she replied. Again, the boys looked at their father.

"Uh, well. Uh. Cause I wanted to make sure the printer still worked?"

The boys and their mother all flashed Mr. Z looks of confusion. Something fishy was going on, and Mrs. Z could sense it.

"What in the world are you talking about, dear? You didn't have any work to do today, right? I mean, it's Christmas. Nobody is working. I don't understand." Mrs. Z was utterly baffled at the moment, as were Charlie and Michael. "And what's that you're holding behind your back?"

"Well, it's a bunch of information I just printed out."

"Information?"

"Yeah, information."

Mrs. Z's head was spinning. "Information for what?"

Mr. Z replied with a straight face, "All the details for our trip to Walt Disney World."

"Details? Disney World?"

Just like that, the look of confusion on their faces morphed into great, big, happy smiles, as Mrs. Z and the boys broke into celebration. Jumping, rolling, screaming, cheering. "We're going to Disney World! We're going to Disney World!" Mrs. Z ran over to Mr. Z and gave him a big hug. Charlie was hugging him as well, around his left leg, and Michael had his arms wrapped around his father's right leg. What a wonderful surprise for the whole family. Mr. Z had pulled off a true Christmas miracle.

"So when are we going dear?" asked his wife.

"We leave the day after school gets out for summer break," he answered, his voice filled with excitement and joy. "We will be there for seven days and six nights, and are staying at the Beach Club Resort."

To Charlie, it did not matter where they were staying, or really even for how long. All that mattered to him was that they would be going to his favorite place in the whole world. The only hard part would be waiting for the school year to end. To a fifth grader, six months could seem like six years. But at least I'm not a third grader like Michael, Charlie thought to himself. That would be way worse.

Another thought crossed Charlie's mind at that moment as well. In fact it was a brilliant idea. "Dad, remember the Disney gift card I told you Johnny gave me for our gift exchange at school?"

"I sure do," his dad replied.

"I was just thinking. I could save it for the trip."

"That's a fantastic idea, Charlie. I was hoping you would say that."

"You were?" Charlie appeared puzzled.

"Yes. Because I'm the one who told Johnny to get you the Disney gift card. And I told him about the trip I was planning for Walt Disney World. Since you love Disney so much, I thought it would be the perfect gift for Johnny to get you."

And instantly, Charlie knew exactly why Johnny had been so excited to watch him open his Christmas gift at school. They had pulled one over on him. Charlie's best friend, and even his own father, had planned this all along. Who could ask for a better friend, or a nicer dad, Charlie thought to himself. Then, he looked at his father and said, with great appreciation. "Thank you, Dad."

"You are very welcome, son."

Mrs. Z shed a tear of happiness.

Chapter Three

The remainder of the school year was a blur of homework, recesses, and sleepovers for Charlie and his brother. All they could think about was what they were going to do, where they were going to go, which characters they wanted to meet, and what they wanted to collect for souvenirs when they arrived at Disney World. Almost every weekend since their dad told them about the trip, Charlie and his little brother would hold secret Disney meetings in Charlie's bedroom, making lists, maps, and anything else they could possibly think of for their upcoming trip to the most magical place on earth. One can only imagine what kind of information an eleven and nine year old could gather. But to Charlie and Michael, it was serious stuff. Anyone who spoke to them would think the two brothers had actually been to Walt Disney World before, when in fact, all their knowledge had come from searching the internet. This would be their first visit. They had questions like, If we go meet Mickey at the Magic Kingdom on Friday, will we still have time for the Buzz ride? Will Mom let us have Dole Whips for a snack? And, who's going to sit with Mom and who's going to sit with Dad on the Peter Pan ride? All these were topics of debate. But at the end of each grueling weekend meeting, which only lasted fifteen to twenty minutes tops, the boys always came to a happy mutual agreement.

As Charlie walked out of the school building for the last time as a fifth grader, his best friend Johnny strolled up beside him.

"Hey there, Charlie. Can't wait to hear all about your trip when you get back. I'm sure you'll have a blast."

"Yeah, I'm so excited, Johnny, I don't know if I'll be able to sleep tonight or not. I can't believe we leave tomorrow morning."

"You still have that gift card I got you for Christmas, right?"

"Oh. Oh yes, I got it tucked away in the backpack I'm taking on the trip. Gonna use it for sure when we're at Disney. "

"Any idea what you might use it for?"

"I have no idea. I'll probably use it when I see something really special. And there's going to be so much to look at."

"Well, I hope you have a good time. And be sure to bring me something back if you get a chance, OK?"

"Oh, you bet I will."

"Thanks, Charlie. See ya when you get back."

"OK, Johnny."

Just then, Charlie's dad pulled up in the van to the loading area, as Michael joined his big brother by the curb.

On the ride home from school, Charlie noticed several things which hinted tomorrow was not going to be any ordinary day. First off, his dad had Walt Disney World theme park music playing on the van stereo. Second, his father was dressed like he was already on vacation. And finally, the back of the van was loaded up with large suitcases, which were tagged for the Magical Express service. Charlie's parents were very keen on the shuttle service Disney provided between the airport and resorts for guests staying on property. Yes, tomorrow was going to be an incredible day. Charlie took it all in as he stared out the window of the van, Disney music playing in the background, Michael and his dad singing, and the sun shining on his smiling face, as their van traveled down the road toward home. Tomorrow was only a dream away.

That evening, the Zastawits home was buzzing like a beehive, with everyone preparing for the next day's travels. Charlie's mom was double-checking the kids carry-on luggage, to make sure they had everything needed for the first day since they would be going straight to the Magic Kingdom from their resort as soon as they arrived and checked in to their room. This was a perk of using the Magical Express service. The rest of their luggage would magically arrive in their room later that day, even though they would be at the Magic Kingdom. A pretty cool thing, Charlie thought.

While Mrs. Z was going through the luggage checklists, her husband was busy making sure he had all the documentation in order that would be required for the trip. This included their MagicBands, shuttle passes for the Magical Express, and boarding passes for the plane. All other important information, like resort and dinner reservations, were loaded onto their MagicBands.

"Honey, what do you and the boys want for dinner?" Mr. Z asked, as he was scurrying around the house to make sure everything was in order.

"Oh, I don't know. I haven't really thought about it. Boys, any ideas for dinner?"

"Can we have burgers from Roxy's?" Michael asked. Roxy's was one of their favorite local burger joints, and was a fast, easy solution for days like this.

"Sounds good to me," Michael's father replied. "Is that OK with you, Charlie?"

Charlie answered with a simple "yep."

"How about you, honey?"

"I'm good with it," she replied.

That was all Mr. Z needed to hear. Orders were taken and he was out the door to fill the van up with gas and get dinner.

It was getting late, and the sun had nearly set below the horizon. Charlie and his brother were eager to get to sleep in expectation of what tomorrow's wake up would bring. Everything to be carried on the plane was packed and sitting in the kitchen, ready to be loaded in the van first thing come morning. Charlie and Michael's parents came around to wish each boy good night and to sleep well, although they knew deep down, there wouldn't be much sleeping going on tonight.

"Alright, Charlie, we'll see you bright and early tomorrow morning," his dad said.

Charlie acknowledged his father with a smile.

"Actually, since we're leaving so early, it will still be dark out. So I guess it won't be very bright out," his dad said with a chuckle. Mr. Z liked to get going early for family vacations. Every day counted, in his opinion. So, he had the family booked for an 8:15 morning flight, which would get them to Orlando by 10:30, and into their resort before noon. This would give them a good, full first day to enjoy the magic. Working backwards, this meant they needed to arrive at the airport by 6:15. And it was an hour-and-a-half drive to the airport, so everyone needed to be in the van, ready to roll, by 4:45am. Pretty early for any normal day. But this was not going to be any normal day. The adrenaline was already flowing through Charlie's body. Morning could not come soon enough.

"Good night, sweetie," Mrs. Z said to Charlie, as she peeked into his room and turned off the light.

"Night, Mom," he replied. Rolling over and pulling the covers above his head, Charlie shut his eyes, ready to ride, ready to explore, ready to dream, ready for all the magical things he would experience the next seven days.

4:15. Morning had arrived. Charlie's alarm was beeping away like a bird on caffeine. He rolled over and shut it off quickly, shook his head, and fell out of bed—disoriented yet excited at the same time. He could hear his brother, already downstairs in the kitchen, wound up and ready to go.

"Sweetie, are you up?" Charlie's mother shouted.

"Yes, Mom." Charlie replied, as he turned on his light, grabbed his clothes, and headed for the shower. Within ten minutes he was cleaned, teeth brushed, and downstairs—ready to go. Wow, that has to be a record time, he thought to himself.

It was dark, very dark. The cats, sensing that everyone was leaving, were meowing for attention, curiously wondering why they now had enough food and water to keep them fed for at least a week. Charlie's father was loading up the rest of the luggage while his mother finished up her hair and makeup.

"OK, everybody ready to go?" Mr. Z asked, as he scanned the kitchen for any loose items.

The boys hopped off the kitchen stools, grabbed their back packs, and headed for the van. Their mom was right behind them as she quickly took one last look around and said goodbye to the kitties. Everyone buckled up as Charlie's father backed out of the garage. Charlie put in a Disney movie for he and his brother to watch on their ride to the airport. The movie started, Mr. Z turned out of their neighborhood, and they were off.

The drive to the airport went smoothly, as well as their check-in and boarding. Take-off was a piece of cake, and for that matter, the entire flight down was a quick and easy experience, thanks to the wonderful staff on board. Charlie and Michael enjoyed their flight to Orlando. It was filled with soda, peanuts, crackers, two very funny flight attendants, and a selection of Disney games and movies that their parents had stored on devices to keep the boys entertained. It was just about 10:20 when their flight touched down in Florida. They were all appropriately dressed for the occasion. Mrs. Z was wearing a bright pink sleeveless polo with khaki Capris, brown sandals, and white-rimmed sunglasses. Her hair was pulled back into a ponytail, held by a white hair band with a pink floral pattern. Her husband was wearing a bright red polo shirt, khaki shorts, brown sandals, and sunglasses. Charlie and Michael were both wearing bright-colored t-shirts, with khaki shorts and sneakers. The bright shirts were a special request of their mothers, making them easy to spot amongst all the people if they became separated at any time.

As they got off the plane and headed through the airport, Charlie's level of excitement continued to rise, as did his brother's. Backlit signs promoting the parks were everywhere, one for Epcot, another for Animal Kingdom. There was even a Disney Store. And this is only the airport, Charlie thought to himself as they pushed on toward the Magical Express.

"This way, honey, I believe the Magical Express service is downstairs," Charlie's father said, as he led their family through the airport. "Charlie, make sure you stay close to me, OK, buddy." Mr. Z had looked back and seen that his wife was watching Michael closely, which reminded him to keep track of his older son. An escalator ride took them down to the lower level, and as they made their way toward the end of the B side, Level 1 walkway, Charlie could see it. He could see the Magical Express Welcome Center. After just a very short wait, his family made their way through the check-in line and onto the bus that would take them to their resort.

In Charlie's eyes, the Magical Express buses were no ordinary buses. The exteriors were covered with a retro blue and beige color scheme, a cluster of grey stripes, and on top of the stripes were the words Disney's Magical Express. To add to it, there were images of a retro Mickey wearing a bus driver's hat on the sides and front as well. Inside the bus were staggered monitors above the seats that played a variety Disney-related videos to keep passengers occupied on their ride to Walt Disney World from the airport, which Charlie and his family were more than thrilled to watch. Everyone had a smile on their face, as the bus carried them closer and closer to the place Charlie's parents had only dreamt of taking their children. That is, until this very moment.

The Zastawits family had checked into Beach Club Reort, dropped off their carry-on luggage in the room, and grabbed a quick snack at the Beach Club Marketplace. Now that all the technicalities and hungry tummies had been taken care of, it was time for them hit the park, and Charlie and his brother couldn't wait another second.

"Everyone have their MagicBands on?" asked Mr. Z.

Charlie, Michael, and their mother all replied simultaneously, confirming they had their bands on.

"Alright then, let's go find a bus to take us to the Magic Kingdom."

Within minutes, a shuttle bus marked for the Magic Kingdom arrived at their resort, picked them up, and took them on their way. On the ride over, Charlie and his family started discussing strategy. Mr. Z spoke up first, as he felt it was his responsibility to act as the family tour guide since he had visited the parks more times than his wife, and the boys had never been here at all. "I think, since it's already the middle of the day, and pretty hot out, we should start somewhere that will keep us out of the sun. Somewhere classic. Somewhere that won't seem too overwhelming after our long trip down. Something like, 'it's a small world?'"

"Sure, sweetie, that sounds good to us," his wife replied as she looked at her two red-cheeked boys who had already started to overheat from the hot Florida sun. Charlie and his brother nodded their heads in agreement. "But on the way, Ed, I think we should stop at the Plaza Ice Cream Parlor for a cool treat, don't you, boys?"

And without hesitation, Charlie and his overheated brother replied, "YEAH!"

"OK, then. I guess the majority has spoken. Ice cream it is," proclaimed Mr. Z.

Minutes later, the bus pulled up to the drop-off station in front of the Magic Kingdom, and the doors opened. The sounds and smells of the park welcomed Charlie's family as they stepped off the bus and started to make their way for the park entrance.

"Have a magical day, folks," the bus driver kindly said.

Charlie, being the last one off the bus, looked back as he exited through the door and said, "Thank you."

The driver gave him a wink, closed the bus doors, and drove off.

Just the short walk from the bus drop-off to the front gate was a chore in the Florida summer heat. Mom's plan to stop for ice cream really was a good idea, Charlie thought, as they made their way through the bag-check area and up to the entry tunnel that passes under the train tracks. While passing through the tunnel, Charlie and his father made sure to grab park maps for quick reference. A true staple of any Disney park enthusiast. Not only that, Charlie's dad collected the maps. He made sure to get at least one from each park, on every trip he made to Disney World.

As they exited the tunnel and into Town Square, Charlie couldn't believe his eyes. It was like he had traveled back in time, a simpler time, a happier time. Everything was themed to the turn-of-the-20th century. Horse-drawn cars, omnibuses, jitneys, and fire trucks carried passengers up and down Main Street. Cast members adorned the streets, selling balloons and popcorn. Others provided photo services or direction. A quartet of colorfully dressed men sang in harmony on the west corner. Several other cast members, dressed up as early 20th century citizens of Main Street, were walking around making every guest feel welcome. And there to greet him and his brother, in the center of Town Square, was Pluto.

Charlie's face lit up like the Fourth of July as he and his brother turned to pose for a picture with one of his favorite canines—who put his arms and paws around their shoulders, like they were the best of friends. This was to be the first of many character encounters to come throughout their stay.

"OK, guys, it's time we headed for the ice cream parlor, don't you think?" asked Mrs. Z.

"You read my mind," her husband replied.

Charlie's mom took the lead as the entire family headed down Main Street, past the bakery, and into the ice cream parlor for a cool snack.

Three ice cream cones and a chocolate shake later, Charlie and his family had made their way past the hub, through the castle to Fantasyland, and into the Small World queue. Luckily, the line was not too long and Charlie's family did not have to stand in the sun. As the line moved along, Charlie and his brother studied the white, silver, and gold clock tower. The smiling clock face and multiple moving parts occupied the boys' imaginations as their family patiently waited in line. Before long, it was time to board one of the boats.

Charlie's family was in line number one, which meant they would be in the front row seats of the boat. As their teal-colored boat approached, Charlie became more and more excited. His first Disney World ride. Ever. The people on the boat exited to the right, and Charlie and his family made their way into the front row seats. They entered in the order of Charlie, Dad, Michael, and Mom. This arrangement allowed Charlie to have an unobstructed view and kept his younger brother securely between his parents, though Michael wasn't too thrilled with it. As the boat slowly started on its way, a young female cast member smiled and waved from the control tower above. Everyone in the boat waved and smiled back as they began their journey around the world.

The water surrounding the boat shimmered from the coins people had tossed in it for good luck. As the boat banked to the left, above to the right people dining at Pinocchio's Village Haus waved to the passing boats. And straight ahead, a dark tunnel. The passageway to a harmonious small world.

As the boat broke through the darkness of the tunnel, a world of brilliant color, motion, and music came into view.

Charlie could not believe his eyes. All the children from so many different countries, dancing, singing, and skating. There were lions, monkeys, and so many other animals. Big Ben, cuckoo clocks, pots of gold and flying carpets. Each section of the world, magnificently represented, with endless motion, colors, and song. And in each section, one sun. Charlie noticed, as their boat passed through each area of the world, a single sun was always present. This was a detail, Charlie's father had told him, that "supported the lyrics of the Small World song." A song his dad had great respect for.

As their boat exited Africa and entered South America, the one sun lay straight ahead at the waterway's bend in Mexico, just above the sombrero hat dancers. It immediately caught Charlie's attention. The pointed flames that surrounded the parameter of the sun were in two layers. The top layer remained stationary, while the bottom layer spun around in a clockwise motion, creating the illusion of a shimmering sun. And though Charlie looked around at all the animated magic that was surrounding their boat, he kept going back to the sun. As the boat banked left, Charlie's eyes locked in on the Mexican sun, while he studied it from a closer view, mesmerized by its animation.

And then, something very unusual happened, something that ordinarily doesn't happen. The sun opened its eyes, focused on Charlie, and began to speak.

Nobody else in the boat heard a thing. They just continued to point and talk about all the details of the attraction that surrounded them as the boat slowly moved along.

Charlie continued to focus on the animated sun as it spoke to him:

> To you a riddle I shall speak, so listen very well.
>
> Take your younger where the sun sets, next to a post you will see.
>
> And there, a bird's tale that's not for sale, will be told by a tree.

Charlie took his phone out and immediately typed the sun's riddle into his notes, not paying any attention to what people were doing or saying around him. When he was finished, he looked to see if anyone else had heard the sun speak. Not one person had seen nor heard what Charlie had just experienced.

As their boat wound through the South Pacific and into the final room, Charlie just sat back in his seat and stared off into the vast array of animated Small World figures, merry-go-rounds, and Ferris wheels while trying to make sense of what he had just experienced. Did it actually happen, or was it his imagination? And if it was real, what in the world did it all mean?

Charlie was on the biggest vacation of his life, but at the moment, he felt like he had been transported into another dimension, a place that only he and the talking sun of Mexico were aware of. He needed to find a place to process the message he'd typed into his phone. Somewhere he could concentrate. Maybe an attraction where he could sit down for a long period of time? Somewhere quiet. Somewhere with air conditioning. Somewhere nearby. And then, it dawned on him. He knew just the place. A place he had seen when researching the Magic Kingdom park online. The Hall of Presidents.

As the Zastawits family exited the Small World attraction into the heat of the day, Charlie made a strong suggestion for the Hall of Presidents.

"You know, Mom, since it's so hot out, we should find things to do that are inside. At least until it cools down this evening."

Mr. Z jumped into the conversation before his wife could answer Charlie.

"I was thinking the same thing. What do you think, honey?"

"Yeah. I think that would definitely be the right thing to do."

"Mom, I gotta use the rest room," Michael chimed in.

"Why sure, honey. I think there's one on the way to the Hall of Presidents, right Ed?

"Yes, right up here by Rapunzel's tower."

"Perfect. Can you please take Michael in?"

"Sure, honey. C'mon, Michael. We'll be back in a sec."

Charlie and his mother went and sat down nearby in the shade to wait for his dad and brother. His mom started researching the parks on her phone, which gave Charlie a few minutes to work on the riddle the golden sun in Mexico had given to him.

He opened the notes on his phone and read the riddle again to refresh his memory.

> Take your younger where the sun sets, next to a post you will see.
>
> And there, a bird's tale that's not for sale will be told by a tree.

Charlie sat and stared at the riddle, reading the first part over and over again: "your younger"? The only one younger than him in their family was Michael. That's gotta be it. Now, where does the sun set? Where is west, here in the Magic Kingdom? Back home, Lake Michigan is west. So the sun always set on the lake's horizon. Easy. But I'm not back home. Where is west? Charlie looked for the sun, which was easy to find since it was early afternoon. The sun was right above them, shining down on top of their heads. That wasn't much help. And since it was early afternoon, and it was summertime, the sun would not be setting for at least seven hours or so.

"Hey, guys, ready to get moving?" Charlie's dad and brother had returned.

"Oh my goodness, yes," replied Mrs. Z. "I really need a break from this heat."

Charlie and his mother stood up and joined the other two, as they made their way through the portal from Fantasyland to Liberty Square and over to the Hall of Presidents.

Inside the attraction queue was a circular waiting area which contained many paintings and historical artifacts around its perimeter. Very cool stuff that Charlie, being the age he was, really wanted to look at. However, he was consumed with trying to solve the riddle. So, while waiting to enter the attraction, Charlie's family walked around, reading and looking at many of the historical materials the queue had to offer, as Charlie sat down and continued to work on the riddle.

Where the sun sets? That was the next piece of the riddle. The sun sets in the west. Yes, I known this already, Charlie thought to himself. But what direction is west? West... West...

The doors started to open. It was time to stand up and get ready to enter the hall. The rest of the family quickly came over and joined Charlie in line.

Within a few short minutes, all the people waiting to see the show had shuffled into the hall and found a seat. While they were waiting for the show to begin, a discussion began on where Charlie and his family would go next, a well-practiced procedure for many park goers.

"Hey boys, any ideas where you might want to go after this attraction?" their father asked.

"How about the train roller coaster, Dad?" Michael blurted out. He had seen it on the Disney Vacation Planning DVD and was really excited to check it out. Michael loved any kind of transportation: cars, trucks, trains, planes; it didn't matter. So when he saw the Big Thunder Mountain attraction on the DVD their dad had shown them months ago, he made sure he wasn't going to miss it.

"That would be a lot of fun, son, but it's probably a little too hot out right now for the train coaster. I promise you, we will definitely ride the train coaster before our vacation is over."

Charlie silently agreed with his father, and was impressed how he handled Michael's demand. Now, back to the riddle, he thought to himself.

"Actually, I believe...wait, just a sec." Mr. Z was checking his phone. "Yes, we have FastPasses for the Country Bear Jamboree shortly after we finish with this attraction. So, that will work out perfectly." Charlie's dad was always thrilled when a plan came together. "Looks like we'll be headed out west after we're finished here with the presidents."

That's it, Charlie thought. Out west. Like in the Wild West. Not the direction west. That could mean only one thing when it comes to the Magic Kingdom...Frontierland. Yes. Charlie was so excited he could hardly wait for the Hall of Presidents show to end, even though it had not even started yet.

As the lights dimmed, all Charlie could do was think of how and when to tell his brother. After all, he was included in the riddle. But when to tell him? It would have to be when we walk to the Country Bear Jamboree show. Yes, that will give me time, Charlie thought. But how to get Michael away from our parents so I can talk to him? There's the challenge. The answer would have to wait until after the Hall of Presidents.

Forty-three presidents and a spectacular story of America's history had made the time pass quickly. It was time to exit the Hall of Presidents.

Charlie's father started up a conversation as they were exiting. "What an incredible show, eh, boys?"

"Oh, that show gets me every time I see it," said Mrs. Z, as she wiped her eyes with her finger.

It wasn't long before Charlie and his family were back outside in the sweltering heat.

"How long until we can use our FastPass at the Country Bears, Dad?" asked Charlie.

"Let's see. It's 3:15 now, and our FastPass is good for the 3:55 show. So we have a good half hour to kill. Any ideas, honey?"

At that moment, Charlie spotted the perfect place to talk with his brother. He pointed to a nearby store. "How about the Ye Olde Christmas Shoppe over there, Mom?"

"Awwww. Yeah, that's a great idea, Charlie." There wasn't a Christmas store on the planet that Mrs. Z would turn down an opportunity to look at. And her oldest son knew that.

"Alrighty, then. Let's go check it out," said Mr. Z.

Charlie and his family marched over and into the store without hesitation, taking relief, once again, from the humid Florida air. Now was the chance for Charlie to break off with his brother. He only needed a minute. Two, tops. He spotted an opportunity and went for it.

"Hey, Michael, you still like Stitch?"

"Yes, of course I do, Charlie," he answered.

"Well, take a look behind you."

"Where?"

"Not there. Over there by the ornaments."

"Oh, yeah. Cool. Mom, can we go look at the ornaments?" Michael asked.

"Sure, honey. Just make sure you stay where we can see you. And Charlie, don't leave your brother alone over there. Ok?"

"Sure, Mom. No problem," Charlie said with a smile.

His plan had worked perfectly. As soon as he and his brother reached the ornaments, Charlie started filling Michael in on what he had experienced.

"Michael, I know you want to look at the Stitch ornaments, but that's not why I really brought you over here." His brother gave him a quizzical look. "I've got something really important to tell you. Something you have to promise you'll keep secret from Mom and Dad. And I really, really mean it. OK?" Charlie stared his brother down for confirmation.

"Secret? What kind of secret?"

"The kind that, if you told someone, they probably would think you were bonkers. And they'd think I was a raging lunatic. They would most likely lock me up for good, send me to a psychologist, and who knows what else." Charlie made sure to keep his voice down, almost to a whisper, so nobody around them could hear what he was saying.

I'm sure it's not that bad," Michael said without interest.

Charlie continued to stare at his brother intensely, without a blink. "Promise me, Michael."

"OK, I promise. So tell me what it is." Michael stopped looking at the ornament he had in his hand and gave Charlie a quick look out of the corner of his eye.

"You promise. You're absolutely one hundred percent sure?"

"Yes. Yes, I'm sure."

"Alright...here it is. Remember the Small World ride?"

"You mean the ride we were just on less than an hour ago?" Michael said sarcastically.

"Yes, of course. Duh. Well, when our boat reached Mexico, and was banking left around the turn, there was a golden sun with flames that moved. Do you remember that?"

"Sort of."

"Anyway, as the boat was passing the sun, and this is the freaky part...it opened its eyes and spoke to me," Charlie said in his best whisper shout.

"What?" Michael started to chuckle quietly, not believing what Charlie had just told him.

"No, seriously, Michael. It's not funny. The sun in Mexico really did speak to me."

His brother continued to chuckle. "OK...OK. If the 'sun' spoke to you, what did it say?"

"That's what I needed to tell you, ya know-it-all. It told me a riddle. A riddle you and I have to solve together."

"Why do I have to help?"

"Because Michael, the sun told me I needed to include you."

"Really? How did the sun know my name?"

"The sun didn't know your name, silly. It just referred to you as my younger brother. And told me you needed to come along. So are you going to let me tell you the riddle or not?" Charlie shouted quietly to his brother.

"Geez, Charlie, OK, OK. Tell me the riddle."

"Alright, then," Charlie said, as he located the riddle on his phone, while at the same time shaking his head, frustrated by his brother's behavior. A common thing between the two of them.

"OK, I found it."

"Good. So what does it say?" Michael was pushing his luck with his big brother.

Charlie gave him a look, then went back to reading the riddle. "It says, 'Take your younger where the sun sets, next to a post you will see. And there, a bird's tale that's not for sale, will be told by a tree.'"

"So what does it mean?" asked Michael.

"That's why I'm talking to you. I need your help to figure it out."

Michael, still not believing what his brother had told, asked. "So, you're sure you're not making this up as a joke?"

"No. I told you, it really did happen. I'm not going to lie to you about something like this."

Michael stared at his brother out of the corner of his eyes and sighed. Then he said, "OK, what are we supposed to do?"

"Well, I already solved the beginning of the first sentence. The "younger" is you and "where the sun sets" is referring to the west, as in the Wild West. You know, Frontierland. So now we need to figure out the second part of that sentence. Understand?"

"Yes, but..."

"But what?" asked Charlie impatiently.

Michael turned his head right and nodded. It was Mom and Dad headed straight for them.

"I guess it will have to wait. So, Frontierland. We'll figure out the rest when we get there. Got it?"

Michael nodded.

"Hey, boys. Find any ornaments you like?" asked Mrs. Z.

The boys acted surprised, as if they had not seen their parents walking toward them.

"I think Michael found a few that he likes. I haven't found any Donald ornaments yet, but I still need to look in the other room," said Charlie.

"Well, looks like we gotta start heading toward the Country Bears show, Charlie. Maybe later, if you'd like, we can stop back here to look for a Donald ornament." Mr. Z knew Donald Duck was Charlie's favorite character, so he wanted to make sure his son had the opportunity to finish looking.

"Sure. That's fine, Dad," Charlie replied, appearing to be uninterested.

Charlie's mother and father both looked at each other, a little bewildered by their son's lack of enthusiasm for something they knew he truly enjoyed. But then, as was usually the case with their boys, they quickly dismissed it. With no more time to spare, the Zastawits family headed for Frontierland. Mom and Dad set a quick pace, eager to make it to the show, while Charlie and Michael brought up the rear, determined to solve the next part of the riddle.

Charlie and his family had walked so quickly to make it in time for the Country Bear Jamboree that he and his brother never had a chance to study the details of Frontierland. The show was nothing short of incredible. Even though Charlie kept running the riddle through his mind during the entire thing, both boys enjoyed the Country Bears. As they exited the attraction out into the Frontierland walkway, Charlie nudged his brother and gave him a look, like he was getting ready to do something that Michael needed to pay attention to.

It was a little past 4:30, almost evening. The temperature and humidity had finally started to drop, making it more tolerable to stay outside. This was Charlie and Michael's chance to look for clues that would help solve the riddle. Charlie just needed an idea to give them time to do so.

"What did you say we were doing for dinner tonight, Dad?" Charlie asked.

"We have a reservation for 7:30 at the Crystal Palace."

"So we have plenty of time to explore the park, right?"

"Absolutely. We do have a 6:00 FastPass for the Jungle Cruise, but we still have plenty of time to do other things. It's just a short walk from here."

"What do you and your brother want to do, honey?"

"Do you and Dad think we could hang out in Frontierland for a while? It looks like there's a lot of fun stuff to do here," Charlie said.

"Sure, that's fine with us," his mom replied. "Where do you want to start exploring?"

"Can we go back toward Liberty Square and start at the beginning of Frontierland?"

"Absolutely. Let's go," replied Mr. Z, as he started to lead the way followed by Michael, Mom, and a smiling Charlie whose plan was working perfectly.

As they were walking, Charlie was looking to his left, toward Tom Sawyer Island. He assumed most of their search would be on the other side of the walkway, where all the buildings were. So by scanning the lighter side of the Frontierland walkway, as they quickly passed by, Charlie was able to create more time for searching the heavily detailed buildings once they reached their starting point.

"Alright, here we are, boys. This is pretty much where Liberty Square ends and Frontierland begins," their dad said.

Charlie turned and scanned the buildings in front of him. They were standing between the Liberty Tree Tavern and the Diamond Horseshoe. He pulled his phone out to confirm what they should be searching for:

> Take your younger where the sun sets, next to a post you will see.
>
> A bird's tale that's not for sale will be told by a tree.

A post. We're looking for a post. But what kind of post? Charlie wondered. A fence post? A lamp post? Maybe...a post with a bird on it? Regardless, he needed to let Michael know what they were searching for, but without his parents hearing him.

"Well, Charlie," his mother said as she was looking around. "I don't see anything here for you to really look at. But, just to the left up ahead is something you and your brother might like. The Frontierland Shootin' Arcade."

"Ooh. Where is that at, Mom?" asked Michael.

"Just right up ahead, on the left."

Charlie could see that his brother was distracted. Not hard to do to a third grader. He needed to remind him about their search. Quickly. But how was...

"Yeah, that's a great idea, Mom," said Mr. Z. "The boys and I could do a little shootin', while you go next door and check out the trading post.

"Oh. Yeah. That sounds perfect, Ed," she replied. Like most moms, Mrs. Z was always up for a little shopping.

Wait, did he just say "trading post"? Charlie asked himself. "Dad, did you just say there was a trading post?"

"Yes. Right next door to the shootin' arcade is the Frontier Trading Post. They have lots of collectible trading pins and other cool collectibles you can buy. We can stop in there, too, after we get some target practice at the shootin' arcade."

"Yeah, sure. That's sounds good to me." Charlie replied, in his best fake-excited voice. What he really was excited about was that he had found the "post." And furthermore, the Shootin' Arcade was next to the post. As good a place as any to start looking for clues, he thought.

Their mom had ventured off to the trading post and Dad was getting change for thirty dollars at the end of the arcade. Charlie seized the moment to talk with his brother about the riddle. "OK, we've reached the spot "next to a post." I need your help here in the shootin' arcade to solve the second part of the riddle: "A bird's tale that's not for sale will be told by a tree." You get it? Michael, are you listening to me, or not?"

"Yes, I get it," he replied. Michael was more interested in playing with the arcade rifle than anything else at the moment.

"OK, just so you understand," Charlie replied, as he thought: typical third grader.

"Yes, Charlie. I. Get. It. But right now I want to shoot some stuff."

"Fine," replied Charlie, who was a little frustrated with his brother's attitude. Their father was on his way back with change in hand. Their conversation had run out of time.

"Here you go, boys. Ten dollars of rootin' tootin' fun apiece." Mr. Z was really into the arcade attraction. You could tell. "OK, guys, where do you want to shoot from?"

There were a slew of rifles lined up in a row. Depending on where you shot from, your selection of key targets could be quite different. Michael, being extremely excited, had already claimed ownership of a rifle down on the left end of the arcade. Charlie and his father looked at each other and decided that's where they should shoot from as well.

Gun fire filled the air with excitement as Charlie, Michael, and their father lit up the vast array of western-themed targets like covered wagons, tombstones, a bank, and a mine. Their dad was pulling off trick shots to impress his boys. Charlie was imagining he was the town sheriff, protecting the common folk, while Michael imagined he was a gunfighter, pinned down in the hills after just robbing the bank. They were having the time of their lives.

In the midst of all their excitement, something clicked in Michael's mind as he took aim at a trio of vultures on the left side of the range. Two were on separate branches of an old, dead cemetery tree. The other sat atop an old wooden sign that had the word BOOTHILL painted in red across it. It was the sign that caught Michael's attention. Behind the word BOOTHILL were faded letters that spelled out something else. And what it spelled was the very detail that triggered Michael's mind to revert back to the riddle. The letters read: FOR SALE.

"Charlie," Michael whispered to his brother. "Hey, Charlie. I think I found something."

Charlie immediately snapped out of sheriff mode. "What did you find?"

"Look at the BOOTHILL sign."

"Yeah, I see it. And?"

"Look closer. Behind the red letters. See it?"

Charlie turned and looked at his father. He was totally oblivious to the conversation they were having. He turned his attention back to the sign, to study it closer. "Oh. Yeah. I see it. FOR SALE. Give me a minute to figure this out." He quickly reviewed the second part of the riddle on his phone.

A bird's tale that's not for sale will be told by a tree.

With the words still fresh in his head, Charlie began trying to decipher the riddle. Not for sale, but the sign says FOR SALE, he thought. But wait. The word BOOTHILL is painted over the words FOR SALE. So technically, whatever was for sale is now NOT for sale. What about the bird? The bird? Yes. There's a vulture on top of the sign. OK. So we have a bird on a sign that's not for sale. What about the tale? He continued to think in his head. The bird has a tale to tell? That's gotta be it. Right. So, if the bird has a tale...

"Pssst. Hey, Charlie. You figure it out yet?" his brother asked impatiently.

"No. Not yet. Gimme another minute or two."

"OK," Michael said, as he went back to shooting targets.

Now where was I? Oh yes. A bird's tale. If the bird has a tale, how do we get him to tell it? It's a shooting arcade. The bird has a target under him. That's easy. You shoot the target.

"I got it, Michael. Hit the target under the vulture on top of the BOOTHILL sign."

"Really? That's it? OK. Got it."

The two boys took dead aim at the target for the vulture on the sign, firing almost out of control, in anticipation of what might happen next. For about a minute the two boys tried to hit the target. Neither were successful. Worse yet, there was no more money left, and Charlie had only two shots to go. His brother was down to three. Pow, pow. Charlie was out of ammo. His brother was down to one shot. Their father had twenty-two shots left, but they could not tell him about their secret mission.

"Alright. This is your last shot, Michael. Take your time."

Michael looked at his brother, turned back to aim at the target, exhaled, and squeezed the trigger. A hit. The vulture turned its head toward the dead, twisted cemetery tree and flapped its wings several times.

But nothing else happened. "No tale?" Charlie mumbled.

His brother was looking at him, getting ready to make a sarcastic remark, when, to his and his older brother's surprise, they noticed the old dead tree had started to move.

Charlie looked again to check his dad, who looked like he still had another dollar or so to use. Yep, that would hold his attention for a little while. Then Charlie turned back to the tree. He and Michael watched in amazement as the old tree twisted and shook off layers of dead bark. At the same time, two of the branches changed into arm-like appendages. The center hole, where the owl normally sat, became a mouth. And a pair of squinty eyes developed on the two vertical center branches. The tree had taken on human-like qualities in only a matter of seconds and turned its attention to Charlie and Michael as it began to speak in a slow, deliberate manner, triggering Charlie to hit the voice-to-text button on his phone. It would be the best chance he had to capture the message.

> Hear me now, for the vulture cannot tell. A tale of his I share today, to unfold a secret spell. This story has no beginning, no middle, or an end. It has but a simple rhyme, a rhyme I dare to lend.
>
> Set way on your journey, not land or big like sea.
>
> Where brown is wet, you'll find the place, a place where he shall be.
>
> It's here a life in shaded stone, awaits in ruins of gold.
>
> Walking, stalking, gleaming eyes, his story shall be told.
>
> Truth it carries, a sacred secret, but beware the darkness bend.
>
> For beyond it lies four mighty kings, seek light to be your friend.

Just as quickly as it came to life, the tree morphed back into its normal petrified state.

"What, what in the world just happened? Did you see that, Charlie?" Michael asked, baffled beyond belief.

"Shhhhhh!" Charlie replied. "We don't want Dad to know." His eyes were fixed intensely on the phone as he finished proofing the riddle of the talking tree in his phone notes.

"Really, Charlie. Did you see what I saw? A talking tree. What...what in the world was that?"

Charlie finally pulled his eyes away from the phone, checked to make sure their dad wasn't watching, then focused his attention on Michael. "Yes, I saw it. That's what I was checking on my phone. I wanted to make sure I had the riddle typed into my phone correctly. Get it?"

"Yeah...sure, I get it. So what do we do now? Tell Dad?"

"Absolutely not. That's the last thing we can do. If Mom and Dad ever found out what we just saw, or what I saw on the Small World ride, they would think we were crazy. Probably take us to the nearest emergency room to be checked out. No, we can never tell them about what we're doing. Understand? Never," Charlie whispered intently.

"Yeah, I understand," Michael replied, with a deep exhale.

"You boys all done down there?"

"Yeah, Dad, we used up all our ammo," Charlie replied with a big smile—doing his best to cover up what had just happened.

The boys and their father went and found Mrs. Z in the trading post, then headed down to the Pecos Bill Cafe to grab something cool to drink. Dad and the boys had worked up quite a thirst at the shootin' arcade.

Charlie and his family found a nice corner table to sit at while enjoying their beverages. Without hesitation, Charlie pulled out his phone and held it so only he and his brother could read the rhyme. Their parents thought nothing of it, as the boys were always sharing games, videos, and such on their electronic devices. Immediately, Charlie realized the first two sentences described "where" they had to go. So he focused his attention on that.

> Set way on your journey, not land or big like sea.
>
> Where brown is wet, you'll find the place, a place where he shall be.

So, based on the first two encounters, we should be looking for an attraction, Charlie thought. And it's not a ride that simulates land, which means it either has to be in the air or in the water. It does say "not big like sea," but there are many different bodies of water besides seas. So it could still possibly be a water vehicle? I guess? Charlie continued to think fast in his own head. There were plenty of attractions that went in the air at the Magic Kingdom, but what would any of them have to do with something that is brown and wet? So, what could be brown and wet? Lots of things. But why the sea reference? Could it possibly be a body of water that is smaller than a sea? And brown? Charlie continued to review the riddle in his mind.

"I think you guys are really gonna enjoy the Jungle Cruise," their father said. "You'll get to see and hear all kinds of cool animals hanging out in the funky brown river water, see head hunters, and best of all, the cast member skipper of the boat tells jokes during the ride. And usually they are hilarious. Right, honey?"

"Oh, yes. You boys are going to love it," she replied. Just don't drink the water.

Charlie's parents and Michael broke into laughter, as they enjoyed their cold beverages.

Charlie was enjoying a good laugh as well. "Ha. Ha. Ha. That's a good one, Mom," he said. "Yeah, don't drink the water. Too funny." Then it clicked. Charlie had the answer he'd been looking for. And the answer came from what his dad had just said. "Dad, did you say there was brown river water on the Jungle Cruise?"

"Yeah. Funky, icky brown river water. Like there would be in a real jungle river. Why do you ask? You're not worried about the water, are you?"

"Oh, no. No. Not at all, Dad. I was just curious, that's all."

"Oh, OK. Just want to make sure you're cool with it." Charlie's dad turned his attention back to his wife as they continued telling Michael about all the fun stuff they had planned for the week.

Charlie, on the other hand, went back to thinking, working hard to solve the latest riddle. That's it. The brown water of the Jungle Cruise. That's the ride we need to go on. And we are. Perfecto. Charlie's eyes lit up, and a big smile came over his face as he knew he had just solved the first part of the riddle.

"Wow, Charlie, you look pretty pumped up. You ready to go cruisin' or what?" his dad asked.

"You bet, Dad," he replied enthusiastically, covering up what really was going on in his head. As their family walked to the Jungle Cruise, Charlie filled Michael in on his latest discovery, keeping his younger brother focused on the task at hand.

During their wait in the long FastPass queue line, Charlie and his brother had plenty of time to decipher most of what remained to be solved of the riddle the tree at the shootin' arcade had told them. They came to the conclusion that the messenger of the next riddle would be located in a shaded area of ruins, with lots of stones and treasure. They will have shiny eyes and like to stalk their prey. Therefore, it won't be an elephant, monkey, or zebra. But, what kind of animal would it be? That was the question they still were trying to answer. And that is why the boys decided they would have to figure out the rest of the riddle during their cruise.

Before long, Charlie and his family boarded the boat. The cruise skipper ran through her welcome aboard spiel, everyone shared a laugh or two, then their journey began—down the river and into the jungle. The next six to seven minutes were a blur of lush jungle foliage, filled with humorous animals, head hunters, and even the back side of water—a favorite of Mr. Z's. But still, there had been no sign of a shaded area where a shiny-eyed messenger may dwell.

The ride had to be almost finished, Charlie thought, while turning to whisper to his brother. "If the messenger does not reveal himself soon, we'll have to take another look at the riddle and try again." But then, just around the corner, past the crocodiles, Charlie spotted something very promising. It appeared to be some sort of dilapidated temple that was built over the river. And it looked like they were going to go right through it. This has to be it, Charlie thought, as he nudged his brother and whispered into his ear. "This it it. Be ready."

The entrance to the temple ruins looked very dark, so Charlie decided to use the audio record feature on his phone to capture any possible riddles within. The boat moved slowly into the temple, and the air became still as they coasted quietly into the darkness. And there, immediately to their left, was a vicious Bengal tiger with gleaming yellow eyes. Everything around the boys suddenly slowed down and became blurry. Voices became muffled. It felt like they had just entered some form of magical time warp or alternate dimension. Charlie and Michael turned their attention to the tiger. His yellow eyes changed to green and grew even brighter. His furry coat glowed bright orange. He turned to face the boys, then began to speak in a deep, hearty voice, as Charlie hit record and pointed his phone toward the mighty beast.

Once beyond the ruins you'll seek, a man in darkness before the peak.

He'll shine and shimmer amongst the crowd, where the center shall be very loud.

Approach him not, for he'll seek you out.

Be patient to learn a secret, to those who live in doubt.

Now continue your magical journey, through ruins and darkness bends.

But take caution beyond my words, for four are not your friends.

The tiger's eyes changed back to yellow and his coat dulled as he resumed his original pose. Immediately, everything around the boys switched back to normal. Nobody besides Charlie and Michael were aware of what had just happened. The boat continued to bank right, and as it did, a very faint sound began to grow.

"What is that noise?" Michael asked his brother quietly. "Do you hear it?"

"Yeah. I hear it. And it doesn't sound very inviting," Charlie replied.

As the boat completed its turn around the dark bend, the source of the sound was revealed. Four giant king cobras, all in attack position.

"These...these are the four kings the tree spoke of," Michael whispered frantically to his brother, while grabbing him by the arm.

In the center of the cobras sat a giant golden statue. And scattered throughout the area lay various smaller golden treasures, all protected by the mighty snakes. But it seemed as though there was obviously something else they were interested in. Something Charlie and his brother had in their procession. Instantaneously, all the people around the boys became muffled and blurry again, as the boat continued on, but at a much slower pace. Without warning, one of the snakes lunged forward toward the boat. With its eyes glowing red and tongue wildly flapping, the snake's mouth opened wide, exposing a pair of venomous fangs—as if it were going to strike. But instead, evil reptile began to speak.

"What sssssss did the tiger tell you sssssss?" the snake asked.

One of the other snakes lunged forward as well, twisting and turning around one of the boat's canopy posts until its intimidating face, also with glowing red eyes, was only inches away from Charlie's.

"Yesssssss, what did the tiger say to you, boy?"

Charlie was petrified. Too scared to move. Too scared to take his eyes off the snake right before his face. He tried to answer, but all that came out was stuttering nonsense. "I I, I d, dddd, don't..."

"C'mon boy, sssssspit it out ssssss." The snake was growing impatient, as though he had very little time to work with.

Just as Charlie gathered up the courage to answer, the snake in front of his face suddenly retreated. Or at least that was Charlie's initial thought. He looked to his left to see the snake flying through the air toward, and eventually hitting, the temple wall. His brother's arm was extended outward in the direction of the discombobulated snake. Michael, without hesitation, had leaped forward, grabbed the snake in front of his brother by the tail, and flung it as hard as he could with one swift athletic move, totally catching the slithering reptile off guard. In response to his actions, the other snake wrapped around one of the poles and made a quick lunge toward Charlie, with fangs ready to strike. Charlie, now recovered from his petrified state, ducked quickly as the lunging snake went right over his head, out of the boat, and into the water. The frustrated cobra quickly scurried to dry ground along the same side of the temple wall as the snake Michael had flung.

Meanwhile, the other two snakes had caught up to the boat as it continued to move slowly through the dark temple ruins. All four king cobras were now following the boat along the right side, hissing and slithering across the vine-filled temple wall ledge. Determined to not let the boys make it out of the temple, they eagerly looked for another opportunity to board the boat and finish what they had started.

"Why is this boat moving so slowly?" Charlie yelled to his brother. During the entire time their boat had been under attack by the snakes, everything else around them, including the boat and the people, had been moving in slow motion. Everyone's speech, their laughs, and even their movements, were slow. Worst of all, they were totally unaware of what was happening to Charlie and his brother.

"I don't know, Charlie!" Michael yelled back. "But watch out behind you!"

All four snakes had managed to climb high up on the vine-covered walls, which allowed them to drop down onto the boat, with each cobra wrapping around a corner post. The snakes now had the boys surrounded.

"You too, Michael! There are two behind you as well!

The snakes moved in to attack. Lunging for the boys, they tried to wrap around any part of Charlie and Michael's bodies they could.

In defense, the boys ran, dove, leaped, or anything else they could to stay away from the cobras, anything to avoid those hypnotic red eyes. But the boat was moving too slowly. Where was the light the talking tree had mentioned? The snakes had taken the advantage, and were now in position to get the answer they demanded. Charlie and Michael dropped to the deck, tired, defenseless, and out of breath.

"You fought well, young boysssssss. But now, you will give ussssss the answer we sssssseek." The red eyes of the snake in front of Charlie began to glow brighter and spin, as they pierced the young boy's mind.

Charlie caught something out of the corner of his eye. Something bright, with a golden glow had interrupted the snake's hypnotic stare. Ahead on the left were several gold statues, shining magnificently. In fact, too much for such a dark place. That could mean only one thing, Charlie thought. There had to be a light source. He signaled his brother to look toward the statues. Michael saw it, too. This was it. The time had come to rid themselves of the snake kings.

As the boat passed the final golden statue and headed toward the light, Charlie and Michael did everything they could to avoid eye contact with the snakes, while trying to muster up enough strength to give the evil cobras one final battle for control of the boat—a boat now exiting the temple and re-entering into daylight.

As the sun's warm evening rays flooded the boat, the four snakes began to smoke and hiss in pain. Unlike the boys, the light was not their friend. And as quickly as they had come, the four cobras fled back to the darkness of the temple ruins. The boys, exhausted and happy that the sun had saved them from one last battle with the snakes, looked at each other and celebrated a silent victory.

Magically, everyone aboard the boat returned to normal, and the boat regained routine speed as it moved ahead into the Indian elephant wading pool. All was clear now, as if nothing had ever happened, though the boys knew better. As the boat motored onward, Charlie and Michael sat quietly, tired and wondering, staring at each other through different eyes than the ones they had seen through before their courageous battle in the temple ruins. It was now clear to both young men that this was not going to be a typical trip to the most magical place on earth.

Chapter Four

The evening was settling in as the Florida sun began sinking toward the western horizon. The temperature had reached a comfortable level with less humidity, resulting in an increase of people in the park. And though it was more crowded, Charlie and his family felt much more relaxed, now that the hottest part of the day had passed. For the last forty-five minutes or so, they had been slowly working their way toward the Crystal Palace, while stopping in some of the Adventureland shops and touring the Swiss Family Treehouse. One could not ask for a more perfect evening.

"Well, everyone, it's almost time to check in for our dinner reservation. What do ya say we start heading over that way?"

"Sure thing, Ed," replied his wife. Surprisingly enough, when she turned to address the boys and get them moving, they had already come to attention and were ready to move on. Food was a great motivator, especially when it came to two hungry boys, who in the past hour had burned up an incredible amount of calories battling four relentless king cobra snakes. Of course, their parents were totally unaware of what had happened. And that's as it should be. At least that was how Charlie felt. And he was willing to do anything necessary to keep his kid brother Michael from blabbing to their parents. Anything.

Dinner at the Crystal Palace was set up like a feast fit for kings. Two L-shaped lines met at the center of the buffet, filled with almost every kind of meat imaginable, potatoes, vegetables, salad fixings, warm breads, pastas, and more. Plus, there was a dessert island in the center of it all, featuring apple cobbler, key lime pie, cookies, brownies, cake, and a soft-serve ice cream machine to boot. The boys could hardly contain themselves. Both had hearty appetites, and having just gone through a hard physical battle with four crazy snakes had elevated their appetites to another level of hungry. They called it the "see-food diet." If they saw it, they were gonna eat it.

In a matter of minutes, Charlie and Michael had each collected mass quantities of food for consumption and back at the table had begun to put on an eating display like only two very hungry boys can. By the time their parents had gathered their food and sat down to eat, Charlie and his brother had cleaned their plates. Not a crumb was left. "Looks like it's time for dessert Michael," Charlie hinted to his brother, hoping to get a moment away from their parents to discuss their next task. At first, Michael appeared a little dazed. Tired from the temple battle and now with a full belly, he was just about ready to pass out from exhaustion. Getting up before the crack of dawn, flying down from Michigan, solving riddles, riding attractions, and battling four large snakes was quite a tall order for a single day. Charlie knew it had to be hard on his younger brother, because he was feeling it as well. But they had come too far to give up now, and big brother was going to make sure they carried on. One way or another. "Michael. Did you hear me? Looks like it's time for dessert. Why don't we go check out the ice cream machine." Charlie nodded toward the desert bar as he gave his brother a look of urgency.

"Uh, OK," Michael replied with a groggy voice. His body looked ready to crash at any moment, and his eyes were at half mast. Charlie needed to work quickly.

"You look like you could use a sugar boost, dude. C'mon, let's go load up on some of those awesome desserts." He grabbed his brother by the arm to help him get up, then guided him toward the desert bar.

"Charlie, I'm sooooo tired. I need to sleeeep," Michael groaned, as he walked with drooped shoulders and floppy noodle-like arms.

"Hang on, buddy. I need your help for just a little longer, alright?"

"OK. I'll try to stay awake."

"Here, take this bowl and fill it with some ice cream. Better yet, I'll do it for you. And grab one of those chocolate brownies over there. Those look good, don't ya think?"

"Yeah, sure. Delicious."

"Start eating your ice cream, while I get myself a little dessert. We need to figure out the tiger's riddle, and I think I found a way for us to talk about our secret mission, even if Mom and Dad are with us."

"Yeah, what's that?" Michael replied,a little more alert now, at least for the moment. The sugar was working.

As Charlie loaded up his plate with goodies, he continued to speak with his brother. "You have your phone with you, right?"

"Yep, got it in my pocket."

"Great, so we can text each other back and forth to figure things out instead of having to talk all the time. Sound good? Mom and Dad will just think we're playing games or something. Like we usually do."

"I guess that will work."

"Of course it will, Michael. Just make sure your phone is set to vibrate and we'll be all set. Got it?"

"Roger that, Charlie-o."

"So I'm texting you what the tiger said now. Not the whole thing, but just the part of the riddle we need to work on first," Charlie said while hitting send on his phone.

> Once beyond the ruins you'll seek, a man in darkness before the peak.
>
> He'll shine and shimmer amongst the crowd, where the center shall be very loud.
>
> Approach him not, for he'll seek you out.
>
> Be patient to learn a secret, to those who live in doubt.

"To me it sounds like we need to be looking for a man, outside where there are a lot of people, after it gets dark out. And the guy we're looking for will be wearing something very bright and shiny. What do you think, Michael?"

Michael checked his phone. "That's sort of what it sounds like to me, Charlie, but for the shiny part…I think the riddle might mean that the man will shine brightly. Sort of like the sun?"

"Oh, yes, that does make more sense, especially since it will be dark out. I think you're right, Michael. Good thinking. We better get back to the table before Mom and Dad come looking for us. We'll figure out the rest after dinner."

Charlie and his brother headed back to the table and enjoyed their desserts as their parents discussed the after-dinner game plan. It sounded like there was a big fireworks show that took place near the castle shortly after it got dark, and that his dad wanted to find a place for them to watch it from. As his parents continued to talk, Charlie checked the riddle he had converted from audio into a written note, for quick reference. His mind was racing as he tried to pick apart the clues spoken by the tiger. He texted his brother:

Peak, the peak of what?

"We need to make sure wherever we watch the fireworks from, that we have a good, clear view. The boys really need to be able to see everything well. Especially since it's their first time seeing the Magic Kingdom's fireworks show. Wouldn't you agree, honey? I mean, it is the grand finale of the entire day, right?" Mr. Z stated in bold fashion.

Michael replied to Charlie's text:

Grand finale? Is that like a peak?

"Oh, absolutely, Ed. We have to make sure they can see everything, including the castle."

"Then we'll probably need to hang out around the Partners statue after dinner, since that is basically right in the middle of everything. Don't you agree?"

Charlie shot his brother a text back:

YES... U R right.

"Certainly. That would be perfect honey," Mr. Z's wife replied.

Charlie looked at his brother with a smile and sent Michael another text:

The middle is like a center. Good place to start.

Make sure m & d take us there.

"That sounds good to me, Dad. Don't you think so, Michael?" Charlie blurted out, while winking at his brother to agree.

Michael played along. "Sure. Yeah, that sounds great."

"OK, then. After dinner we'll head for the hub and hang out until fireworks start," Mr. Z proclaimed.

Charlie shot his dad a smile, and his brother a nod, before getting back to his dessert. It was going to be a great night.

Dusk was upon the kingdom as the Zastawits family made their way to and around the hub. The castle lights had come on, highlighting its magnificent details with subtle changes in hue from purple to blue, then green, golden yellow, burnt orange, and back to purple again. It was truly a sight to behold. The photos Charlie and his a brother had looked at online didn't do it justice. It was amazing, it was spectacular, it was almost too hard to explain—unless you were actually there to see it. They both stood in awe, as the music of the park surrounded their senses. Their parents watched and enjoyed the expressions on the boys' faces while enjoying the moment as well.

Soon the sun had all but disappeared beyond the horizon. Night had settled in. That's when it suddenly dawned on Charlie—he and his brother were supposed to be looking for a man in bright clothing. He snapped out of his obsession with the castle and elbowed his brother, who looked at him with a blank stare until Charlie pointed to his phone and gave Michael a look of urgency, while sending him a message:

Need to find bright man now.

Michael read it, then quickly shook his head, before frantically beginning to scan the hub area crowd with Charlie for a bright, shiny man.

It wouldn't be long before the show started—they needed to work quickly. The boys scanned left toward Adventureland. Nothing. Then they looked right, toward Tomorrowland. No luck. What about by the statue of Walt and Mickey? Nothing. And the stage area in front of the castle? Nothing there, either. Time was running short, as the anxiety inside of Charlie began to elevate. Where could he be? Charlie thought, as he and his brother continued to look in all directions. He began to lose hope, wondering if they were in the right place. Then, suddenly, like a bolt of lightning, it struck him. An elbow, that is. From his brother. Right to the rib cage.

"Ow! What did you do that for?" Charlie shouted in response to his brother's actions.

This immediately got his parents' attention.

"Michael, what did you do to your brother?" his mom asked in her serious parenting voice.

"Nothing, Mom. It was an accident," he said, while trying to get his big brother's attention using funny facial expressions.

"An accident, eh?" his mom replied.

Finally, Michael got his brother to catch on to what he was trying to do.

"It's no big deal, Mom. Michael was just spinning around and bumped into me. That's all," Charlie told his mother, in order to protect his brother from any possible scolding.

"Is this true, Michael?"

"Yeah, Mom, nothing happened. It was an accident."

"Alright, then. Just be more careful from now on."

"OK, Mom."

Now that the emotional storm had passed, Michael finished what he originally intended to do in the first place: get Charlie to look behind them, toward Main Street, U.S.A. Putting his hands on Charlie's shoulders, he spun his big brother around to show him what he had discovered. Whispering quietly in Charlie's ear he said, "Look down the left side of the street."

Charlie scanned the left side, past the mom who was sharing an ice cream cone with her three-year-old son, past a family of eight who were all wearing yellow shirts that read "Our first visit." Farther and farther down the left side of the road, Charlie's eyes continued to search through the sea of spectators, all waiting for the fireworks to begin.

"I don't see anything, Michael."

"Keep looking. Just a little farther. In front of the bakery. You see him?"

"The bakery, the bakery? Oh. The bakery. Yes. Yes, I see him now."

"Shh! Not too loud, Charlie. Mom and Dad might hear you."

Charlie and Michael had spotted a man, an older gentleman, average in stature, wearing oversized glasses covered with LED lights. His vertically striped vest was lined with alternating colored lights which changed in hue from one minute to the next. The pants he wore flashed in patterns of purple and blue. Atop his head sat a tall hat with Mickey ears, also covered with flashing lights of various colors. And the cart he was pushing along the left side of the street was filled with a large assortment of light-filled toys, hats, and balloons—all of which shown brightly against the shadow-covered crowd. It appeared he was working his way toward the hub, as if he knew right where the boys were, without even looking.

"We're supposed to wait, right?" Michael asked.

"Yep. That's what the tiger said. So that's what we'll do."

The boys looked back to make sure their parents were still nearby. It was getting pretty dark out, making it difficult to tell one person from the next in the crowded hub.

"You boys alright?" their mom asked.

"Yeah, Mom, we're fine," Charlie replied.

"OK, just make sure you stay near us."

"Don't worry. We're not going anywhere. Right, Michael?"

Michael nodded, as the two of them turned their attention back to the brightly lit man making his way closer and closer to the hub. Finally, the man covered in lights reached a spot near the west side of the hub, where he stopped and set up his cart. He was only about ten feet from where the boys stood watching. They both looked at each other, wondering what to do next, hesitant to look at the stranger they had code named Mr. Bright.

Mr. Bright pulled some of the light spin toys off the cart and began to play with them as he smiled. A voice came over the speaker system and announced that the fireworks show would be starting in just a few minutes. They were short on time. Charlie was thinking they might have to approach the well-lit man, even though they were told not to. He gathered up the courage, then looked over at the stranger. The older man was still smiling as he handed out brightly lit items to paying customers who were anxious to make their children happy. While counting out change to a heavy-set man who had just purchased a Buzz light toy, Mr. Bright glanced over at the boys and said with a kind smile, "I'll be with you in just a second." The boys curiously looked at each other, then back at the man they were about to meet.

"So what can I help you with tonight, gentlemen? A lighted sword? Perhaps a couple of luminary spinners?"

"Uh, I'm not, I mean, we're not sure," Charlie responded, not knowing if they were supposed to give the man some sort of secret code-like answer.

The brightly lit cart had caught their father's eye, and their conversation had peaked his interest. "What do you boys think? Those spinners look pretty cool, eh? If I were your age, I'd definitely be into those," Mr. Z said. His inner child was shining through.

"Well, sir, you have a very sharp eye. Those are our biggest seller, night after night. Very popular among the kids," the shiny stranger replied.

"Yeah, they sure are cool. You boys want one?"

"Sure, Dad, that would be awesome," Michael said, being the third grader he was.

On the other hand, Charlie was a little hesitant, still trying to make sense of the situation.

"What about you, Charlie, you want a spinner, too?" his dad asked.

Charlie was still finding it a difficult question to answer. And time was running out; the show was about to start.

"Well, if the spinner isn't your thing, I do have a very special item in the bottom drawer below," said Mr. Bright with a subtle grin. "Something I've been saving for a situation just like this. Might be just what a smart young man like yourself would be looking for." The man reached down, slowly opened the bottom drawer, and pulled out what appeared to be some sort of magnifying glass wrapped in a purple velvet cloth. It had a very ornate handle which looked like two inverted, silver sea horses with emerald green eyes. Their tails were elongated and wrapped around the glass, forming a frame. Connecting the glass to the frame were two spindles, one at the top and one at the bottom. This allowed the glass to spin horizontally. Charlie had never seen anything like it before. There was a button between the sea horses on the handle. When the old man pushed the button, the glass spun rapidly, making it appear as if it weren't even there. Like it had disappeared. As the glass spun, a lime green light glowed brightly around its perimeter.

"That looks really neat. What do you call it?" asked Charlie.

"We call it Merlin's magic looking glass."

"Wow, that's an amazing toy," said Mr. Z.

"Oh, yes, it's very unique. Very unique indeed. In fact, this is the first one we've ever given away."

"Well, we have to pay you for it, right?" asked Charlie's father.

"Actually, you don't. It's a gift from me to your son."

"But I don't understand," his father said.

The man looked down at Charlie with a soft smile. "Talking with your son, I could tell he was someone who would appreciate a gift such as this. Someone who truly believes in the magic we create here in the parks. We'd be honored to have him except this gift."

Mr. Z stood speechless, as he stood looking at Charlie.

"So, what is your name, young man?"

"It's Charlie, sir."

"Well, Charlie, on behalf of everyone here at the most magical place on earth, I present to you a token of our appreciation." The man held the toy with open hands and offered it to Charlie, who gladly accepted with a smile so big it could light up the night sky.

"Thank you," Charlie said, as he held the toy up, admiring its detail.

"Yes, thank you very much, sir," I'm sure Charlie will treasure it for quite some time. We really appreciate your generosity," said Mr. Z.

"It has been my pleasure. I hope you and your family enjoy your stay with us."

"Yes, I'm sure we most definitely will. Thank you again."

On that note, Charlie, his father, and his brother turned and started to walk back to where their mother was standing. As they were walking, Mr. Bright called out to Charlie.

"Oh, Charlie. I forgot. There's one more thing I need to tell you about your toy. That is, if your parents don't mind?"

"Dad?" Charlie said to his father.

"Sure. Yeah, go ahead, Charlie. We're only a few feet away."

Charlie walked back over to see what the kind man had to say.

"So I assume by now you realize this is no ordinary toy, right, Charlie? Especially after all that you've been through today."

"All that I've been through?" Charlie asked.

"With the sun, the tree, the tiger, and those pesky snakes?"

Charlie looked at the man and said, "So you do know. You're the person my brother and I were supposed to seek out."

"Oh. Right-right-right. Absolutely. I guess you could say I'm a friend of sorts who has come to help. And that's *all* I can tell you about myself at this time. Now, about the magic looking glass I gave you. It has...well, it has special powers."

"It does?"

"Shh. We have to be very quiet. Yes, it has magical powers. Now listen carefully, we haven't much time. Near the end of the fireworks show, you need to make sure and take a close look at the water, over near Sleepy Hollow Refreshments." Mr. Bright hinted with his eyes, to the boy, which direction the building was located.

Following the old man's eyes, Charlie began turning his head toward the refreshment building.

"Stop," the senior cast member said, in a frantic quiet tone of voice. "Keep looking at me. Eyes on me, and me only. We can't afford to give anything away. Make sure to use your new toy when you look at the water. And you must press the button for it to work. OK?" He gave Charlie a wink.

"How will I know when the show is almost over?"

The narrator will let you know when it's time for the finale. That's when you'll want to go look at the water."

"What am I looking for?"

"I can't tell you right now. Others may be watching or listening. You'll know when you see it. Oh, and another thing. And this is very important. Make sure nobody is watching you when you do it. Understand?"

Charlie answered quietly. "Yes, I understand."

"And after you've used your toy, Charlie, what you discover can be viewed again through the looking glass just by pressing the button on the handle. Got it?"

"Yep, I got it."

"Very good. Now, I have to exit the hub before the show starts. Part of cast member rules, you know. Management doesn't want anything distracting from the show. So, you're feeling OK about this, right, Charlie?"

"Yeah, sure. I guess?"

"Alright, then, with any luck, I'll see you soon."

The brightly lit cast member turned and walked quickly toward an employee exit behind the buildings on the west side of Main Street. At the same time, Charlie went back to join his family, as a voice came over the air. The street lights dimmed, and all heads turned toward the castle. The fireworks show was about to begin.

The brightly lit old man's instincts had been right. Someone had been close by. A couple of spies up to no good had been lurking just beyond the shadows of the west gazebo. They had been looking through the crowded area in front of the castle and down Main Street, searching for the messenger—a messenger who had been selected to make contact with someone outside the secret circle of Patrons. The only problem was, the spies had no idea who the messenger was. They had only been instructed to look for people acting in an unusual manner, or who stuck out in a crowd.

"Do you see anything, Grim?"

"No. Nothing. Nothing at all. This is like trying to find a needle in a haystack, if you ask me."

Both men were dressed to blend in with the crowd—colorful polo shirts, khaki shorts, and sandals. Their hair was neatly trimmed and their faces were clean shaven. The perfect disguise for any spy in Disney World. Only two details may have given them away. The first was their unusually designed wrist bands. Unlike the MagicBands many of the other people were wearing, Grim and his partner Duke were wearing large brushed steel bands with thick, circular faces that displayed large blue LED codes that had nothing to do with the time of day and everything to do with map coordinates. But for where?

The second detail that may have given them away was much more obvious. As the two men were searching around the hub for the messenger, they would disappear in one spot then reappear in another. But they did it with such precision and timing that none of the guests even noticed. It was as though they knew exactly where the disappearing and reappearing points were. They would disappear into a hidden nook by Casey's Corner, then reappear on the opposite side of Main Street near the Plaza Restaurant. Vanish on the front porch of the Crystal Palace, then pop in on the right rear corner of the castle stage. But their last transportation put them only thirty feet away from where Charlie and the old man had been talking. Their re-entry point was right next to the west gazebo.

"You see anything yet, Duke? Our window of opportunity is about ready to close. The captain said the meeting between the messenger and outsider would most likely take place just before the fireworks show. So if we can't find them in the next ten minutes, we'll be out of luck."

"Yeah and worse than that, we'll have to go back without any intel for the captain. You know how much fun that will be."

"Right. We better get back to looking."

Just then, Duke spotted and pointed at something he thought was suspicious. "Speaking of which, what do you make of the guy right over there dressed up like a firefly, Grim? See, over there near the water. Talking to a kid."

"Nah, I don't think so. No way a Patron would be dressed up like that. I mean, look at him. C'mon. And as far as the kid goes, he's just buying a light toy, like every other kid his age here in the park is doing. No, believe me, there's nothing going on between those two that we need to worry ourselves with."

"Yeah, you're probably right, Grimsly. Let's go look elsewhere, before we run outta time."

Grim agreed and the two stepped back through the gazebo, disappearing once again to somewhere else. Little did Mr. Bright and Charlie realize, the old man's mastery of disguise as a cast member selling light toys had saved them from a night of certain peril.

The nighttime grand finale show was nothing short of breathtaking. The skies filled with fireworks, the castle lighting changed in hue to fit the moods of the show and was blanketed at times with amazing visual effects. The air was filled with the combinations of uplifting music and narration, followed by responses from the crowd. Charlie and his family were captured by the moment which surrounded them. It was then that the narrator hinted of a finale, the cue for Charlie to go look at the water in front of Sleepy Hollow Refreshments. Fortunately, it was only fifty feet from where they were standing.

Charlie looked at his parents, who were currently hypnotized by the show, as was his brother. It was the perfect moment to slip away toward the water without them noticing. He slowly inched himself backwards, away from his family. Then he turned and took about fifteen quick steps to the water's edge. Nobody else was near the water, as most of the crowd had gathered toward the center of the hub for the show. Perfect, Charlie thought, as he pulled out the magic looking glass and pushed the button. The frame glowed brilliant green as he began to scan the water. For the first ten or fifteen seconds, nothing appeared through the looking glass, which made Charlie start to worry. He needed to get back to where his parents stood before they realized he was missing and started to freak out. Luckily, he could still see them from where he stood, and it appeared they still had no clue he was gone. He turned his attention back to the water, and something amazing happened. As he was staring through the looking glass, his eye picked up a scribbled purple letter along the right edge of the glowing perimeter. Quickly, he moved the looking glass to the right to reveal the rest of the letters, which formed the word "At." As the fireworks changed, so did the words, which matched the colors in the sky. The next word was "midnight," followed by "enter," then "the." Eventually, a full sentence had formed, which Charlie memorized.

> At midnight enter the Chapeau near the square to discover a friend's advice.

After the final word disappeared, the magic looking glass immediately stopped spinning as the lens snapped back into place. Charlie stuffed it back in his pocket and rejoined his family, who were unaware that anything had happened. As the show came to a conclusion, Charlie looked up to meet his mother's kind eyes as he typed the message he had just read through the magic looking glass into his phone.

As the crowd dispersed, Charlie's mom announced that she was taking Michael back to the resort for bedtime. It was easy to see why; just looking at his brother, Charlie could tell the sugar from dinner had worn off. Michael could barely keep his eyes open.

"OK, honey, we'll see you and Michael later. Charlie and I are gonna go hit some attractions, since the park is open late tonight. Do a little father-and-son bonding while you and sleepy eyes get some rest. Sound good to you, Charlie?"

"Oh, yes. That sounds great, Dad." Charlie couldn't have been happier.

"Alright, you two have fun. Michael and I will see you later. C'mom baby, let's go so you can sleep. We have a long week of fun and excitement ahead of us."

Michael showed his approval with one tired nod.

As they turned and started to leave, Charlie sent his brother a text:

> Discovered something during show. More to find out tonight.
>
> Talk tomorrow. Night night.

"Well, Charlie, what do you want to do first? We've got almost three hours of fun ahead of us."

"I don't know, Dad. Could we go check out Pirates?"

"Aye, aye, captain. If it's adventure you seek, then adventure ye shall have."

Charlie and his father headed toward Adventureland, full of energy and ready to begin a late night of fun.

It had been a fun-filled evening of thrills and excitement for Charlie and his father. Two mountainous adventures, a close encounter with a raucous lot of pirates, a run-in with nine hundred and ninety-nine ghosts, and to top it off, a tasty treat at Aloha Isle. Midnight was fast approaching as Charlie and his father sat on a bench, enjoying their treats while discussing all the magical fun they had just experienced.

"Well, that was cool, don't you think, Charlie?"

"You bet, Dad. That was great. Pirates of the Caribbean and the Haunted Mansion were so much cooler than I expected. We definitely gotta make sure to go on those again with Michael and Mom. And the Big Thunder Mountain ride was awesome. I know you promised Michael he would get a chance to ride it while we're here. We definitely need to make sure that happens. I think he'll go crazy over that attraction, don't you?"

"Yes, you're right. I did promise him, didn't I. Don't let me forget, OK?"

"Don't worry, Dad, I won't."

"Looks like we should start heading toward Main Street and Town Square. It's eleven forty. That still gives us time to check out some of the stores on our way out. Sound good?"

His dad's words threw Charlie into a panic. Amidst all the fun he and his father had been having, Charlie had uncharacteristically lost track of the time, not realizing midnight was so near. Immediately he looked on the park map to locate the Chapeau. Please be on Main Street, he frantically thought to himself. His eyes quickly scanned the map. Where are you, where are you. His mind was racing. Ah. There you are. It was off to the side of Town Square, just as the magic looking glass had told him. Which meant it was on their way out of the park. Now he just needed an excuse to visit the Chapeau. The two of them had already begun their journey toward Main Street. Charlie continued to think fast as they walked.

"Hey dad, what is the Chapeau?"

"Oh, that's a good one, Charlie. They have a great selection of head gear. Hats, caps, head bands, and best of all, lots of ears to choose from. If you want something for your head, that's the place in the Magic Kingdom to go."

"Do you think we could look there first, Dad? I'd really like to check out the ears."

"That's my boy. Looking for a classic set of ears. Nothing says Disney like a set of ears. Sounds good to me. I know exactly where that's at. We can start there and work our way around Main Street."

"OK."

Charlie kept up with his father's pace as the two of them marched their way down Main Street, past the bakery, past the crystal shop, then a left at the candy store and into the Chapeau at eleven fifty four. Six minutes to spare.

"Wow, we made good time, Dad. You really do know your way around here."

"I've had plenty of practice, son. I love this place. In fact, I dream of this place. Know it like the back of my hand. There's nowhere else like it."

For a brief second, Charlie just looked up and admired his dad, who was taking in the details of the shop as he spoke to his son. At that very moment, he knew exactly why he loved Disney so much. He was just like his father. The dreams, the passion, the love for this magical place. And not only the physical place, but a place that can only be found within your heart.

"OK, Charlie, go ahead. Look around. Explore. Seek out that perfect set of ears. You know, the ones you've been dreaming about."

Charlie looked at his father, smiled, then turned and began his search. While browsing the shelves of the store, he heard the twelve chimes of a clock on the wall. It was midnight. Someone was to meet him in the store. At least that's what he thought. As he continued to look at all the hats and ears, he kept wondering when his special friend was going to show up. Slowly he made his way up into a smaller room to the right of the main entrance. While entering the room, he scanned the wall straight ahead. Nothing there he wanted. Then he panned to the left, just to the right of the checkout counter, where Charlie spotted a set of shelves full of classic ears, which he liked a lot. But, he continued to search. Looking for something special. Something unique.

As he peered up and beyond the checkout counter, he noticed a shelf which held upon it a small selection of deluxe-styled ears. There were six shelves. Each held three sets of ears. Eighteen sets of ears in all. The top shelf was well lit, but as his eyes worked their way down toward the bottom, the shelves and the items on them became more shaded, making them harder to see. The ears on this particular set of shelves seemed different compared to those throughout the rest of the store. The materials used to make them were of better quality, and the attention to detail was set to a higher standard. This was it, exactly what he had been looking for.

He politely asked one of the cast members if he could look at a set of ears, pointing to the center one on the top shelf. The cast member obliged and handed Charlie the ears for a closer look. The caps center felt like smooth velvet. The ears were made of a softer, rubber-like material with a dull finish. The stitching was a thicker quality black thread, which would hold up through the years. And the logo in the center of the cap was a finely aged patch that had been sewn on, giving the ears a greater sense of quality. On the back, the word "Sample" had been sewn on using a brilliant, brushed-gold type of thread, as an example of how someone's name would appear if desired.

"A very nice choice for such a young man. You must really be a huge Disney fan like me," the cast member said as she admired watching how much Charlie enjoyed looking at the ears.

A look of pure admiration painted his face as Charlie remained speechless. He looked up with a smile in response to the friendly cast member's comment. His father curiously walked up to see what his son had discovered.

"What do we have here? It's looks like you may have found something you like, eh, Charlie?"

"I'd say he most certainly has, wouldn't you, Charlie?" the cast member replied, as she played along with Mr. Z.

In response to both, Charlie nodded yes, while continuing to study his big discovery.

"So how much does a set of ears like this cost?" his father asked.

"Our special deluxe-styled ears run about fifty dollars. I know it's quite a bit more than our standard ears, but these are special, and the quality is well beyond our standard ears. Most of our guests buy them to collect and display, not wear."

"Oh, I see. So, Charlie, if you're looking for a set of ears to wear, you'd probably be better off getting a set of regular ones. But, it's totally up to you."

Charlie stood in thought, weighing his options, while holding the deluxe-styled ears.

"How long are you visiting?" the cast member asked Mr. Z.

"Seven wonderful days, and this was only day one. We're so happy to be here."

Charlie continued to think while his father and the young lady carried on a friendly conversation. After a brief two minutes of thought, he made a decision. Charlie walked over to the regular ears and chose one off the shelf. He compared the two sets of ears he held in each hand, then reluctantly gave the deluxe ears back to the cast member to return to the shelf.

"I guess I'll get the regular ears, Dad," Charlie said, as he placed them on the counter to pay for.

"Oh, it's OK, sweetie," the cast member said, in an attempt to cheer Charlie up. "I'm sure you'll find plenty of other wonderful things to collect during your stay. Would you like us to embroider your name on the back?"

"Sure," he half-heartedly said, still wanting the other ears, but trying hard to look happy.

"Well, I'm not so sure about that. Are you, young man?"

The three of them quickly looked to see who had just spoken.

"Mr. Wellington. Well, this is a surprise. So nice to see you, sir," the cast member said.

Behind Charlie and his father stood a man, mature in age, rather thin and average in stature. He had wavy grey hair, bushy eyebrows, and clear-rimmed glasses. His button-down shirt was untucked, very playful and filled with color. He wore khaki pants with white sneakers. Perfect for walking the grounds. And underneath it all, he carried with him an air of kindness and sincerity, mixed with deep wisdom.

"Oh, now-now, Lori, you know you can call me Frank. I'm no different than you are. In fact, we are almost the same. We both share a deep passion for Disney, do we not?"

"Yes. Yes, sir. I mean, Frank. Sir. We do. Heh-heh."

"And who do we have here, Lori?"

"Well, Frank, this is Charlie. A very big Disney fan. And this is his father, Mr...?"

"Zastawits. Ed Zastawits. Nice to meet you, Frank."

"So very nice to meet you as well, Ed. And what about Charlie here. From what I've observed, it appears you have a dilemma on your hands. Am I right, young man?"

"No. Not really, sir. Well, I guess not."

"Sounds to me like you're still in doubt. What does your father think?"

"Oh, I agree with you, Frank. I think Charlie really wants to get the deluxe set of ears, but they're a little bit more than he can afford."

"Really. Is that all that's holding you back, Charlie? Money?"

"Yes. Yes, sir."

"Well, I think I may have a solution. And it's sitting right here in this room."

"You do?" Charlie said with a bewildered look on his face.

"Lori, would you be so kind as to retrieve the tan box sitting on top of the shelf, next to the plant, please."

With a quizzical look on her face, the cast member got a small step ladder and brought down one of the decorations from atop the deluxe ears shelf.

"Now, if you would please open the box."

Miss Smith opened the box and they all looked inside. The box was empty. They all looked up at Frank, wondering what he was trying to do.

"Oh," he said with a chuckle. "All of you assumed something was going to be in the box. No-no-no. I just want to use it so I can put what I'm about to show you into the box."

"Aghhhhh," they all collectively responded.

Frank pointed toward the shelves. "If you look down on the fifth shelf, in the shadows behind the left set of ears, you'll find another set. If you could pull those out, please."

Lori found the ears and brought them out, with a surprised look on her face. "I didn't know those were even back there. How did you know about those?"

"Just a hunch, dear. As you know, here at the parks, anything is possible." Frank smiled for a moment, as he looked at Charlie, while handing the ears to the boy. "So what do you think, Charlie?"

The ears looked different than any of the others he had seen in the store, including the deluxe versions. They were deep black with subtle metallic flakes, while the cap section was made of an aged black velvet, with a recessed, subtle Mickey head in the center. There was no visible stitching around the edges, yet everything was fully intact. Not only did the ears look different, but they felt slightly heavier as well. There was definitely a special quality about them.

"Wow, these are really awesome. Even cooler than the others on the shelf. What do you think, Dad?" Charlie looked at his father, hoping he would agree and let Charlie get the magnificent set of ears.

"Yes, I have to agree, that is one incredible set of Mickey ears. Something an avid fan would love to have. But, I'm not quite sure they would fit into our budget," his father replied, in an attempt to not hurt his son's feelings.

"Oh, I'm pretty sure you'll find the price *quite* affordable," replied Frank.

"There's no price listed. But, it looks like they do have a tag I can scan, Mr. Zastawits," Lori said.

"That's a wonderful idea, Lori. Scan it in and see what you come up with," Frank said, while he stared at Charlie with raised brows.

Charlie found Frank's gesture to be very peculiar. It was as if Mr. Wellington already knew the answer. And his voice...it seemed so familiar.

"The ears scanned in at only...eighteen dollars? Well, that's, that's quite a bargain," Lori said, while giving Frank a look of disbelief.

"There, you see, Charlie, well within your budget."

Mr. Z was also quite surprised, as he tried to find his words. "Well, er, uh...it, it looks like you'll be able to get the ears you really wanted after all, Charlie. I guess we have Mr. Wellington to thank. Go ahead son and thank him. It's the least we can do."

"No, really. It was nothing. Nothing at all, Ed."

"Please, Charlie. Thank Mr. Wellington for his generous knowledge. Without it, we would never have found this set of amazing ears."

Charlie looked at the ears, then up toward the wise man. "Yes, my dad is right, thank you, Mr. Well..."The boy paused for a second as he stared into the kind stranger's familiar eyes.

"Go ahead. Finish what you were saying, son. It's OK, don't be shy."

Charlie shook his head to free his mind from deep thought, then continued. "Yes, thank you, Mr. Wellington, for pointing out the ears. I'll cherish them forever. I promise."

"Please Charlie, call me Frank...and, you're welcome. But, we're not done yet. You still need to add your name to the back. Make the ears your own. Right? Lori, I think that a special set of ears such as this calls for our custom gold thread, don't you?"

"Wonderful idea, Frank. It would compliment the style of the ears perfectly," she said, while pulling out the thread from the drawer below. "Here it is. What do you think Charlie? Pretty snazzy, eh?"

Charlie just looked and nodded with a smile.

"Alright then, give me a minute or two to spool the machine and we'll get your name on there."

And it literally was only about a minute or two. Lori was quite the expert when it came to stitching names on ears. She probably did it at least twenty to thirty times a day. "Here you go, Charlie. All finished. These ears are now officially yours."

He took the ears from Lori and turned them around to admire his name, stitched in brilliant gold thread on the back. Then he handed them back so Lori could place them in the box, then into a bag for Charlie to carry.

"Well, son, I think it's time we start heading back to the resort. It's been a full day. Besides, the park will be closing soon. Thanks for all your help, Frank, and you too, Lori." Both acknowledged Mr. Z with smiles and waved goodbye as Charlie and his father headed out the door.

Just as they exited into Town Square, Frank called out to them. "Wait, Charlie, wait! Come back! There's something I forgot to tell you."

The two of them stopped in their tracks and turned around, surprised the old man had called them back.

"Go ahead, Charlie. See what Mr. Wellington wants. I'll wait here on the bench and do a little people watching."

"OK, Dad," he responded, while walking back toward Frank.

"Charlie, I almost forgot. And this is really important. Tomorrow. Where are you and your family going for the day?"

"Oh, we're going to Hollywood Studios. Why?"

"You don't recognize me, do you? Look closer," Frank said, as he leaned towards the boy.

Charlie stared closely, looking over the older gentleman's facial features. "It's you. The man who gave me Merlin's magic looking glass."

"I told you I would see you soon. Don't you remember?"

"Yeah, that's it. You're Mr. Bright. I knew your voice sounded familiar."

"Mr. Bright? That's what you called me? Ha. Ha. Ha. Well, I guess that, that makes sense, based on the disguise I was wearing." Frank gathered himself, then continued. "Anyway. Back to what I was saying. I need you to take note of what I'm about to tell you."

Charlie pulled out his phone, ready to type. "OK. Ready."

"Tomorrow. Wear your ears to the park. Find the man in white. Both you, and your brother, need to touch him until the ears begin to glow. Then repeat these words, while continuing to touch the man in white:"

Ears of virtue show the way, a place of hope we'll find today.

"Did you get all that, Charlie?"

"Yes, sir. I mean, Frank. Sir. I, I got it."

Frank looked at the boy with a look of nobility. "Good luck, young man. I'll see you when you get back. At that time I will tell you more."

"OK. I guess I'll see you later?" Charlie asked, not really sure how to respond to what he had just been told.

"Yes. See you later, young man," Frank replied, as he shook the boy's hand, then turned and quickly walked away.

Charlie returned to his father, who got up from the bench. The two began their way back to the resort. The bag Charlie held in his hand swung to and fro as they marched down the sidewalk toward the bus pickup line. And unbeknownst to either one of them, the box inside the bag began to glow, illuminating the bag, for a brief moment.

Chapter Five

The rising sun pierced the gap between the curtains, just as a family with noisy children passed by the room of the Zastawits family. The combination of both events triggered Charlie's eyes to open and his brain to waken. His brother, being a morning person, was already up, sitting in the bedside chair and playing a game on his phone. Their father was not in the room. He had woken up an hour earlier and was out taking a walk. Their mother was up as well, sorting through her clothes, trying to decide what to where on their second day of magic and adventure.

"Good morning, sweetie, did you get enough sleep?" Charlie's mom asked him.

He rubbed his face, and in the middle of a yawn replied, "Yeah, I guess so."

"Great. Now that you're up, I guess we can all get ready to go. Michael, do you want to clean up first, or should I go first?"

"You can go, Mom," he replied, not even taking one second to pull his attention away from the game on his phone.

"OK, then. I'll go first, but be ready to jump in the shower as soon as I'm done. And that means having your clothes out, ready to go. You know how your father is. As soon as he gets back from his walk, he'll expect us to be ready to hit the parks."

"We know, Mom, don't worry," Charlie replied in an effort to keep his brother, who he knew was barely paying attention, out of trouble.

"Alright, it's going to be another wonderful day," she said, heading into the bathroom.

"Pssst, Michael. I've got something I need to tell you. Wait until Mom starts the shower, then I'll fill ya in on what I found out last night.

Michael gave him a short and sweet, "OK."

Within a minute or two the shower water had started to run. All clear.

"OK, I think it's safe now. Last night, during the fireworks, I snuck over by the water and used the magic looking glass Mr. Bright gave me to read a secret message."

Michael looked at his brother like he was making no sense at all.

"No, really. I used the magic looking glass to read a secret message that formed over the water on the left side of the castle during the fireworks."

"So what did it say?" Michael asked.

"Well, basically, it told me I needed to meet a stranger at a hat store around midnight. So Dad and I went on a bunch of rides and stuff until it got close to that time. Then I tricked Dad into taking me to the hat store."

Michael gave his brother a look of disinterest.

"Yeah, Michael, but this is where it gets weird. I was looking at the ears, pretending that was what I came to the store for, when this older guy shows up and has the cast member pull out these special ears that were hidden behind the others. He told me I need to wear the ears when we go to Hollywood Studios and find the man in white.

"Who's the man in white?"

"I don't know. That's what we have to figure out. Oh, and he also said, once we find this man, we both have to touch him and repeat these words, until these ears I'm wearing glow:

Ears of virtue show the way, a place of hope we'll find today.

"Then what happens?"

"How would I know, Michael. That's what we have to find out. Get it?"

"I guess?"

"And there's one more thing he told me. He said he would see us when we get back, and that he'd tell us more at that time. But don't ask me where we're going, cause I have *no* clue. All I know is he didn't seem too worried about it."

"So who is this guy that told you all this stuff?"

"Oh, that's right. This is probably the best part of all. Remember Mr. Bright?"

"Yeaaaah."

"Well, it was him. But he was dressed differently. And I learned his real name. It's Frank Wellington. He seems really nice. But kind of strange, too. Like he knows more than everyone else around him. I think he's a wacky scientist or something. Anyway, he was really nice to me and Dad. You'll meet him soon, I'm sure. But for now, as in today, we gotta find this mysterious man in white at Hollywood Studios. Got it?"

Michael nodded, as the door to their room opened. Their father was back from his morning walk, chock full of energy and ready to go.

"Hey, boys. Good morning. Where's Mom?"

Charlie pointed toward the bathroom.

"Oh, OK. I guess I'll, uh, I'll kick back and check out some Disney TV while you guys get ready. We're headed to Hollywood Studios today, right boys?"

The boys looked at each other and smirked as they both said, "Yes."

Meanwhile, somewhere on Disney property, the two Thorn spies who had been searching for the messenger the night before were arguing over how they were going to break the bad news to their captain.

"So, which one of us is going to tell him? We've got about thirty minutes before we meet the captain for breakfast."

"Well, to tell you the truth Grimsly, I'm more worried about what we're going to tell him than who's gonna do it. Cause if he don't like it, it won't matter who tells him. We'll both have our gooses cooked."

"Right, right you are, Duke. So I'd say we need to get our story straight and we'd better do it quick."

Like all other Thorns, Duke and Grim didn't have much to offer when it came to thinking. In fact, they were really only good at following orders, and even that was challenging at times. Thus the reason they were Thorns in the first place.

Mr. Fibs was captain of Segment Two, better known as Epcot. He wasn't exactly the kind of person one would care to meet, and definitely not someone any normal human being could ever work for. He was a short, round man, with a partially bald, sunburned head. His appearance was that of a tourist who lacked any respect for how he looked. The shirts he wore were two sizes too big for a man of his stature, but were necessary to fit around his equator-like waist. His shorts were equally out-sized. Half the snacks he constantly consumed ended up on his shirts, which were always covered in busy floral patterns to help conceal the food he spilled on them. On his feet he wore a pair of overworked flip flops which could barely hold the weight laid upon them.

Fifteen minutes had passed like five, as Duke and Grim wrapped up their strategy, or lack thereof. They decided the best thing to do was to tell the captain exactly what had happened, or at least what they could remember, which was that they had had no luck in spotting the messenger, and then hope that Fibs didn't lose control and have them locked up, stretched out, or even worse, fed to the crocodiles. Telling the truth was usually not the best of ideas when talking to Captain Fibs. All the Thorns that worked for him knew he had a short temper. Usually, they would cook up any kind of little lie possible to avoid having to deal with that temper.

"Alright then, Grimsly, the truth is what we'll tell him."

"And if he goes red-faced on us, blows his top, or decides to have us thrown in chains, then what, Duke?"

"Well...then I guess we'll have to come up with a quick lie, won't we."

"Huh, huh. Yeah, and a really good one at that. Otherwise, it'll be a rather unfortunate day for us, I tell you," Grim replied, as he nervously stared off into nothingness."

The two young men adjusted their transporter bands, which gave the term "park hopping" a whole new meaning, then walked through a low-traffic resort doorway and vanished, before reaching the other side—a valuable skill Thorns had to master before they could achieve spy status.

Charlie and his family were standing out by the Crescent Lake lighthouse, waiting for the boat to Hollywood Studios. The early morning sun was already heating up the air, as Charlie and his brother sought out the only relief available, within the shadow of the lighthouse. Their parents, fully exposed to the early morning rays, patiently stood in line to assure they would get a good place to sit on the boat. This was an opportunity for the boys to discuss their plan of attack for the day's mission: find the man in white.

"So Michael, any ideas who this man in white might be? I've been thinking about it since I got up, but so far, I haven't come up with any possibilities."

"I don't know. Are there any characters in Hollywood Studios that dress up in all white?"

"Hmm. None that I can think of."

"What about the people who work in the park?"

"Like the people who work in the stores, in the food places and stuff like that?"

"Yeah, someone like that."

"I'm not really sure. I guess we'll have to keep our eyes open as we're walking around. Could be. I don't know. Sounds like we're just gonna have to make sure we have Mom and Dad take us around the whole park. What do you think?"

"I think you're right."

"This could be a long day. But at least it should be a fun day. After all, we're at Disney World."

"Yeah. We're at Disney World."

As the boys finished their conversation, the boat pulled up and docked for boarding. The Zastawits were almost the first to get on, as the captain welcomed them aboard with a big smile and a little early morning humor. Their father played along as he headed straight for the back right seats. Charlie followed quickly behind, then Michael, and finally Mrs. Z, who secured the tail end of the family line. It was as good a place as any to enjoy the relaxing morning cruise down the calm, sunlit waterway which would lead them to a day of big fun, great food, and memories to last a lifetime.

The two spies, Duke and Grim, reappeared in a hidden corner on the left side of the Norway Pavilion in Epcot, near the Viking ship. They were to meet Captain Fibs for an all-you-can-eat breakfast at the Akershus Royal Banquet Hall.

"Only three minutes to nine, Grimsly. We need to step on it or he's gonna be toss'n us outta the place."

"Don't get your knickers in a bunch, mate, we're almost there," Grim replied as the two frantically made their way to the Norwegian breakfast hall. In less than a minute, they reached the entrance where they saw Captain Fibs perched at the end of a long table. And to their surprise, the other four captains were also present, along with more Thorn spies. Immediately, Grim and Duke slipped into a nervous panic, quickly looking at each other. Neither had any idea what to do next. They had no intel, nor did they have any lies thought out to appease their short-tempered captain. Worse yet, there were now others who would bear witness to their fate.

"Ah, there they are now. Come and join us, lads. I'm sure you've got plenty to talk about. At least, I hope so, for your sake. Ha-ha-ha-ha-ha."

As Captain Fibs burst into laughter, so did the others sitting at the table. And while everyone enjoyed a good chuckle, Grim and Duke stood and stared at each other, laughing half-heartedly, knowing the laughter might be ending all too soon.

"Well, c'mon gents, and have a seat. Food will be get'n cold soon and we don't want that to happen, now, do we?

Grim and Duke slowly took their seats.

Fibs leaned in toward the center of the table, his eyes peering over the rims of his sunglasses and focused with intent upon his spies, his mouth chewing on a piece of breakfast sausage while grease ran down his chin. He slowly raised his left hand off the table and pointed directly at Duke. All eyes at the table went to him.

"Now, then, what do you have to tell me," the captain said in a lower and more serious voice.

"Well, well, Captain. It, it was, uh, it was quite a long night. Me and Grimsly followed your lead on the messenger and searched the Magic Kingdom from corner to corner, and then some. With the permission of Captain Planks, of course."

Everyone at the table turned to Captain Planks, who acknowledged Duke's statement. Then all eyes were quickly back on Duke.

"We must have covered the entire park six times over, we did. Started first thing at park opening and carried on 'til they closed the gates."

"Well, that's good to know, that the two of ya spent sooooo much time look'n for the messenger."

Fibs skewered another sausage with his fork and stuffed it in his mouth, chewing slowly as he stared down Duke with a piercing gaze. The table went silent.

"But what that tells me, is that you never found the messenger. Now did you?"

"Uh, no. No, Captain, we didn't. I tell ya, we did exactly like you said, right down to the very last detail. But..."

The captain motioned Duke to stop speaking, then turned his attention to Grim.

"Tell me now, Grim, is this true? You couldn't find the messenger? No sign of them? Anywhere?"

The captain's face began to turn red. Sweat began to run down the sides of his cheeks, and his jaw grew tight as he stared down Grim, waiting for the answer he already knew.

"No, Captain, no luck at all."

On those words, Fibs flew into a silent fit of rage, shaking the chair he was in to the point that he almost tipped over while losing the sunglasses off the top of his head. Slowly, he worked his way back to calm by drinking a large glass of ice water and wiping off his sweaty forehead. He rolled his eyes and placed his face in his hands, then looked up toward the ceiling, contemplating what to do with the miserable failures that sat before him.

Grim, knowing they were in deep water, seized the moment of silence and started pleading their case with one bad excuse after another, which he eventually began to spin into a fabricated web of lies. It was their only chance at getting out of the mess he and Duke were in.

"You see, Captain, there was a moment, just before the fireworks, when we thought we were getting really close to finding the Patron's messenger. Duke and I had spotted a man who appeared to be walking, all nervous-like, around the Magic Kingdom hub. This guy really fit the bill."

Duke caught on immediately to what Grim was doing, and jumped in to help with the fabrication.

"Yeah-yeah, Captain. This fella was look'n over his shoulder about every two or three steps he took. And he had this look on his face, like he was searching for something. Something like, you know, an outsider."

Grim jumped back in, as he could see the lie was working on the captain. Fibs' face was slowly changing from beet red back to blotchy white. He appeared to be gaining interest. "And we were just starting to sneak up close on the guy, but then this crazy old man who was selling light toys, dressed up like a one-man light parade, jumped into our line of sight to talk to some stinking kid."

"That's right, Grimsly. That wacky old man dressed up like a firefly boogered up our whole plan of attack. We would have had him for sure, if it weren't for that crazy old cast member talk'n to that kid."

"Wait. Back up a second there, Duke," Fibs said calmly. "Tell me more about this old man in the light suit."

"Well, Captain, this old man was covered in lights from head to toe, and not just one color, they were changing into all sorts of colors. He was wearing a really tall hat with Mickey ears that was lit up as well. Not only that, he had on these big, funny glasses that were lit up, too."

"So what was this guy doing, did you say?"

"He was pushing a cart full of all sorts of light toys, balloons, hats and stuff, which he was selling to the kids and all."

"Let me ask you, Duke. In all the time you've been working as a spy for me, have you ever seen this cast member before?"

"Uh, no. Uh, nope. No, not that I can remember, Captain."

"And would you and Grimsly say that this man, a man dressed up like a human spectacle of lights, stuck out in the crowd?"

"Why, yes, yes, I would."

"And did I not tell you before you left for your assignment what you should be looking for?"

"Oh, yes. Yes, you did, Captain," Duke replied, as he was trying to figure out in his mind what the captain was getting at.

"Please tell, Duke."

"Uh, let's see. Well, um. Oh, yes. You told us to, uh, to look for someone acting in an unusual manner, or...or who stuck out in a crowd. Yeah, that's it. Right, Grimsly?" Duke looked at his partner for confirmation. And then it dawned on him as to what he had just said. Five key words rang in his head. "Stuck out in a CROWD." He quickly turned to face the captain, his heart in his stomach and his palms sweaty.

"That's right, Duke. I specifically told you to look for someone acting in an unusual manner. Or who stuck out in a crowd. And this old man dressed up like a human light show definitely stuck out, in, a, crowd..." Fibs' face began to turn red as he yelled under his breath and slammed his fist on the table. Quickly, he caught himself and returned to a calm state, not wanting to attract attention in the restaurant.

"Yes, you're right, Captain, you did tell me and Grimsly those exact words. I remember now. We're terribly sorry, Captain. Really, we are."

"I know you are, boys, I know you are."

Fibs paused for a moment as he stared into an empty corner of the room before turning his attention back on his spies, while slowly cutting through a breakfast sausage with a knife.

"But, if this ever happens again, it'll be more than breakfast sausage I'll be cutting next time. Understand me, boys?"

"Yes. Yes, sir, Captain, sir," Duke and Grim responded in relief.

"Now then. What else can you boys tell me about this man—who, from the sound of it, is our messenger."

"Aye, what else ye be tell'n us?" asked another captain toward the other end of the table. His name was Reginald Plank, and he was in charge of the busiest segment of all, Segment One, also known as the Magic Kingdom. He too sported sunglasses—but mainly to conceal his left eye, which was blind. His brown hair was long on top, yet tight on the sides, with bleached highlights. Five o'clock shadow covered his face, while faded t-shirts and khaki shorts with deck shoes were the norm for his wardrobe. Plank's voice was soft, but gravelly, and he spoke like someone who had just walked off a pirate ship. While he was medium in stature and very fit, the opposite of Fibs, it was easy to tell they had two common traits, which all captains of FOTO shared: their lack of patience, and their tempers.

"Well, uh, let's see," said Grim. "The crazy-looking old fella who jumped in front of us was carrying on about some 'special' light toy that he was trying to sell to this kid."

Duke jumped into the conversation, to add more detail. "Yeah-yeah. He had this crazy-looking magnifying glass thingy that spun around and lit up that he was showing to two young fellas and their father. The old man even called the older kid back to tell him a little more about it."

"Was there anything else you remember the old man doing?" asked Fibs.

"No, I don't think so," replied Duke.

"The water, Duke. Tell them about the water," Grim said.

"Oh, right-right-right. Just before the old man left, the boy started looking over toward the water near Sleepy Hollow Refreshments, and the old man turned the kid back quickly. Like he didn't want him looking that way or something. Don't know what that was all about."

"Well, there ya have it, ya bloom'n buffoons. I'll tell you what ye'r young matey was up to. He was confirming with the shiny man where he needed to go, so he could read a secret message, he was."

Duke looked at Plank with a blank stare.

"That's right. Ya heard me, matey. That there magnify'n glass ya spoke of...well, it ain't no toy, ya see. It ain't no toy at all. That there was Merlin's magic looking glass. And it's used to read secret messages. It was imagineered by the Patrons many years back so they could pass messages along without us find'n out. Back when WONDER was just being developed. Ya might say it's a pretty important piece of the puzzle we're trying tuh put together."

"So, Plank, what da ya make of it?" asked Captain Fibs.

"I think ya already know what I'm thinking there, Fibsy. There's only one reason the Patrons would be handing out somethin' like that to an outsider," Plank said, while lowering his sunglasses to look at Fibs with a glimmer in his one good eye.

"Yeah," replied Fibs with a sinister smile. "Only one good reason."

Charlie and his brother had had a busy and exciting morning, ever since their family passed through the gates of Hollywood Studios. It had been one incredible experience after another.

Rush to an attraction, stand in line, take a ride, check out a store, get their photo taken by a cast member, then start all over again. And woven between all of that, the boys had been searching long and hard for a man in white. Unfortunately, they had not had any luck so far, and it was just about lunch time. At least that's what their stomachs were telling them.

"Well, guys, and gals," Mr. Zastawits said. "Looks like it's just about time for lunch. What do ya say we head over toward the Muppets 3D show. I have us scheduled for lunch at Mama Melrose."

"What's that, Dad?" asked Michael.

"It's a tasty little Italian restaurant tucked away back in one of my favorite little nook and crannies of the park. There's even a small Christmas shop next door that your mom likes to browse in. "So what do ya say? You boys ready for an Italian-style lunch?"

"You bet we are," they both enthusiastically replied, feeling the need for food before continuing their search for the man in white.

Charlie and his family headed for Mama's, visions of Italian food dancing in their heads—and stomachs, too.

At that very moment, hidden deep in the shadowy woods near the center of a deserted chunk of land that was once known as Discovery Island, a meeting was taking place—a meeting with dark intentions. The captains of the Forest of Thorns Order had called for an urgent gathering of Thorn spies and soldiers. It was quite the display of some of the roughest and scariest looking rabble-rousers ever to set foot on Disney property—even more frightening than the looters and plunderers over on the Pirates attraction. In fact, many of the Thorns went to great lengths to be as disgusting as they possibly could. Not bathing or brushing their teeth for months, wearing dirty clothes and shoes with holes, sleeping in mud, and eating with their bare hands were just a few repulsive characteristics each Thorn possessed. Rules and structure did not usually apply to them, unless, of course, it was a captain's orders. Only a Thorn captain possessed the leverage to earn a Thorn's respect. As it was, the Thorn captains provided each Thorn with a very powerful masking device, used to help them carry out their daily duties. The device, a hi-tech belt buckle, allowed those wearing it to walk amongst Disney guests as a common tourist. It had a brushed silver appearance with the letter "T," for Thorn, in the center, surrounded by an ornate circle of thorns. When activated by pushing the "T," a digital disguise quickly blanketed the one wearing it, instantly making them look like any typical guest. It was a brilliant piece of technology, developed by a former Disney imagineer gone bad, who now went by the name of Lucideous.

On an old dilapidated stage made of wood were five chairs, and sitting in those chairs were four of the five captains of the world: Plank, Fibs, Wontdo, and Rued. Captain Plank, a true pirate at heart, ran the crew for Segment One, the Magic Kingdom. Fibs, the king of slobbery, took care of Segment Two, better known as Epcot. Segment Four, also known as the Animal Kingdom, was run by the corrupt Captain Wontdo. And Captain Rued, a master of thievery, kept the Thorns in line for Segment Five, now known as Disney Springs.

The four men had been sitting in their chairs, leaning over and quietly speaking amongst themselves. But now it was time to address the Thorns. All four Captains stood up and approached a wooden podium which displayed the same logo that was on the belt buckle devices of all Thorns.

"Alright laddies, it's time we call this meetin' to order!" shouted Fibs, as he slammed the top of the podium with his fat hand, producing a thunderous crack. "The reason we called all of youz together was to tell ya we've got some really big news."

"Like what, Cap'n? Did ya find us some pretty ladies?" one of the Thorns up near the stage shouted, followed by laughter from his fellow Thorns.

Then another hollered out from the other side of the crowd: "Or maybe they dug up a hundred barrels of rum!" Again, more laughter from the crowd.

"Quiet, you knot-headed dopes!" yelled Fibs, with a beet-red face. "Agh. Would somebody get rid of these two so we can continue on with our meeting?"

It only took a second. Two of the larger Thorns grabbed one of the jokesters, while two more grabbed the other funny guy.

The two were carried away kicking and screaming as they disappeared into the surrounding woods. Where they were taken, or what was going to happen to them next, was no concern for any of the Thorns. In fact, they preferred not to know, or even care, for that matter.

"Now, then. Where was I? Oh, yes. The really big news. We just found out this morning that an outsider has been chosen by the Patrons to begin the search."

The entire crowd burst into cheer. Then one of the Thorns asked, "The search for what, Cap'n?"

Fibs and the other captains cast their evil eyes immediately upon the Thorn who had dared to asked such a foolish question.

"You don't know what we're talking about, matey?" Plank asked in a low, grumbly voice. All four captains continued to stare right through the poor soul who had been foolish enough to ask such a question.

"Oh, yeah, yeah, yeah. Right, right. The search. Of course, I know about the search," replied the Thorn, who was quick to back-pedal his way out of the jam he had just gotten himself into.

"That's right, the search," answered Plank. "Go ahead, Fibs. Tell 'em the rest of it."

"Because of this, we need each and every one of you to go to your segments, split up into pairs, and stake out all the Dream Dots. You'll be looking for a young lad. Not sure what he looks like, or how old he is, but keep your eyes peeled for any kid acting strange around one of the dots. Oh, and he might not be alone. If you see anything, anything at all, report back to your captain immediately. Understood?"

The entire gathering of Thorns responded in unison. "Aye-aye Cap'n!"

"Good!" Now get a move on, you bunch of yellow-livered ninnies! We're burning daylight!" shouted Plank.

Lunch at Mama Melrose had been delightful for Charlie and his family. They were leaving the restaurant and heading to the Christmas store, It's a Wonderful Shop, located just around the corner.

"Well that was delicious, don't you think, honey?" said Mr. Z.

"Oh, I can't eat another bite, I'm so full. The food was delicious, I couldn't stop eating it," his wife replied with a little chuckle.

As they continued to walk toward the Christmas store, Charlie began to think about the man in white again, wondering if he and his brother would ever find him. Half the day had already passed, and still they had no idea who they were looking for.

"Hey, boys, check it out," their father said with a big-kid smile. "That's probably the only snowman you're gonna see in Florida during the summer. What do ya think? You guys should go take a closer look, so I can take a picture."

At first, Charlie thought it was a cheesy idea. A picture with a snowman. Really? That is, until it all clicked. Snowman? Man in white? The snowman is white. Could it be? The man they had been looking for all morning? I guess there's only one way to find out. "Sure dad, that's a great idea. C'mon, Michael. Let's go stand by the snowman so Dad can get a picture."

Michael acknowledged his big brother, who gave him a look like he had just discovered something really important as the two walked up to the snowman for a photo op.

While their father fiddled around with his phone to take the picture, Charlie whispered quietly to his brother. "This is the guy. The man in white."

Michael turned and gave his brother a surprised look.

"That's right, you heard me. Now smile for the camera so Dad can take his photo, and they can go into the store."

"OK, smile, boys," their dad said. With the click of a button, another memory had been created.

"Oh, that was a great idea, Ed. Now let's go in and see what's new," said Mrs. Z. It's a Wonderful Shop was one of her favorite hidden gems of Hollywood Studios. And again, another opportunity for shopping.

"You boys staying outside? It's starting to get hot out."

"Yeah, Dad, Michael and I are gonna hang out with the snowman for another minute or two, then we'll come inside to cool off."

"Alright, we'll see you guys inside. I gotta get out of this heat."

"OK, Dad. We'll be right behind you."

As his dad headed into the shop, Charlie started in with his brother. "Ok, now that Mom and Dad are inside, we can check to see if this really is the man in white. Place one of your hands on the snowman and I'll do the same."

"Does it matter where we place them?" Michael asked.

"No, I don't think so. Mr. Wellington said we're just supposed to touch him."

Charlie and his brother touched the snowman, then recited the words:

Ears of virtue show the way, a place of hope we'll find today.

The boys looked at each other, waiting for something to happen. And it did. Within seconds, the ears atop Charlie's head changed from a metallic black to a brilliant crystal blue. Within each ear, spark trails of silver, gold, and white spun round and round like pinwheels of mini firework-like bursts. The cores of each ear grew brighter and brighter with each passing second, engulfing the boys and snowman within an orb-like spectrum of light. As the orb grew more and more radiant, the boys looked at each other, still touching the snowman. They frantically looked around, then back at each other, not knowing what to say. A gust of wind began swirling around their bodies as the cascade of sparkling trails and firework bursts became larger and more rapid, until the entire orb had become so bright that it hurt their eyes to look at. And then, in a brilliant flash of light followed by a loud shooooop, they were gone. Only the snowman remained where they had stood just seconds ago.

The air had become still and quiet. No longer could Charlie and Michael hear the background sounds of people, the attractions, or the park music. The lights returned to normal intensity, revealing an unfamiliar place. The boys moved their heads in all directions, side to side and up and down, taking in an environment neither had experienced before. Slowly they turned and looked at each other, realizing they were no longer in Hollywood Studios. Nor were they in human form, but instead, wooden animated figures in a toymaker's shop.

"Cha-Cha-Charlie. You look like, like a cartoon," Michael stuttered out, as he tried to find his words.

"Yeah, so do you. What just happened to us? I mean, you look like you. Well, sort of. But you're made of wood. You look like a wooden toy."

"You, too. You look like a little wooden boy with Mickey ears."

Charlie felt the top of his head. "Whew. At least I'm still wearing the magic ears. But I don't know how to use them to get back."

Michael's jaw dropped. "Are you saying Mr. Wellington didn't tell you how to get back?"

"No. No, he didn't. And I forgot to ask him about it. Oh, boy, now what are we going to do?"

Looks like we're stuck here, Charlie. Way to go. Now we get to spend the rest of our lives as little wooden toys."

"Oh, and I suppose you would have remembered to ask how to get back?"

"Yeah...well, maybe. I don't know."

"Exactly. You don't know."

"So what do we do now?"

"Well, there's a reason Frank sent us here. I don't know what it is, but there is a reason. So I say we start looking around for it."

"What about getting back to Mom and Dad?"

"The way I see it, Michael, Frank wasn't too worried about sending us here. So I'm sure we'll find our way back, just fine. Since we're here, what do you say we just take our time and have a look around. I'm sure that's what Frank would want us to do anyway."

"Yeah, you're probably right," Michael said, rolling his eyes in agreement.

Charlie nodded to his brother, then the two of them slowly and carefully began to explore the toy shop, but from a much different perspective. Since they were small wooden toys, everything in the room was much larger than if they had been normal-sized humans. The chair near the fireplace was so large, they would need a ladder just to climb up into it. On the foot stool next to the chair lay an old wooden tobacco pipe, about the size of each boy. The dozens of intricate cuckoo clocks hanging on one of the walls were almost large enough for the boys to fit into. And the carved wooden animals up on the shelves were big enough, that if the boys wanted to ride them, they could.

An iron kettle hung suspended in the fireplace, above a large cluster of red-hot coals, which cast a golden glow and deep shadows throughout the room. One of the small, ornate windows was slightly open allowing the excess heat from the coals to escape. The work station bench was covered with small, messy cans of paint, paint brushes, and wood-working tools. Just in front of the bench was a wooden vice, a bucket full of wood shavings, and yet more shavings scattered on the floor. To the right of the bench sat a small, narrow pedestal table, on top of which, sat a fish bowl.

It was at that moment Charlie began to realize where he and his brother actually were. This wasn't just any ordinary toy maker's workshop. They were in Geppetto's workshop.

"Do you realize where we are Michael? We're in Geppetto's workshop!"

"Really? Why do you think this is his workshop?"

"Well, just look around. Doesn't a lot of this stuff look familiar? The cuckoo clocks, the music boxes, toys, marionettes, and the fish bowl?"

"Yeah, but I don't see Geppetto, Pinocchio, the cat, or even the fish."

"Well, maybe they're out somewhere on an adventure, or..."

"What? What is it, Charlie?"

As he was arguing with his brother, Charlie caught sight of a bed over in a corner of another room. At first glance, it looked like someone may have been in it. But after a second glance, Charlie could tell it was empty.

"Oh. It was nothing. False alarm. For a minute there, I thought someone was in the bed behind you. But there's not."

Michael turned and looked over his right shoulder, then replied in a wise tone. "Yep, you're right. Nobody in the bed. Glad you figured that one out."

"Alright, alright. Enough with the sarcasm. We need to figure out how to get back to the park. And how to change back to normal. Being a small wooden toy isn't exactly working for me, and I'm sure you're not enjoying it either. Right?"

"Uh, no."

"OK, then, there has to be a reason Frank wanted us to come here. We just need to figure out what it is. You go look by the work bench and I'll check the area over by the fireplace."

The two split up and began searching. Michael stumbled through the giant wood shavings on the floor as he made his way to the small pedestal table with the fishbowl on top. The intricate carvings of sea horses on the side panels were perfect for climbing on, as Michael made his way to the top of the table where he peered into the fishbowl, his face appearing comically distorted on the other side of the bowl. "Nothing in here," he mumbled to himself. Eventually, he worked his way to the top rim of the fishbowl and established an athletically balanced position before leaping forward and landing in a full somersault, then back into a perfect stance on top of the workbench.

Over near the hot coals, Charlie had managed to work his way up onto a brick ledge by climbing the log pile just left of the fireplace. On that ledge sat two more kettles, one large and one a little smaller. But he found nothing there that was of any help. The only thing he noticed was how much hotter it was than just a few feet away, in the middle of the room. To a small wooden toy, the fireplace was the size of a house, and the hot coals intimidating. With no more to see on the ledge, Charlie jumped down and ran back to the center of the room, trying to get a better look at what sat atop the fireplace mantle. From what he could see, there appeared to be several ornate bowls, two or three decorative plates, a stein, and a music box with three large figures on it. But the mantle on which they sat was so high up, Charlie did not think it would be possible to reach. So he shouted out to Michael, to see if he had found anything.

"Hey, Michael, you having any luck over there?" Charlie's words echoed through the shop. To them it was the size of a large toy factory.

"Nothing over here on the work bench but a bunch of paint, brushes, and bowls!" Michael yelled back.

"Alright, c'mon down and we'll try a couple other spots."

Michael jumped and sprang off the blade of a saw, like a diving board, going into a triple, mid-air somersault, before making a perfect landing on the floor.

"You know, Charlie, I kind of like being a toy now," he said with a big grin.

Charlie just shook his head and rolled his eyes in response to his brother's sudden inflated ego. It appeared Michael possessed tremendous athletic abilities as an animated character, which had gone straight to his head.

"Are you done gloating over yourself?" Charlie asked, while giving his brother a look of disgust.

"Oh, I guess so, Charlie. Geez, can't we have any fun?"

"We're not here for fun, Michael, we're here to learn something. I just haven't figured out what yet. Anyway, why don't you go check out the counter and shelf full of toys over by the front window, and I'll go take a look in the bedroom."

"Alright, lots of toys to play with."

"Yeah, lots of toys. But see if any of them can help explain why we're here, or how we can get back to the real world. You know, smart things. We need to stay focused, so we can find our way back to Mom and Dad." Charlie realized it was going to be challenging to keep his younger brother from getting carried away in a shop full of toys. But he also knew it had to be done; a rare quality for a boy of his age to possess.

"I got it, Charlie. Focus. Blah, blah, blah."

"Good, now go check out the stuff by the front window while I look in the bedroom."

"Got it, brother," Michael said as he took off darting toward the front window, like a deer running through the woods.

"And be careful!" Charlie shouted at his brother.

His brother raised his hand, then continued on his way.

Charlie shook his head, then ran off toward the bedroom.

There was a chair next to the front window counter which allowed Michael to easily climb up and reach his destination. The window counter was filled with all sorts of animal toys, such giraffes, camels, ducks, and pigs. There was also a little wagon, a man in a top hat, a conductor, and a push-and-spin toy that looked like a ride from the traveling fair. Flanking the counter were two small shelves, which sat about a foot higher. On one, a dog and ceramic jug. On the other, a portly woman with a jolly smile, and another jug. But what caught Michael's attention was what he saw when he looked out the window. Or rather, what he didn't see. Remembering back to scenes from the movie, he expected to see a quiet little Italian village, fast asleep. But instead, all he could see was white, like a dense fog, so thick the human eye could not penetrate it. Michael became so consumed with the fog that he tripped over the pig behind him as he was backing away from the window. Quickly, he jumped to his feet, then over to the shelves filled with toys that were just left of the window counter. Within a few brief minutes, he had combed the entire shelf unit of toys and found nothing unusual to report to his brother. Eager to tell Charlie what he had seen out the window, Michael made his way down to the floor and ran toward the bedroom, repeatedly yelling his brother's name.

Charlie was having no luck either as he searched the bedroom for something that might help them return back to their parents in the real world. By the time Michael came running and shouting into the bedroom, Charlie had already searched the dresser with shelves that sat against the wall opposite the bed. Upon it sat many wooden toys and music boxes, just like the shelves near the front window. He had also searched the cat's bed, the night stand, and was just getting ready to step onto the ornate headboard of the large bed when he heard Michael shouting his name. This made him lose his grip and tumble out of control, bumping his head, then his rump, and finally landing on the soft bed mattress in a tangled mess. Not exactly the way he had planned it out. Aggravated with the results, Charlie stood up quickly, fighting to get good footing on the cushy bed. He peered down at his brother with a look of disgust, while shouting out in his best quiet voice: "You need to keep your voice down. Someone might hear you."

"I know. I know, Charlie. But I saw something. Or actually, I saw nothing. I don't know what I'm trying to say. Ah. Just wait 'till I get up there, then I'll explain."

Charlie just looked at his brother with a quizzical expression. Before he knew it, Michael had climbed and leaped his way onto the mattress—panting like a dog who had just chased a rabbit.

"So what were you saying about not seeing something?"

"When I climbed up on top of the front window counter and was looking around, I noticed something odd about the view.

When I looked out the window, all I saw was, well, nothing. No quiet village, no cobblestone streets, no people, nothing."

"Not even white mountain tops, highlighted by a starlit sky?" Charlie asked.

"No. Nothing but a dense, white, endless fog."

"OK. OK. keep it down," Charlie said, as he nervously looked around for an answer. Then he spotted one. "Looks like we need to get to the window above the bed and open it up, so we can see what's on the other side."

"Right," his brother replied. "That's a good idea."

"If we can climb to the top of the bed post just under the window ledge, we should be able to get up there."

"OK, let's go, Charlie."

The two small, wooden boys struggled to make their way across the fluffy bed, then up the bed post and onto the window ledge. It took all their strength to pull the window into an open position that was wide enough to look out. Charlie, remembering a scene from the movie, expected they would see a starlit sky with a magic wishing star shining brightly. But when they peeked around the window frame, all they saw was white. The boys just stood and stared in silence. Neither knew what to say. That is, until all the cuckoo clocks in the shop started to sound off. There must have been fifty to a hundred of them. All different sizes, shapes, colors and sounds. There was a pair of ducks, a mom spanking her son who had gotten into the jam, a tipsy man hanging out a window while hiccuping, another man attempting to behead a turkey, and a momma bird in a nest with her three baby birds. The sights and sounds were endless. Almost too much to bear.

"I wonder if this is a sign, Michael!" Charlie yelled.

"I think it is, Charlie!" His brother shouted back, pointing at the ears atop Charlie's head. The ears had started to glow brightly, just as before. And like before, the boys became engulfed by a large orb of lights and wind. As the orb grew more radiant, Charlie looked at his brother and shouted: "Yep, I guess we were right! It's time to go!"

Charlie's words were followed by a brilliant flash of light. Then a loud shoooop. And just like before, they were gone.

Chapter Six

Earlier that day, prior to the FOTO meeting on the deserted island, a message of great importance had been passed down through the ranks to the five evil Thorn captains. The Dark Thorns had given notice to Planks, Fibs, Shivers, Wontdo, and Rued that it was very likely the outsider chosen for the search would be entering the World of Natural Dream Enhanced Realities (also known as WONDER) later that day in Hollywood Studios. And that they would be carrying one of the Objects of Magic, which had not yet been identified. Their orders were to seek out the outsider, capture them, and bring them to Thorn Castle, where they were to be held captive.

As Shivers was responsible for Segment Three, Hollywood Studios, the Thorn captains had quickly determined it would be in their best interest if Shivers and his crew skipped the island meeting and headed straight there. They all felt this would increase their chances of capturing the outsider, which would keep them in the good graces of the Dark Thorns and help avoid any possibility of being shackled in chains, dunked in the well, or turned into warty toads. The Thorn captains were not scared of much, but one fear they all shared was facing a Dark Thorn who had just received bad news.

Somewhere near the Tower of Terror exit in Hollywood Studios, a hidden door suddenly swung open, smashing against the wall. Fourteen Thorn spies and their ruthless captain burst into daylight and headed toward the south end of Sunset Boulevard. The door slammed behind them, completely masking its existence. Each spy was wearing one of the wrist-band devices used to transport from one location to another by way of secret portals, known as Dream Dots. Each Dream Dot on Disney World property was marked in the map on their devices. To get from one dot to another, all a spy had to do was tap the screen to activate the dot nearest them for departure, then tap the location on the map of the the dot they wished to go to. Instantly, they would be transported to the other location. The shorter the distance between dots, the less time it took to locate an arrival destination, simply because it required a shorter period of time to find on the Walt Disney World map. For longer distances, a spy might even decide to make multiple, shorter jumps before reaching their final destination, in order to simplify their map searches. It was truly an ingenious device developed by FOTO techies and refined by the Dark Thorns for spying on the Patrons.

Leading the spies was Captain Marty Shivers. Tall and gangly, with a slightly bulging belly and oversized flippers for feet, Shivers was nothing good to look at. His sly smile was trained to hide a poor excuse for teeth, and was surrounded by four days of stubble. His eyes were cloaked by greasy bangs, a pair of hippie-style, circular sunglasses, and an oversized sun hat. The linen shirt and pants he wore were in dire need of ironing and his sandals revealed a pair of hideous feet, featuring yellow toenails in desperate need of a pedicure. He also carried with him a temperamental personality that was just as ugly as the way he looked. He fit in perfectly with the other Thorn captains.

Shivers barked out orders as he and is crew marched down the Sunset Boulevard toward the center of the park. "All right, you bunch of misfits, now listen up. Smith and Tanner, I want you to stay back here and keep an eye on Sunset Boulevard, the tower, and the coaster. Wess and Johnson, you two take the entry gates and Hollywood Boulevard. Jones and Triddle, watch the Animation Courtyard. And so it went, Shivers assigning two spies to each section of the park, until all were covered. There would be no possibility of missing the outsider now, the captain thought to himself, as he paced the courtyard of the Great Movie Ride.

An hour had passed, and yet, still no sign of anything suspicious. Shivers was getting antsy—to the point that he was madly chewing on a straw acquired from a nearby popcorn cart. Where in the world was this outsider? He couldn't take the wait any longer. Grabbing the shortwave communicator out of his pocket, he quietly spat out: “Any of you nitwits seen anything yet.”

“Nothing yet, Captain.”

“Us either, Cap’n. No signs of ’em near any of the Dream Dots we’ve checked out.”

“Well, keep look’n, we don’t want anything slip’n by us.”

“Yes Cap’n. We hear ya, loud and clear.”

“And remember, boys, we don’t want them escaping from WONDER. We gotta keep them in here. I don’t want to attract any unnecessary attention from the Patrons. If we can capture the outsider inside WONDER, it should make for a smooth transition. Understood?”

For fear of what might happen to them if they failed, multiple confirmations spilled in over the communicator airwaves in response to Shivers’ question.

“Very well then, boys. Let’s keep our eyes peeled and our ears open.”

The bright light faded and a calm silence settled in. Charlie and Michael had returned to where their journey began, in front of the Christmas shop at Hollywood Studios, next to the snowman. The boys looked to their left, looked to their right, then at each other, and smiled. Everything was going to be fine.

“Let’s go find Mom and Dad, Michael,” Charlie said, eager to see his parents and confirm they hadn’t missed them.

Michael agreed, and the two of them rushed into the Christmas shop to find their parents. When they went in the store, something seemed amiss. There was no sign of their parents. Furthermore, when they asked the cast member behind the counter if she had seen two people that fit their description, the cast member just smiled big and told them she had not, then asked the boys if they needed help finding anything—as in merchandise to buy. An odd answer for a cast member, being that two young boys had apparently just lost their parents. The cast member continued to stare and smile at them.

Charlie grabbed his brother by the sleeve and pulled him away from the counter, out of earshot of the cast member who he continued to look at with bewilderment. Quietly, he mumbled to his brother: “There’s something weird going on here. I don't know what it is yet, but something's not right. I mean, I can understand that we may have been gone long enough for Mom and Dad to start searching for us. But if that were the case, then the cast member in the store would have most certainly expressed her concern. And she didn't. We need to get to the bottom of this and figure out what's going on."

"Are you saying you don't think that lady over there is a real cast member?"

"Exactly, Michael. Let's go outside and see if we can find Mom and Dad."

"OK."

Charlie thanked the cast member for her help as the boys calmly left the store. Upon returning outside, both boys looked to their right, which led to the Muppet Courtyard, then left, which led back to where they had lunch, at Mama Melrose. But for some strange reason, when they looked left there seemed to be more beyond the Italian restaurant. Before their magical journey to Geppetto's work shop, that area been fenced off for park expansion.

"Charlie, what's going on here?"

"What do you mean?" Charlie replied, as he stared with a look of disbelief toward the area beyond the restaurant.

"You know. That," Michael said, pointing in the same direction that Charlie was staring.

"Oh, yeah. That. I don't know. But something is definitely not right."

"What do you mean by, not right?"

"I don't really know yet, but something just feels...different to me. The cast member's strange reaction, that area over there. I think we need to have a look around. I got a feeling Mom and Dad aren't, well...actually here."

"What? Why wouldn't they be here? They were here before we were sucked away by that giant ball of light to the toy shop. Why do you think they'd leave us?"

"I don't think they left us either, Michael. Let's go look around, then I'll tell you more about what I'm thinking."

"Whaaaat? I don't get it."

"I don't really get it either, but I'll explain further as we look around."

Charlie and Michael headed toward the back of the park, past Mama Melrose and into an area of the park that had been fenced off for construction. To their left was a stage show with a Hunchback of Notre Dame theme. All the people they passed while walking were dressed nicely, perfectly groomed, and smiling from ear to ear. No crying babies, no whining children, no angry or tired parents. The buildings and signage all looked freshly painted, the walkways spotless. The birds nearby were chirping in perfect rhythm with the park music. The sky was a pretty blue with only a small touch of pure white clouds, and it was no longer hot out, but rather a comfortable seventy five degrees. Even the trash cans were spotless, with no signs of use. It was as though everybody and everything in the park was absolutely perfect, as if they had come right out of a Disney vacation planner video or an Imagineer's concept drawing.

Stranger still were the attractions the boys passed as they continued searching for their parents. To their right was a fake cityscape, to the left, a quiet residential area that had not existed in the park for at least fifteen years. Next came a Honey, I Shrunk the Kids play area, where everything was blown up to a scale which made you feel like the size of an ant. Behind the residential area, the park expanded even farther back, to what sounded like a stunt show—a stunt show which, according to Charlie's recent study of the park online, should have been closed to make way for the new Star Wars and Toy Story-themed lands. It was like the park had somehow magically expanded beyond its defined boundaries and now included not only attractions that had recently been closed, but also extinct attractions which had been removed from the park many years ago. As the boys continued on, Charlie was now certain they would not find their parents in this odd and mysterious place. He decided it was time to explain to his brother why.

"You thirsty, Michael?"

"I guess so. Why?"

"Cause I think we need to take a break and rest for a minute. Besides, I really need something to drink."

"Can we go over there to get something?" Michael asked while pointing to the Studio Catering Company. "It looks like they have orange pop there. I could sure go for one of those."

"Sure, sounds good to me. Let's go."

After they got their drinks and sat down, Charlie started explaining his observations, telling his brother why he didn't think they would find their parents in the curiously odd version of Hollywood Studios they currently were in.

"What's that? A couple of kids came through one of the Dream Dots? Which one?" Shivers asked two of his spies over the communicator, while pacing in front of the Great Movie Ride. "Over by the Christmas shop, you say? They must have used the snowman, I presume? So which way did they head?"

"They took off toward the back of the park, Captain. So what's next? You want me and Jones to follow 'em?"

"Yes. Yes, keep an eye on 'em. Let's see if they lead us to the Patron's messenger. But don't give yourselves away. Keep a safe distance. We'll want to catch 'em off guard when the time is right, if you know what I mean."

"Alright then, Captain. We'll follow the two little brats."

"And once they settle in somewheres, you boys let me and the others know."

"Why's that, Captain?"

"Uh. You're not too sharp between the ears, are ya mate? Let's just say we're gonna throw a little surprise party for our two little guests. As well as anyone else that may show up to help them. Understand?"

"Oh, that's bloody brilliant, Captain. Brilliant.

"Yeah, yeah, yeah. Just be sure to tell us when the two little boogers settle down somewheres. Then we can rendezvous at that point. In the meantime, I want half the men to go around the left side of the park and half around the right side. Then slowly work your way toward the back. I don't want these two slip'n through our fingers. Understood?"

"Yes, Captain!" the crew answered through their communicators, as if they were standing right in front of him.

"Good. Goooood. Now stay on your toes and keep your eyes peeled tight for those two boys, ya bunch of knuckle brains."

"But, but, Captain. How are we supposed to keep an eye out if we don't know what they look like? Only Jones and Triddle know that."

The airwaves went silent. All the crew expected Shivers to blow his top at such a silly question as this.

"Well. Ya got me this time, Mr. Smith. Jones. Triddle. How in the world do you two block heads expect us to keep a lookout, if we don't even know what these two chaps look like..."

"Uh, uh, uh. Well. Uh. Let's see. Uh."

"Well, go on. Spit it out, for Pete's sake."

"Ok. Let's see. The older boy was about eleven or so, with brown wavy hair and medium build. He had a bright orange shirt on, khaki shorts, and white sneakers. The little one was wearing a blue shirt, with grey shorts and grey sneakers. He looked to be about eight or nine, and also had brown wavy hair, a slim frame and was much shorter than his brother."

"Well, there you go, gents. Be on the lookout for two boys, one wearing an orange shirt, the other blue. And both with brown wavy hair. Easy enough."

The crew confirmed their understanding and headed off to find their prey.

"That's why we aren't going to find Mom and Dad in this park."

Michael just sat and stared at his older brother, like he was nuts.

"What, Michael? You think I'd lie to you about something like this?"

"No, Charlie. I just think you've lost your mind. I mean, a talking sun on Small World and the snakes from Jungle Cruise were one thing. But to think we are in a completely different place than Mom and Dad is just, well, that just doesn't make sense."

"It's not really a different place, but rather the same place at a different time. Or maybe even a combination of different times in the park's history? Sort of like a combination of all the best ideas Disney's Imagineers have ever had for Hollywood Studios, all wrapped up into one super park. I really don't know how else to explain it. But I do know this isn't the same time in the park's history as when we left Mom and Dad. Just look around, if you don't believe me."

"You know, Michael. You really should listen to your brother. He's on to something, I tell you."

Slowly, Michael and Charlie turned their heads to see who had interrupted their conversation. It was a small portly man with red hair, khaki pants, and a green polo shirt. He had a kind, friendly face—a face Charlie swore he'd seen somewhere else before. Yet he couldn't remember when or where. So he asked.

"Have we met before?"

"Well, not exactly," the man responded with a chuckle. "But we have crossed paths in your dreams."

"How is that even possible if we've never met before?" Charlie asked.

"Well, it's actually quite simple. You see..."

"No time for explanation now, Ben. We don't want the boys getting caught."

"Who said that?" Michael shouted, as he and Charlie rapidly turned their heads in all directions, trying to pinpoint who had just spoken.

"You'll have to look a little higher if you want to see me, young squires."

"Where? I still don't see anyone," Charlie said, while continuing to look.

"Look behind you. Up in the rafters."

The boys both turned and looked up. What they saw with their eyes, their minds could not believe.

"No. Really? Charlie said in disbelief.

"Are you seeing what I'm seeing Charlie? Is...is that an owl? A cartoon owl?"

"Looks like it to me, Michael."

"But cartoons aren't real. And they sure can't talk to real people."

"Well it looks like this one is real. And it can talk to us," Charlie replied, while continuing to stare in disbelief.

"And why is he wearing glasses?"

"I don't know, Michael. Why don't you ask him? Obviously he can answer you."

The majestic white owl bowed and shook his head as he listened to the boys argue with one another. Finally, he'd had enough. "Boys. Boys. Boys. Enough with the bickering. Now hush up and listen carefully. We haven't much time."

The boys instantly snapped to attention.

"Urrrrrr-urrrrr-urrrrr-m-ahemm." The owl cleared his throat, then spoke. "Now, we haven't much time for explanation or introductions. So I'll get right to the point. Your brother is right, Michael. This place you're in. It's not the same place as where you left your parents."

"Then where are we?" Michael asked.

"Well young lad, at the moment, you are somewhere between Geppetto's toy shop, which you just visited, and reality. You see, you were trapped here by the FOTO captains."

"The who? And where is here?" Charlie asked in an excited, but confused voice.

"FOTO captains. No time to explain now, lad. We'll get to that later. All you need to know now is that you and your brother are in danger. You're trapped in a place, other than reality, and there are evil-doers headed this way to try and capture you."

"Why would they want to capture us?" Charlie asked.

"For two reasons. First, because you have in your procession one of the Objects of Magic. And second, they see you as a threat to their existence."

"But. I...we don't. We don't understand," Charlie stuttered out nervously.

"The ears you're wearing. Well, obviously you already know. They have magic powers. Powers that can be used to seek out one of the crystals."

"Crystals?" Charlie questioned, having no clue what the owl was speaking of.

"Yes, the Kingdom Crystals. But enough of that for now. We're losing precious time. I need the two of you to listen closely. These evil-doers, we'll call them Thorns."

"Thorns?" Michael blurted out.

"Yes, Thorns," The owl hooted back. "Now quiet down and listen. The Thorns are headed straight for us, from both sides of the park. So getting the two of you out of here and back to your parents safely isn't going to be an easy task. But, with a little knowledge and a lot of effort, we should be able to succeed. My friend Ben Glimmer here is going to act as a distraction. This will allow me to guide you and your brother through the park, avoiding as many Thorns as possible so you can reach the nearest Dream Dot. If all goes well, this will get you back to your parents, who will be completely unaware that you were ever gone. Any questions?"

Michael acted confused, while Charlie gathered up his thoughts for a question. "So, Mr. Owl. I do have a couple questions."

"Fire away, lad."

"How do you plan on directing us? And what is a Dream Dot?"

Oh. Yes, of course. Good questions, both of them, young man. You know what a hidden Mickey is, right?"

"Yes," Michael said.

"Well, I'll be leaving behind a trail of invisible hidden Mickeys that only you and your brother will be able to see. Like a trail of bread crumbs. Just follow the Mickeys and they'll lead you to the Dream Dot. Oh, and Dream Dots are portals used to pass back and forth between reality and WONDER. And sometimes, even areas within either one. For now, just think of it as a doorway back to reality. It's how you and your brother transported to the toy shop, then to here. So you should already be familiar with how the Dream Dots work. And WONDER is something we'll have to explain later. No time to do it now."

Most of what the owl said made sense to Charlie. Still, he had one more question. "So you said the hidden Mickeys were invisible. How are we supposed to see them if they're invisible?"

"Well, now, you really are as sharp as a tack, aren't you, young squire. Very impressive, I must say. I can see now why Frank chose you. Yes, now where was I? Oh yes, the invisible Mickeys. Ben, please give the boys their glasses."

The kind little man handed each boy a pair of silver-framed sunglasses with unusually tinted purple lenses.

"Now, put your glasses on. These will allow the two of you to see the hidden Mickeys I leave behind, which are created using a special oil that comes from my feathers. Now, the Mickeys will not be perfect in shape, but seeing them through the magic glasses Ben just gave you will make them glow. So, as you might say, they will stick out like a sore thumb. Understand, lads?"

"Yes, Mr. Owl. We get it," Charlie answered. "By the way, you look familiar as well. Just like your red-headed friend, here. Have we met before?"

Somewhere off in the distance, loud voices of two cranky men could be heard arguing. Ben and the owl directed their attention toward the noise.

"OK. I think it's time you and your brother get a move on. Trouble is near," Ben said, as he anxiously looked over his shoulder.

"I don't know, Benny. I'd say it's a little too late for warnings, wouldn't you? Ha. Ha. Ha. Ha-ha-ha."

It was too late. The two spies trailing Charlie and his brother had already radioed in to Shivers, describing the boys' location and who they were speaking with. Captain Shivers and his Thorn spies had the boys and their new-found friends surrounded.

"It's you," Charlie said. "The mean man in my dream that was chasing..." Charlie paused, then turned and pointed at Ben. "You were chasing him. And you were trying to get the box he was carrying. And-and, the owl. He was there, too."

"What in the world are you talking about, Charlie?" his brother asked.

Slowly, Shivers and his crew inched their way closer toward the boys and their friends.

"The mean man, eh, boy?" Shivers growled to Charlie, as he stared him down. "What makes you think I'm mean? Why, we've never even met before. Maybe you've got it all wrong. Maybe they're the bad guys and I'm the good guy," he said while pointing at Ben and the owl.

"No, I don't believe that. I don't believe that for one second," Charlie snapped back.

"Well, if you really feel that way, then I guess that leaves me no choice. I'll just have to take you, your brother, and your little friends, and lock you up until you change your mind."

"Pssst, I say, gentlemen," the owl whispered to Charlie, Michael, and Ben. "I feel it's time we make a run for it. Ben and I will stir up the pot, so to speak, giving you and your brother a chance to make a clean getaway. Head toward Pixar Place and keep a watchful eye for the hidden Mickeys. Understood?"

"But..." Charlie started to whisper back.

"We have no time for questions! Just get ready to run and follow the Mickeys," the owl snapped back.

"Hey. What are you four whispering about over there?" Shivers demanded, while signaling his spies to close in and capture their prey.

"OK, now!" the owl shouted.

Ben took off like a shot, heading straight for four of the spies. Splitting the group of four down the middle, he went into a baseball slide and under one of the Studio Catering Company tables. The four spies all collided into each other as they dove over the top of the table in an attempt to grab Ben. The table tipped over and chairs flew everywhere, creating a big racket. At the same time, the owl had taken off and was flying in low, random circles around the other spies, causing their bodies to get twisted up like pretzels and eventually fall down.

"Drat! You blockheads! Get back on your feet and grab the boys and those Patrons!"

"But, Captain!."

"No buts!"

"But, Captain!"

"Oh, What is it you fool?"

"The boys, sir. Well, they've escaped."

"What do you mean, they've escaped! They're right over there!" Shivers shouted, as he pointed without looking.

"Sorry, Captain, but they're not."

Shivers spun his head to where he was pointing. "Why sure they...huh? Ohhh... Why didn't you tell me they were gone!"

"We just did, Captain."

"Ohhh.... Well, get up and go find them! Don't just sit there ya, knuckle heads!"

Captain Shivers had become so enraged with the boys escape that he totally forgot about Ben and the owl. By the time he came to this realization and looked to see where they were, Ben and the owl had managed to escape as well. They were nowhere to be found. And this just added to the frustration Shivers was already experiencing.

"And where'd the other two go?"

"They, they got away, too, Captain."

"Whaaaat! Got away?" With his face turned fire-engine red, and his patience shot to oblivion, Shivers screamed, "Now listen, you meddling fools!. We need to find them before they get out of WONDER! Otherwise, it'll be our heads! Do you understand?"

"Yes, Captain!" The crew replied.

The Captain spat, shouted, and pointed out directions on where he wanted his spy teams to search within Hollywood Studios. Each group paired up and quickly took off, to seek out Charlie, Michael, Ben, and the owl.

Charlie and his brother had already made it to Pixar Place and were moving quickly through the imagined crowd of picture-perfect guests, their eyes on the lookout for the owl's hidden Mickeys.

"I don't see anything yet, Charlie."

"Me either...wait a sec. Look over there," Charlie said, while pointing upward.

"Yes! I see it!"

Sure enough, Charlie had spotted a hidden Mickey on one of the green army men props on top of the roof.

"Looks like we're headed in the right direction, Michael."

As the boys pushed on, they spotted a hidden Mickey on the Pixar Studios sign. Then another in a star on the One Man's Dream sign. The more they spotted, the more their confidence grew. And then, just as they were approaching the Little Mermaid attraction, Ben went sprinting by, right in front of where they were headed. It was like he just materialized between the pillars of the Animation Courtyard entryway arch. And only fifteen quick steps behind him were six nasty Thorn spies, all easy to spot by their sloppy appearances. In WONDER they weren't concerned about fitting in using their belt buckle devices, since all the guests around them were only visions or dreams of the Imagineers. In other words, the guests weren't real and paid no attention to the Thorns or how they looked.

As Ben continued sprinting, he turned his head and winked at the boys with a smile. It was as if he knew the Thorns had no chance of catching him. He ran in a large figure-eight pattern within the Animation Courtyard, confusing the Thorns who were chasing him. Eventually, it caused all six to collide with one another and fall to the ground. But of course, Ben didn't stop there. He laughed and laughed, while pointing at the six men who had fallen. This made them even angrier, and motivated the Thorns to quickly get up, which was exactly what Ben had hoped for—the perfect distraction to keep Charlie and Michael safe from the hostility of the evil Thorns. Within a matter of seconds, all six had managed to regain their footing, and their obsession to catch the little red-headed fellow continued. With a barrage of unfriendly words, Ben led the evil spies around the Hollywood Brown Derby Restaurant and down Sunset Boulevard, far away from where the boys were headed.

Just as the boys turned their focus back to finding hidden Mickeys, the animated owl swooped down quickly like a blur of white and silver. Right before their eyes, in mid flight, the great owl's movements immediately switched into slow motion. With his beak moving slowly as well, he turned and spoke to Charlie and Michael.

"Foooolllooooow thhhhhhe trrrrraaaaaail!"

Without hesitation, the great owl switched back to blazing speed, shooting off with a sonic boom followed by a sparkling trail of silvery-white fireworks and stars. Within the dissipating boundaries of the trail were at least two hundred hidden Mickeys, all leading past the Great Movie Ride, over Min and Bill's Dockside Diner, across Echo Lake, and disappearing near the large structure of Gertie the Dinosaur's ice cream stand.

Momentarily captivated by what they'd just seen, the boys cleared their heads, then took off in full sprints toward the dazzling trail the majestic owl had left behind. As they approached Echo Lake, something alarming came to their immediate attention. To the left of the lake were four of the Thorns, heading at full speed right toward them. And to the right of the lake, Captain Shivers and four more Thorn spies were also headed toward the boys. Charlie's mind began to spin uncontrollably as he and his brother continued running. But to where, was the question at hand. A decision had to be made. Shiver's evil-spirited crew was closing in from both sides of the lake, and the boys had no time to spare.

"What do we do, Charlie?"

"I don't know! I'm thinking, I'm thinking," Charlie responded, as his eyes scanned the landscape, frantically searching for a way out.

And then it came to him. The owl had told them to follow the trail. Obviously he meant the trail of hidden Mickeys. Yes, that's got to be it. "We need to head that way, Michael." Charlie said, pointing directly at Min and Bill's Dockside Diner.

"What? Are you crazy? We can't go that way, Charlie! What are we going to do, walk on water?"

"I don't know, but we were told to follow the trail and that's what we're going to do. We have to trust the owl. What other choice do we have? It's the only chance we have to reach the Dream Dot that will get us out of this mess."

Michael had no choice but to agree. The boys looked at each other, then darted straight toward Min and Bill's, following the trail their owl friend, Alexios, had left behind.

"Get 'em, boys! Looks like they've run into a dead end!" Shivers shouted.

"Yeah, we've got 'em now, Captain!" one of the Thorns confidently replied.

As the boys closed in on Min and Bill's, something rather strange happened. It appeared they were gaining altitude as they approached the diner, rising off the ground, higher and higher, with every step they took, until they were eventually high enough to run right over the building.

Shivers and his crew stopped in their tracks, staring and trying to figure out what in the world was happening. "Well, don't just stand their you, block heads! Go get 'em! If those two little brats can do it, so can we!" Shivers yelled impatiently. His crew took off toward the diner, which the boys were now right above. Their only problem was, the Thorns could not see the trail left behind by the owl. So they were unsuccessful in their attempts to run up and over the diner as the boys had. This frustrated Shivers even more, as he continued to yell louder and louder at his crew and their pathetic failures to achieve what Charlie and Michael had done so effortlessly.

As Charlie and Michael stopped for a brief second to look back, now suspended in mid-air over Echo Lake, they noticed that the trail behind them was slowly starting to fade away.

"Looks like we need to keep moving before we end up getting wet," Charlie said to his brother.

Michael agreed, as the two of them turned and quickly headed down the trail, over Echo Lake and around the dinosaur ice cream stand, leaving Shivers and his frustrated crew far behind.

No longer able to see the boys, Captain Shivers fell to his knees and began to scream uncontrollably. It was going to be a long evening for his crew.

Meanwhile, Charlie and his brother had reached the end of the trail, which led right down into the well by the Indiana Jones Stunt Spectacular show.

"Are you sure, Charlie?"

"You see it, don't you? The trail leads into the well. So that's where we're going."

"Right you are Charlie," came a voice deep within the shadows of the brush. Just beyond the well sign. It was the owl. Only his big yellow eyes were visible. "Have faith in my words, lads. Believe in the magic," Alexios said, as he looked toward the well.

"Oh, I get it," Charlie said. "And I do believe. Come on, Michael, follow me." Charlie climbed the fence, jumped feet first into the well, and was gone. His disappearance was followed by a flash of light and a gust of wind, which shook the surrounding foliage.

Scared of being left behind, Michael quickly looked at the owl to confirm it was okay, then climbed through the fence and jumped in as well.

Ben and Alexios' plan had worked.

Chapter Seven

Charlie and Michael awoke the next morning to the sound of their mother's blow dryer, exhausted and confused from the previous day's events. Strangely enough, upon their return from WONDER the night before, the boys had discovered that their parents had no recollection of them ever being gone. Apparently, while Charlie and Michael were in WONDER, someone had placed their parents under some form of memory spell which prevented them from noticing their boys had been missing for that entire period of time. For the rest of that evening, the Zastawits family had carried on with their vacation as if nothing had ever happened, though Charlie and Michael knew better.

"Good morning, boys," Mrs. Z shouted over the noise of her hair dryer. One of you needs to jump in the shower. Times a-wasting."

Michael, being more the morning person than his brother, grabbed his clothes and headed for the bathroom.

"Hey, Charlie, your dad found a letter under the door this morning with your name on it. Looks like a pretty fancy envelope. You should open it. It's over on the table."

Charlie's head was still a little foggy from just waking up, but his mother's words somehow penetrated through it all and peaked his curiosity. He rolled out of bed and managed to stumble over and find the letter, which was inside a metallic purple envelope with gold script lettering and an ornate border, sitting on the table next to the mirror. The envelope read:

Charlie Zastawits

You're invited to a special character lunch.

Charlie tore open the letter and quickly read through it:

All of us here at the most magical place on earth are excited to invite you and your brother for a Magical Kids

> Lunch down in Boatwright's Dining Hall today. Parents, please bring your children for check-in between 12pm and 12:15pm. Lunchtime activities for your children begin at 12:30pm and end at 2:00pm. Bring your appetites and your imaginations. It's going to be a magically terrific time!
>
> Hope to see you today,
>
> Mickey & Friends

The letter was signed by Mickey and all his friends, and included an illustrated image of several characters enjoying lunch in a playful manner.

"Mom, did you read this? Michael and I are invited to have lunch today with some of the characters."

"Oh, really. Let me see that letter," she said in a curious voice. Their mother already knew about the lunch. Her husband had set it up months ago and had secretly told her about it on the trip down. She decided to play along and build up the excitement for Charlie and Michael.

"See, look. It's today, Mom," Charlie replied as he danced around the room, too excited to sit down after handing the letter to his mom.

Mrs. Z quickly glanced at the letter again, then replied, "Why, you're correct, Charlie. It is today. I guess when your father returns from his walk, we will have to check and see if he thinks it's OK for you and your brother to go to the lunch alone. You know how protective he is of his boys," she said in a curiously doubtful tone, still stringing the boys along to maintain their level of excitement.

On her last word, the lock clicked, the handle turned, and Mr. Z walked into room, returning from his morning stroll. He was full of energy and ready to go. "Good morning, everyone. Ready for another magical day in the parks?"

"I'm just about ready, dear. The boys still need to clean up. And Charlie has something to show you."

Mr. Z took the hint from his wife and ran with it. "Oh, really.? What do you have to show me, son?"

"It's a letter from Mickey and all his friends. They invited Michael and I to a lunch party."

"Really? Well, when is it?" his father asked, in a semi serious tone.

"It's today, Dad. Can we go? Please. Please. Please."

"What about your mother and I? Are we invited?"

"Uh, no, Dad. It's just for kids. No adults allowed."

"I don't know. Sounds kind of scary to me," Mr. Z jokingly replied.

"Please, dad. Pleeeeease!"

"Yeah. Please, Dad!" Michael chimed in, as he burst out of the bathroom to give his brother support.

"I don't know. What does Mom think? Honey?"

At this point the boys were bouncing up and down on the floor and beds, unable to control their emotions, their bodies filled with restless energy and excitement.

"Pleeease, Mom. I promise we'll be good.," Charlie said.

Their parents looked at each other, started to smirk, then looked at the boys as Mrs. Z blurted out, "Of course you can go. You didn't really think we would say no, did you?"

"Really?" Charlie and his brother responded with great big smiles.

"Why, of course, boys, it's Disney World!" Mr. Z shouted.

The entire family enjoyed a good laugh, then the boys rushed to clean up so they could all begin the third day of their magical vacation.

Morning passed quickly for Charlie and his family, which was filled with a trip to Disney Springs where they enjoyed fabulous stores like Once Upon a Toy, Goofy's Candy Company, and the World of Disney, the largest Disney store on the planet. Mrs Z. was taking mental notes all along, keeping track of future gift ideas for the boys, and her child-like husband as well. Eleven fifteen came quickly. Charlie and his family headed out for lunch where, after a short bus ride, the boys were taken for their big, spectacular event with Mickey and friends. They were so excited, they could hardly wait.

The line was long, almost endless it seemed, as parents waited patiently with their children to check in for the lunch event. As the children said goodbye to their parents and entered Boatwright's Dining Hall, they were greeted by happy cast members and escorted to tables throughout the character-filled restaurant. Donald, Goofy, Stitch, Snow White, Cinderella. Belle, Beast, Captain Hook, and others were there, already mingling. There must have been at least twenty characters. Normally, Boatwright's served character-free dinners only. But this was a special occasion. Charlie and his brother were escorted to a corner table toward the back of the restaurant. His mind was filled with so much excitement that he had completely forgotten his parents had left to go eat somewhere else. It was going to be a fantastic lunch, indeed.

Before long, all the children had been seated, food brought to the tables, and the grand announcement made, which welcomed in special guests Mickey and Minnie. The lunch party had begun. Characters and cast members danced around the hall from table to table, interacting with the children who were enjoying their delightful meals. Music and balloons filled the air, giving the party an energetic charge of happiness. At that moment, amidst all that was going on, Tigger approached Charlie and Michael, encouraging them to follow his lead. The two boys gladly obliged, hopping up from their table and skipping along to the music as they followed Tigger around the room and through a doorway into a smaller room. The door suddenly closed behind them. Charlie, sensing it was a trap, yelled to Michael, who lunged for the door. But it was too late. It was securely locked from the outside, leaving the boys no way to escape.

The boys quickly focused their attention back on Tigger, who was gesturing for Charlie and his brother to come over and sit down. Both boys walked cautiously up to the table and sat down. Tigger held up a finger, signaling the boys to stay where they were. Walking to another door, the big orange cat struck a pose and opened it up. And out came a friendly face. Right away, Charlie and Michael recognized the jolly little man. It was Ben Glimmer. The short, red haired fellow they had just met the day before in Hollywood Studios.

"Why, it's you. Ben. What in the world are you doing here?" Charlie asked.

Ben's smiling face quickly turned serious. He signaled to the boys to be quiet as his eyes locked in on the two youthful faces, and spoke: "I'm here because there's something I must tell you.

Both you and your brother need to listen carefully, and speak to nobody of what I'm about to say. Is that understood?"

Charlie and Michael both looked at Ben and agreed.

"Very well," Ben replied. "I just learned today that one of our most valuable Patrons has been captured by the evil forces of FOTO. We need you, Charlie and Michael, to help rescue our loyal friend before the Thorns are able to extract vital information from his mind that would lead to the destruction of WONDER."

"I'm sorry, Ben. But what is WONDER and why is it so important that we save this Patron friend of yours?" Charlie asked.

"You see, Charlie, many years ago, when Disney animation was making a name for itself and Disneyland was on the verge of opening, a select group of Imagineers secretly developed a magical world, a world created by their dreams and ideas. They called it the World of Natural Dream-Enhanced Realities, or WONDER. In this world, both reality and dream-like fantasy coexist. The deeper one travels into WONDER, the further removed from reality they become. For example, yesterday you and your brother first transported into Deep WONDER, and then were trapped by the Thorns in an outer level of WONDER, on your way back to reality."

"What? I don't understand," Charlie replied.

"Well, let me explain further. You see, there are three levels of WONDER. The first, simply called WONDER, is a world that looks just like the parks, but really isn't. It's what you might call a perfect vision, or a simulated version, of how the imagineers think the parks should look. This is where Alexios and I met you yesterday. Which brings me to my next point. In the first level of WONDER, animated elements, both 2D and 3D, plus real people and other things, can coexist within these simulated realities. Hence the reason you and your brother were able to meet and interact with Alexios, a 2D-animated character. Understand?"

"Oh, yeah. I get it." Michael responded.

"Yeah. Yeah, I understand, too. Go on," Charlie said.

"After the first level comes Deep WONDER. In Deep WONDER, everything is animated, including those who travel there. And again, the animations can be either 2D or 3D. Or even both. I believe you and your brother were able to experience a tiny bit of Deep WONDER yesterday, just before we met you?"

"Right. Michael and I were turned into 2D-animated wooden figures. We were in Geppetto's work shop. Hey, how did you know we were there?"

"Well, I didn't really know where you went, just that you had transported into Deep WONDER. Thanks to Frank."

"Frank? You mean Frank Wellington?" Charlie asked.

"Yes, Charlie. Frank Wellington," Ben replied with a sad expression. Which brings me to my next point." Ben paused and sighed. "As it turns out...unfortunately, well...Frank is the Patron. He's the one FOTO captured."

"Oh, no!" Charlie shouted. But why would somebody ever want to harm a nice man like Frank?" Charlie was beside himself. "And what or who is this FOTO thing you keep speaking of?"

"Shh. I know it's hard, Charlie, but we need to keep our voices down. You never know who might be lurking about." Ben leaned in toward the boys and whispered quietly, "And when I say who, I mean members of FOTO."

"Oh, yeah, so what is it?" Charlie replied back to Ben in a quiet tone.

"FOTO is the dark shadow that hangs over all that is good in the Disney community. Its proper name is the Forest of Thorns Order, and what it consists of is a conglomeration of all those who are evil and villain-like in the magical world we live in. It was started by a budding artist who attended drawing classes provided by Walt many, many years ago. His identity is still unknown to this day. Evidently, through the years, as the success of the Disney company grew, so did the jealousy of this unknown artist, to the point where the jealousy turned into spite and anger. And eventually led to the formation of FOTO, an organization whose name was inspired by a quote from Maleficent:

A forest of thorns shall be his tomb.

Borne through the skies on a fog of doom.

Now go with the curse, and serve me well.
'Round Stefan's castle, CAST MY SPELL!

As years have past, this dreadful order has grown larger, stronger, and more threatening to all the good that Disney tries to instill upon the world. And now, led mainly by the Dark Thorns, supreme leaders of FOTO, this evil and terrible force is determined to find, and gain control of, all the Objects of Magic which are key to preserving the happiness Walt spent a lifetime creating for the world."

"That doesn't sound good," Charlie said. "So those men, the ones that were chasing us in the park yesterday. They were members of FOTO?"

"Yes, indeed they were. It was mostly a group of FOTO spies who belong to the lowest level of the order and are often referred to as Thorns. The Thorns are led by captains. There is one Thorn captain for each segment, or park, in Walt Disney World, plus one for Disney Springs. Marty Shivers, the tall, skinny fella with the bad temper that you had the unfortunate experience of meeting yesterday, is the captain for Segment Three, better known as Hollywood Studios."

"Yeah, that was unfortunate. How come he was chasing us? We didn't do anything to him."

"You're right, Charlie. You and your brother didn't do anything to him. But, you have something he wants. Something the Dark Thorns need."

"And what's that?" asked Michael.

"The ears Frank gave you. They are one of the Objects of Magic. FOTO captured Frank because he was the one who gave you the ears. FOTO figured they could use Frank to get to you."

Charlie's eyes lit up.

"And by the way, make sure you always, ALWAYS wear those ears durning your stay here at Walt Disney World, except when you're sleeping, of course. Or taking a shower. Anyway, you know what I mean."

The boys confirmed their understanding.

"You never know when you may need them to get out of a fix. You'd be surprised what those ears are capable of doing," Ben said while pointing at the ears on top of Charlie's head.

"Yes. Yes, sir," Charlie replied.

"I have a question," Michael said.

"Sure, lad. What is it?"

"You said there were three levels of WONDER? You've only told us about two. So, what's the third level?"

"Ah, yes. Good question, Michael. So glad you were keeping track. I don't know much about the third level. But what I can tell you is this. Lying even deeper within WONDER is what we like to call the Dream Core. This is the center of WONDER, an area most of the Patrons, including myself, know little about. And for good reason. It is there, in the very heart of WONDER, where Walt's most cherished secret is preserved."

"Cherished secret? Whoa, that sounds important," Charlie said. "Do you know what it is?"

"Sorry, lads, I don't know anything about it. And even if I did, us Patrons, the guardians of WONDER, have sworn to never reveal our secrets to outsiders."

"Aw. After all we've been through, you still think of us as outsiders?"

"I'm afraid so, laddie. But, on the positive side of things, there's still more I can tell ya."

"Well, go on then, get on with it," Michael said.

"In a recent chain of events, it has come to our attention that the Thorns have obtained information vital to finding one of five Kingdom Crystals. If FOTO finds all five crystals, it will dramatically increase their chances of penetrating the Dream Core, something the Patrons cannot allow to happen. Ever."

"And why is that?" asked Charlie.

"Um. You see. Well. I...I don't exactly know. So sorry."

"And what are the Kingdom Crystals?" Michael blurted out.

"Now-now boys, no need to get all worked up."

"That's alright. Tell us what you do know, Ben," Charlie said in a kind voice.

"Alright, then. Let me see. Where was I?"

"The Kingdom Crystals," said Michael, as he rolled his eyes.

"Michael, take it easy, will ya," Charlie said. "Go ahead, Ben. Please continue."

"Ah, yes. Right. So. What I do know about the Kingdom Crystals is that there is a catch. In order for FOTO to find them, they will need to use the powers from all five Objects of Magic, as each object is magically connected to one of the crystals—one of which you have in your procession, the Ears of Virtue. If we can keep the Objects of Magic away from FOTO, their chances of succeeding will be greatly reduced."

"Wait a minute. You said reduced? So even if the Patrons keep the five objects away from the Thorns, which would prevent them from finding the Kingdom Crystals, there's still a chance FOTO can succeed?"

"I'm afraid so, my boy. How? I'm not quite sure. But Frank told me it would still be possible. And that's why he needs you."

"Needs me?" Charlie said with a baffled voice.

"Yes, you and your brother."

"Needs us for what?"

"To help the Patrons, of course."

"And how are we supposed to do that. I mean, what do we know? This sounds crazy."

"I know. It does, doesn't it, Charlie. Now you can see why it is so critical that we succeed in rescuing Frank Wellington from FOTO. Without him, we haven't a chance. So, are ya with me, lads?" Ben said, as he leaned in closely, looking deep into their eyes for the answer he needed so desperately to hear.

"Well, I guess we have no choice. Right, Michael? We need to help Frank, so he can help us," Charlie said, while looking at his brother.

"Right," his brother replied.

A tear ran down Ben's cheek as he pulled the boys closer for a hug. Then, in a quiet tone of voice, he told the boys his plan to rescue Frank.

When Ben and the boys had finished with their meeting, the lunch party out in the larger rooms of Boatwright's still had a half hour to go. Ben quietly slipped out the door he entered from, while Tigger (who had patiently been guarding the room) opened the other door and walked the boys back out into the fray of happy, dancing children. Still hungry for lunch, Charlie and Michael went back to their table to grab a bite to eat, and ponder all they had been told, while Tigger entered the character conga line to entertain the children.

After the lunch event had ended and the boys were picked up by their parents, the rest of the day continued on like any other ordinary day at Disney World. Charlie and his family enjoyed a variety of attractions, food, fun, fireworks, and laughter, creating a multitude of family memories that would last a lifetime—though neither boy could stop thinking what might lie ahead for day four of what had become a most unusual vacation.

Chapter Eight

Day three had filled their heads to the point that neither boy slept well that night. Charlie's dreams had been vivid and focused on what members of FOTO might be doing to Frank Wellington. Over and over, Charlie's mind replayed images of Frank being poked, prodded, and mistreated by a group of grungy Thorn toadies. It was a thought his mind never escaped through an entire night of restlessness and sweaty pillows.

"Charlie. Charlie, wake up. You're having a bad dream," Michael said as he shook his brother's shoulders in an attempt to wake him.

Charlie's eyes suddenly opened, startled by the abruptness of his return to the reality of morning.

"Earth to, Charlie. Come in, Charlie. Can you hear me?" Michael said.

His brother sat up quickly and shook his head as he gazed toward the sunlit balcony doors. Another day had come.

"Hey, Charlie, you need to snap out of it before Mom or Dad walk in the room and see you this way. You don't want them to start thinking something is wrong," Michael said, trying to talk his brother back to a normal state. "Do you hear me? Mom and Dad went out to grab coffee from the food court. You don't want them to see you like this, do you? Charlie?"

"Mom? Dad? Frank. We have to help Frank. You're right. I gotta...I gotta straighten up," Charlie blurted, as his eyes moved rapidly from side to side. The mention of his mother and father jolted his mind back to reality. He jumped out of bed, opened the sliding balcony door, and stepped outside to awaken his senses.

"What are you doing, Charlie? You need to get ready."

Charlie turned and looked at his brother, then turned back to face the morning. "Yes. You know, you're right, Michael. I do need to get ready. And so do you. It's going to be a busy day. We need to get Frank back."

As Charlie cleaned up, he began to think about the Crystal Palace and the wonderfully delicious breakfast their family would be enjoying that morning. In turn, this reminded him of the secret plan they had discussed with Ben the day before. During their discussion, Charlie had told Ben where their family would be eating breakfast the next day. In response, Ben suggested the two boys be on the lookout for a swallow in a tree. Now, Charlie knew that a swallow was a type of bird. And that birds, for the most part, dwell in trees. But what he didn't know was where to begin looking for a little tiny bird that would be perched up in a tree at the Magic Kingdom. Furthermore, Ben had told them that under this tree, they would find a rock near a wheel of water. And there, under the rock, they would discover a hidden message Frank had left behind. This made the boys wonder why Ben couldn't just tell them what the message. Obviously that would be easier. The truth was, Ben couldn't tell them, because he didn't know. Everything he had told them, every last bit of detail, had been read from notes written by Frank. All Ben could tell them was that Charlie needed to be wearing the magic ears to read the message. Ben had also told the boys, and this was the most important detail of all, that the path to finding Frank will lie somewhere along the path to finding the first Kingdom Crystal.

As Charlie and his family made their way to breakfast, his mind and stomach continued to churn to the point his appetite had all but disappeared. By the time his family reached the Crystal Palace, he was ready to skip breakfast altogether and seek out the swallow in the tree. But of course, he knew better. There was no way their mother would ever let her two growing boys skip a meal. So Charlie quietly carried on with the Zastawits ritual of breakfast: gathering food and drink, sitting, eating, discussing their plans for the day, then claiming to be too full to move. The boys knew the ritual all too well, and recognized when it was about to end. This was their chance to seize the moment.

"Hey, Dad, where can you find trees in this park?"

"What? That's an odd question, Charlie. Why do you ask?"

"Well, Michael and I had a bet whether or not there were trees in all the lands of the Magic Kingdom."

"Of course there are. At least I think so, right, Ed?" their mother replied.

"Oh, I'm sure there's a tree or two in every land, Charlie. At least I think there is. Hmmm. Now you got me wondering, Charlie. Yep, I guess that's something we'll just have to find out. Could be fun."

"Yeah, that sounds great," Charlie replied.

"However, we're only in the Magic Kingdom for the first part of the day. Then we're hopping over to Hollywood Studios for the second half."

Charlie and Michael looked at each other with desperate eyes.

"Oh. Well. We should probably get moving then. Don't you think, Dad?"

"Absolutely. I guess it's time we head out and start searching. Ready, Momma?"

"Oh, yeah," she replied, while getting up from her chair.

The boys jumped up as well, eager to go.

"So where are we headed? You boys seem like you're in a hurry."

"Well, we only have half a day, Ed, and the boys want to do some tree hunting in the Magic Kingdom. So I say we just head straight for Fantasyland and work our way back through Adventureland. There's a lot more trees on that side of the park than the other."

"Great idea, Mom," Charlie said, smiling to his brother.

With their parents under the impression they were searching for trees, the boys searched high, low, left, right, and around every nook and cranny, for the entire morning. Nothing in Fantasyland. No luck in Liberty Square, either. Frontierland showed promise, with all the trees on Tom Sawyer Island. But still, no sign of a swallow in a tree. Had they misunderstood Ben's words? Were they looking in the wrong park? Charlie was beginning to think so. The first half of the day was nearing its end and so were Charlie's hopes. As their family passed into

Adventureland, Charlie's mind began to work at double speed, scanning quickly for any trees nearby. Could it be located on the Jungle Cruise? No. Because it would be impossible to search for clues from a boat. Same was true for Pirates of the Caribbean. One by one, Charlie checked off all the possibilities in his mind. Until, that is, he thought about the Swiss Family Treehouse. Could it be? Quickly, he threw together a plan. There was no time to lose.

"Hey, Dad. We haven't checked out the treehouse yet. Do you think we could go walk through it? It's almost time for us to head over to Hollywood Studios, so I thought that might be something quick and fun to do before we go."

"Sure, buddy. That sounds like a perfect plan. Everyone agree?"

"Oh, yes, I love the treehouse," said Mrs. Z.

"Me, too," answered Michael, giving his brother a thumbs up.

As Charlie and his family approached the treehouse, he read the sign near the entry point out loud:

> On this site, July 17, 1805, the Swiss Family Robinson composed of myself, my good wife and three sons, Fritz, Ernst and little Francis...we're the sole survivors by the grace of God of the ill fated ship SWALLOW.
>
> From the wreckage we built our home in this tree for protection on this uncharted shore. Franz.

"That's a pretty awesome backstory, don't ya think, Charlie?"

"Yeah, Dad. It's very interesting," Charlie said as he looked and smiled at Michael.

Mr. Z was somewhat of a fanatic when it came to the Swiss Family Treehouse. In fact, he was utterly obsessed with its details. Immediately he grabbed his wife by the hand and became her tour guide, leading her off, and up, into the treehouse. It was the perfect opportunity for the boys to search the grounds.

"OK, Michael, what was it that Ben told us to look for again?"

"It was a rock near a wheel of water. I think?"

"Yeah, that sounds right. Look over there. It's a water wheel, used to raise water up into the treehouse. Let's go."

As the boys approached the wheel, the mouse ears on Charlie's head began to hum softly as they gave off subtle, internal sparks of light that only someone up close would notice—in this case, Michael.

"Charlie. Your ears. They're lighting up, like fireworks."

"Yeah. I figured something was going on up there, with all the humming and popping I'm hearing. Look, Michael. There's a bunch of rocks over there."

"I know. I see them. But how are we supposed to know which one has the message under it?"

As Charlie scanned slowly over the rocks, he said. "That's easy. It's the third from the left. The one with three stars on it. It's marked of three, just like Ben told us."

"Where? I still don't see it."

"Right there, on the right corner of the stone. Three little stars," Charlie said as he pointed to the mark.

"Oh. Now I see it."

"Since I'm the one who will be able to read the message using the ears, you will have to pull back the stone. Ready?"

"Sure, I'm ready," Michael replied as he crouched down and got into position to pull back the stone.

Charlie scanned the area, just to make sure no one was watching, then he signaled Michael to lift the stone. What he saw underneath the stone was another stone. But the second stone was far from ordinary. It was relatively flat, black in color, and had a message etched in green lettering. The closer Charlie moved toward it, the more prominent the green glowing letters showed on its surface, which spelled out the secret message Frank had left behind:

> One man's dream becomes a young man's adventure and the beginning begins where the attraction ends.

Charlie quickly reached for his phone and took a photo of the rock before the words faded away. "Got it Michael."

Michael let the larger top stone fall back into place over the smaller black stone. CLUNK.

"What are ya guys digging for under those rocks?" a voice whispered over Charlie's left shoulder, startling him. When he turned to look, he saw two young teenagers curiously staring at the rocks. One was a boy, the other a cute girl with long blonde hair. Most likely they were brother and sister.

"Uh, not much. We're just doing a little exploring. Nothing special," Charlie replied.

"Are ya sure, cause it looked to me like you were reading something under that rock your brother was holding up."

Charlie barely heard what the boy said; his eyes were fixated on the girl.

"Answer him, ya goof," Michael said to his brother, while nudging him in the side.

"Oh, right. Nah, I wasn't reading. Just checking out some bugs, that's all."

The girl looked at her brother, then rolled her eyes. "Nothing to see here, I guess."

Her comment made Charlie feel foolish for what he'd said, causing him to blush.

"Yeah, you're probably right, sis. Let's get outta here," the teenage boy said, as he and his sister turned and headed up into the treehouse.

Charlie, still fixated on the girl, remained sitting on the ground. His brother, on the other hand, stood back up and started walking into the treehouse.

"Well? C'mon, Charlie. Get up. We have to go find Mom and Dad before they leave us. Geez. You'd think you'd never seen a girl before. Hurry up, for Pete's sake!"

Charlie finally managed to get back on his feet and the boys headed up the treehouse stairs to track down their parents.

An hour had passed and the Zastawits family had just finished with a light lunch at the Plaza Restaurant near Main Street. As they headed down the street toward the front gates, Charlie and Michael lagged behind just enough to have a private conversation regarding their latest discovery.

"So what was written on the rock?" Michael asked.

Charlie pulled out his phone and showed his brother the photo he took.

"So, it looks like we're headed to the right park?"

"Yeah. The Walt Disney: One Man's Dream attraction is there. I saw it yesterday when we were there. That has to be where we need to go. Don't you think?"

"I'd say so."

"Good. So we'll worry about the rest when we get there."

Charlie tucked his phone away as he and Michael took in the sights and sounds, and the smell of freshly popped popcorn, while exiting the Magic Kingdom, on their way to an afternoon of fun and unknown experiences at Hollywood Studios.

Since the afternoons were so hot in the Florida summer, Charlie and his family were maximizing their time indoors, and in doing so, had sought out activities or attractions with small crowd levels. This unscheduled chain of events played right into Charlie and Michael's plans, which were to spend a great deal of time in the One Man's Dream exhibit. Their dad was sweating like a faucet, their mom's hair frazzled by humidity. The boys couldn't ask for a better opportunity.

"Hey, Dad, do you think we could grab a couple of snow cones from the stand over there, then head into One Man's Dream? It should be nice and cool in there. And it doesn't look like there's a line, so we should be able to get right in."

"You read my mind, Charlie. That's a great idea. Let's go grab a cool snack and head for shelter." The whole family silently rejoiced as they gathered up cool treats at a nearby stand and made a beeline for the exhibit entrance.

As they entered One Man's Dream, the cool air cast down upon their overheated bodies, a feeling the whole family acknowledged with praise. Once inside, Charlie's parents broke off from the boys as their father immediately went into tour guide mode, eager to show his wife how much he knew about the subject matter that lay before them.

"OK, Michael, let's review the message Frank left for us under..."

"What? What's wrong? Aren't ya gonna finish what you were saying?" Michael said.

Charlie had gone into a goofy stare from mid-sentence. He had spotted the teenage girl they met at the treehouse earlier that day, and her big brother was still with her as well.

"Charlie, what are you looking at? What's wrong with you? Charlie!" Michael said as he turned to see what had stolen his brother's attention. "Oh, geez, not the girl thing again. You gotta snap out of it. We have stuff to do."

"Yeah. Stuuuufff," Charlie replied, in a dumbfounded manner.

"She's a teenager anyway, Charlie. You have no chance."

The girl turned and flipped her hair with her hand, then shot Charlie a sparkling smile across the room, as if she knew he was watching her.

"You see, Michael, she just smiled at me. I mean, just look at her. Nice hair...big brown eyes...and her smile. What a smile."

"OK, whatever you say, Charlie." Michael wasn't buying it. Something just didn't feel right to him, which made him begin to think: is it a coincidence that these teenagers showed up during the two most important moments of the day? First of all, they were there when we discovered Frank's message under the rock. Then, they pop up again? Now? Right when we are about to search for clues that could lead us to Frank, and possibly the first of five Kingdom Crystals? But just as Michael was gaining traction in his thoughts, his brother threw him off course.

"And her skin. So tan and shiny," Charlie said, as he continued to ramble on about the teenage girl.

That was it. Michael had had enough. "Look, if you want to sit here all day and dream about a girl you're too afraid to talk to, fine with me. But I thought we were trying to help Frank. I mean, look at her. Yeah, she's a girl. And yeah, she's pretty. But why would a teenage girl be interested in a younger boy like you? Don't you think that's kind of weird?" Michael said, in an attempt to pull his brother out of the girly daze he was in.

"What? Weird? Why do you think she's weird? She looks pretty normal to me."

"I'm not talking about the way she looks. I'm talking about the way she thinks. As in, why would she be interested in a goofy young boy like my brother."

"Your brother? Oh. You mean me?"

"No. I mean the other brother I don't have. Geez. Of course I mean you."

"Ah. Ha-ha-ha. Of course you mean me. You don't have another brother," Charlie replied with a chuckle of embarrassment.

"Glad to have you back, Charlie. Now, don't you think we should start looking for those clues?"

"Yeah. Right. The clues. Let me take a look at the second part of Frank's riddle. It says here, "the beginning begins where the attraction ends."

"Right. So what you think that means, Charlie?"

"Sounds like whatever it is we're supposed to be looking for will be located somewhere near the end of the attraction. Don't you agree?"

"Yep. That makes sense to me."

"Alright, then, let's head toward the end of the exhibit and start looking there," Charlie said. The two boys checked to see where their parents were. Their father was heavy into his Disney lecture with their mother, so both parents were mentally occupied. Charlie and Michael walked slowly by, letting their parents know they were headed farther down the exhibit. Both turned to look at their kids, and quickly gave the boys approval to venture off toward the end of the exhibit. If their parents had only known what they had just done, they may had never let them go.

Charlie and Michael painstakingly continued their search near the end of the attraction, as the past half hour had given them nothing to go by. Their parents were now within earshot and time was running short. The boys were afraid if they couldn't find something soon, their opportunity to find Frank and help the Patrons of WONDER would be lost forever.

"Let me know if you see something, Michael. Anything at all. Cause I haven't," Charlie said, while frantically searching for any clues that might lead them in the right direction.

"Nope. I don't see anything either. Wait a minute. What's that over by the Spaceship Earth model? Oh, forget it. It was just the lighting or something."

"Oh, just keep looking, Michael. At least we know where not to look."

"I'm going to check by the D23 display, while you look by the Tree of Life model. OK, Charlie?"

"Yeah. Yeah. That's fine. Just do it quickly," Charlie said impatiently. "We're running out of time."

Michael darted over to the D23 display, thinking that this had to be it. The clue they were looking for had to be located in this display. There wasn't much left to see in the exhibit. But all he found was more disappointment. With his head held low, he drug his feet back to his brother and delivered the bad news. "Nothing there either, Charlie," Michael sniffed a couple times, trying to hold back his emotions.

"Well, Michael, I didn't have any luck either. I don't think there's anything left for us to search here, do you?" Charlie said as he looked upwards, seeking an answer.

"Hey, boys. Isn't this place terrific? It's just loaded with all sorts of good stuff. Don't ya just love it?" Their parents had caught up. And their father was beside himself, giddy as a kid in a candy store. "Have you guys looked at everything in here you wanted to? Cause if you have, we can move on."

The boys were afraid to speak, worried if they did, it would be the end of their search for Frank, the end of their search for the first Kingdom Crystal, and the end of WONDER.

"If you're still looking, that's fine, boys, but there's one more thing we still have to see."

Charlie's perked up. "There is?"

"Why, sure. We still have the One Man's Dream film to watch in the Walt Disney Theatre. See?" His father pointed at the theatre doors, which were flanked on both sides by LED displays that let guests know how much time was remaining until the next show started.

"Oh, my goodness. We didn't even notice, Dad. I guess we were too wrapped up in all the cool things here in the exhibit," Charlie said, as he and his brother let out a big chuckle, relieved that there was still more to see, and still a chance to save Frank.

The theatre doors opened just seconds later and Charlie and his family walked in, finding perfect center-row seats. Mr. Z sat on the left, the boys in the center, and Mrs. Z on the right. The doors closed, the room darkened, and the screen lit up with the incredible life story of Walt Disney. As the movie carried on, Charlie kept trying harder and harder to find something, anything, that might help lead them to Frank. But with only a few short minutes left in the show, he still had found nothing. The pressure on his young mind had broken him down to the point of surrender—that is, until he heard something in the middle of Walt's interview about the merry-go-round and the influence it had on him to build Disneyland. Just when Charlie was about to give up, Walt turned, looked him right in the eye, and said:

> If I were you, young man, I'd go give that tree in the other room a closer look. You may have overlooked one of its most important details. Oh. And be sure to repeat these words when you do: "on the eagle's flight we shall see, the true power of this magnificent tree."

Charlie quickly typed Walt's words into his phone, then leaned toward his brother and whispered, "Did you hear that, Michael?" His brother shook his head. Charlie looked at both parents and neither seemed phased. They had not seen nor heard what Walt had said either. When the movie ended and the lights came back up, Charlie persuaded his parents to take them back into the exhibit, which was a common practice amongst guests. As they made their way there, Charlie's father noticed that he still had more to show his wife, at which point Charlie signaled Michael to follow him to the Tree of Life. He was pretty sure this had to be the tree Walt was referring to. Once in front of the scale model, he explained to his brother what had happened during the movie, and to repeat the words "on an eagle's flight we shall see, the true power of this magnificent tree."

As the boys repeated the phrase, Michael noticed Charlie's mouse ears were beginning to glow, just as they had earlier at the treehouse in the Magic Kingdom. "Your ears are beginning to light up again, Charlie. I have a feeling something crazy is about to happen to us."

"I think you're right, Michael."

While scanning the Tree of Life display for clues, something rather amazing happened. Everything in the model came to life and began to move. The deer grazing on the grass began to walk, the miniature people pointed to the tree and were discussing something about its details, using body gestures. Even the animals that made up the tree itself began to move in slow, smooth motions, making the branches sway back and forth in a rhythmic pattern. The tree had come to life right before Charlie and Michael's eyes. And as the boys continued to watch in disbelief, a mighty bald eagle broke free from the detailed animal bark of the tree. Its figure glistened with metallic gold and silver dust while it circled the display with effortless grace over and over again. With each pass the eagle made, the tree became more animated and brighter, and began to glow a magnificent green. Unbeknownst to the boys, the display glass had evaporated into thin air. A strong, freshening wind began to swirl around the tree as though it were following the circling eagle. Over and over, the eagle circled the tree, the wind gaining strength with each pass. And the tree continued to get brighter and brighter.

On the eagle's next pass, a woman's echoing voice called out: "Come, let the journey begin!" The sound of the woman's voice surrounded and embraced the boys from all sides, carrying their thoughts beyond reality. As the wind reached its pinnacle, the eagle came soaring from behind the tree, right at the boys with talons out and screeching, as if it were going to attack. Anticipating the eagle's wrath, the two brothers ducked into defensive positions. Just as they did, the magnificent bird burst into a breathtaking display of sparkling gold and silver dust, followed by a barrage of loud, tingling noises. And then... silence. The boys opened their eyes, uncovered their heads, and slowly looked around. They were no longer in the One Man's Dream exhibit.

Chapter Nine

The eagle had magically transported the boys into an Animal Kingdom vision of WONDER. And like their previous journey into a simulated Hollywood Studios, everything was perfect. All the foliage was lush and green, the buildings perfectly detailed, the sky, a wonderful shade of blue, and all the smiling guests dressed and groomed to perfection.

"So what do we look for now, Charlie?"

"I'm not exactly sure. It looks like we're on Discovery Island, the heart of the Animal Kingdom. Maybe the Tree of Life has something to do with it, or else the magic ears wouldn't have transported us to this location. I guess we start by searching the island."

But just at that moment, there was a small rumble deep beneath the walkway the boys were standing on, followed by a subtle quake in the earth.

"Charlie? Did you just feel that? It was like, I don't know...a mini earthquake or something."

"What? No, you're imagining things. Florida doesn't have earthquakes."

"Yeah, well, what's that noise I hear coming from under the ground? And this really isn't Florida we're in right now, anyway."

Indeed, Michael had heard something. A distant rumbling noise that sounded like it was working its way up through the earth, closer and closer to where the boys stood. The ground began to shake uncontrollably. Charlie and Michael took off running toward a nearby shop for protection.

"Michael, you were right!"

"I told you so! Now do you believe me?"

Nearby trees began to fall. The walkway where the boys had stood broke open, with cracks traveling in all directions.

Strangely, but expected, the simulated guests and cast members acted as if nothing unusual was happening.

"Why aren't the people scared?" Charlie said.

"Well, if they're not worried, maybe we shouldn't be either?"

"No, we need to worry. I don't think they can get hurt, being they're simulations. But we can."

"How do you know it can hurt us, if we've never done this before?"

"I don't know, Michael. But my gut tells me, if you go out there, you're gonna get hurt. And usually, if something feels wrong, that means it is. So stay put. Got it?"

The earth continued to open up in various directions all around them. Steam pushed out through each fresh crack, as the ground continued to shake. And then...it stopped. The boys cautiously ventured out, making sure the ground had stabilized before moving on. As they were looking around, water from the nearby stream slowly crept in to fill some of the cracks created by the earthquake and form what looked like more than just a random pattern.

"Hey, Michael, take a look at this, will ya."

"Letters."

"Exactly. The water is spelling out a message by filling in some of the smaller cracks. S...e...e...k. Seek. o...u...t. Seek out. The water continued, until it had reached terminal points in the cracks, leaving behind the message: Seek out the Ziwani Trader.

"Ziwani Trader? What's that mean, Charlie?"

"Quick, grab a park map from the stand over there. Let's see if we can find it."

"Good idea, Charlie. I'll be right back."

While Michael retrieved a map, Charlie occupied his time by carefully looking around for anything peculiar, like clues, unusual characters, or anything else. But what really caught his eye were the cracks in the ground. They appeared to be fixing themselves. Very slowly, the water in each crack sank into the earth as all the openings sealed themselves up, until no traces were left behind. By the time Michael returned with the map, the walkway was back to being picture perfect.

"Look at the ground, Michael."

"Why would I want to look at that cracked-up mess?"

"Just look, would ya?"

"Alright, alright," Michael said as he turned to see what his brother thought was so incredible. "What the..."

"I thought you'd get a surprise out of that. Guess I was right."

"So where did all the cracks go?"

"They just kinda sealed themselves back up."

"Really? They sealed themselves up? How'd they do that?"

"Disney Magic, I guess," Charlie replied. "Remember, this isn't the real world we're in now. It's a part of WONDER. So anything is possible. Real or not."

"I guess you're right. Here's the map you wanted," Michael said as he handed it to his brother to check over.

"OK, let's see what we can find. Ziwani Trader, Ziwani Trader, where are you?" Charlie scanned over the map, using his finger as a pointer. "Ah! There it is. Ziwani Traders. Looks like we're headed to Africa, Michael. Which is..."

"Over there," Michael replied, while pointing to a sign that showed the way.

Zawani Traders was full of African merchandise, including clothes, instruments, house decor, animal toys, and various other items. Charlie, being an animal lover, was immediately drawn to the animal toys. There were walking elephants made of wood, giraffe kites, zebras with wheel hooves that could be rolled across the floor, and many other interesting toys which the boys had never seen the likes of. But there was one particular item that caught Charlie's attention. It wasn't a toy, but rather a walking stick, in a basket near the back corner of the market store. It was hand carved out of wood and highly detailed with cultural graphics. Atop the stick sat a beautifully carved ostrich head with strong details and welcoming eyes, which called to Charlie. It was almost as if he had been cast under a spell. Slowly, he walked over to the corner and pulled the walking stick from the basket to get a closer look at its amazing artistry.

"How much for this, sir?" Charlie asked the cast member.

"What? You don't have any money to buy that, Charlie," Michael snipped. "Besides, that thing is kind of weird looking, don't you think?"

"Quiet, Michael. You're being rude. How much, sir?"

"Ah. That's is a very good choice, young man. Very good indeed. It was created in one of the most remote villages back in Africa. Very rare and very well crafted."

"Oh. So it's probably pretty expensive then, right?"

"For any normal customer on any normal day, yes, it would be. But you, young man, are very special. We were told you would be coming to visit our market to seek out the ostrich stick," the cast member said.

"So you knew we were coming? How did you know that? I've never been here or met you before in my life."

"A wise man, a Patron of WONDER, informed me almost two months ago that you would be coming to this very market."

"You mean Frank? Frank Wellington? But, but he's only known me for a couple days."

"Ah, but that is only what you know in your brain. Sometimes you need to search beyond your thoughts."

"Beyond my thoughts?"

"Yes, beyond."

"What do you mean, beyond?"

"Look inward, child. Search within your heart. It is there you will find all the answers you seek. You just have to listen."

"Listen?"

"To your heart, young man. Listen to your heart. It will never lie to you. Now, about that stick you hold in your hand."

"Stick? Oh, right. The walking stick. Huh-huh." Charlie had become so mesmerized by the cast member's words that he'd completely forgotten about the ostrich stick he was holding.

"So you wish to purchase the ostrich stick, yes?" the cast member asked with a smile.

"Yes. Yes, sir. That's right. So how much does it cost? I don't believe you ever mentioned a price. Did you?"

"For someone willing to help a man such as Frank, there is no monetary price. Only what you are willing to sacrifice. In this case, your time, happiness, and wellness."

"Really? You mean I don't have to give you money for it?"

"To some, what I've already mentioned to you holds far greater value than money ever could. In time, you may understand as well."

"I'm not quite sure I'm following you."

"In time, my young friend. Now you and your brother must be on your way. And remember, listen to your heart. Go now, before they discover you are here."

"Who's they?" Michael asked.

"The Thorns."

"Right. Thorns," Charlie said, as he looked at his brother with concern. "Thanks for your help, sir. C'mon, Michael, let's get out of here." Charlie paused for a second. "Wait a minute. We don't know where we're supposed to go," Charlie said, as he turned to look at the cast member for one last bit of advice.

"Listen to your heart," the cast member said as he pointed to his chest and smiled.

Confused, Charlie and his brother headed out the door, taking in the scenery while trying to decide in which direction to head. The perfect blue sky, which had been present all along, was beginning to give way to a strong east wind and a wall of storm clouds. And waiting for them, just ahead, were the teenage girl and her feisty big brother, both staring directly at the boys with evil grins and piercing eyes. The boys sensed that their day was about to change as quickly as the weather had.

"I don't know, sis. Looks like our friend found something pretty important. What do you think?"

"Yeah, Troy. I think you're right. Hey cutie, can I see what you bought?" The girl gave Charlie a big shiny smile and batted her eyes in an attempt to sway his better judgment.

Luckily, it had no effect on his younger brother. "Sorry, we're not allowed to talk to strangers."

Michael's words struck a nerve. "I wasn't talking to you, half pint. I was talking to your big brother here," she said, while continuing to smile in Charlie's direction.

"Well, he's not listening, are you, Charlie?"

"Charlie. I like that name. Can I see what you bought, Charlie?"

"Don't you dare do it," Michael whispered to his brother with a nudge.

Charlie finally snapped out of his girl daze and responded. "Sorry. Like my brother already told you, we're not allowed to talk to strangers."

Charlie's words threw the teenage girl into a tizzy. With her face turning red, jaw clenched, and eyes bulging, she yelled, "Troy! Take the stick from that kid! Now!"

Troy lunged forward on his sister's command, grabbing for the stick. With cat-like reflexes, Michael leaped between Charlie and Troy's reaching hand—blocking his path to the stick and causing the larger boy to lose balance and fall to the ground.

"Run, Charlie!" Michael yelled as he tumbled athletically across the ground and back into a stance. "This way!"

"Get back here, you little pretzel boy! I'll tie you into knots!" Troy yelled in frustration after being foiled by Michael's actions.

Charlie took off like a dart, quickly following his brother toward Asia, with the ostrich stick in hand.

"Troy! What are you doing? Get up! Get up, you dimwit!"

Charlie turned to look back while he was running. His brain couldn't believe what his eyes began to witness, as it appeared the Thorn belt buckles could do much more than just act as a source of camouflage. The teenage brother and sister team simultaneously hit their buckles and instantly changed from human form into a pair of very large, animated creatures that were part human and part baboon—known in WONDER as baboonagins, creatures as large as a human that walked upright and spoke like a human as well. But that is where the similarity ended. Baboonagins' heads and facial features were very much baboon-like. Their arms were much longer and hands quite larger than ours. Baboonagin feet were also quite large, with elongated toes for gripping tree branches, since much of the time they traveled through the jungle swinging from tree to tree. Their strength was two or three times that of a physically fit human, making them very dangerous to deal with, especially when they had a particular goal in mind—like chasing down two young boys.

Looking around, they quickly picked up Charlie and Michael sprinting toward Asia. They stared at the boys with their piercing yellow eyes, striking fear in Charlie's mind. His heart began to race as he turned to look back again. The two baboonagins had started to chase them, and were quickly gaining ground as they made noises only baboonagins could. It didn't help that the boys were running straight against the east wind that had just rolled in. Charlie grabbed the magic ears from his head and held them in one hand, while holding the ostrich stick in the other, making it very awkward to run. It was almost as if nature was trying to slow them down so the baboonagins could catch them.

"Michael! We gotta find somewhere to hide before they get much closer!" Charlie yelled, as he was running and fighting for each and every breath. "Turn left here at Yak and Yeti! I think there's a water ride up here we can jump on to get away from them!"

Michael raised his hand while he was running to confirm he had heard Charlie. As if things couldn't get any stranger, the farther the boys ran, the more their surroundings began to change. Trees grew taller, brush grew thicker, vines wrapped their way around anything and everything at an accelerated rate. Tropical flowers grew to enormous sizes. Pathways and buildings began to disappear or blend in as the wild tropical foliage took over. Even the simulated cast members and guests began to vanish into thin air. The park-like atmosphere of the Animal Kingdom was totally gone. The boys found themselves trapped in a ferocious jungle of unfriendly surprises.

Meanwhile, in a dark, evil place, hidden somewhere deep within the real Animal Kingdom, a private meeting was taking place. Kunn, Dark Thorn Leader of the Animal Kingdom, was discussing with his captain how he and his crew planned to capture the boy with the magic ears, as Charlie was the one who possessed the power Kunn and all other Dark Thorn Leaders wished to control—a power created by all Objects of Magic, one of which was the Ears of Virtue.

"Well, Captain Wontdo," Kunn said as he looked into his magic waterfall. "Now that I've cast a spell over the area where those two boys are, what plans have you put in place to capture and bring them here?"

This question put fear into the heart of Captain Wontdo, who normally was not afraid of any man. But the Dark Thorns were not ordinary in any sense of the word. Wontdo feared

Kunn, not only because he dreaded the consequences of an unhappy Dark Thorn, but because of the dark power Kunn had to control an entire simulation within WONDER—in this case, the Animal Kingdom. Furthermore, the small waterfall Kunn was looking into granted him vision for whatever he desired within that park. So anything Wontdo said about WONDER, Kunn could reference using his magic waterfall. Wontdo could not lie.

"Well, sir, we already deployed two of our best soldiers into WONDER to capture the boys you speak of."

"I can see that," Kunn said as he gazed into the waterfall. "And the older boy. He still has the magic ears, yes?"

"Oh, I'm quite certain he still has the ears in his possession, sir. He wouldn't have been able to transport from One Man's Dream into WONDER without them."

"Yes, I believe you're right. It does appear you have things under control. Well, at least for the moment," Kunn said in a snide manner.

The captain nervously cleared his throat. "Yes. Yes, sir. We've got it all under control."

"Excellent. Report back to me once you have captured the boys."

"Yes, dark leader."

"And make sure they have the ears."

"Yes. Of course, sir."

"Very well. You may go now."

"Yes, sir," Captain Wontdo said as he exited Kunn's secret liar.

"Charlie, what do we do? Those big monkey things will be here any second and there's nowhere to hide."

"I know, Michael. Don't you think I know that. I'm trying to figure this out. I mean, look at this stuff. It's growing like crazy. I can't even see the sidewalk anymore."

"Well, hurry up before..."

"Shh. You hear that?"

"Hear what, Charlie? All I hear is stuff growing."

"Water. I hear running water. Don't you hear it? It's coming from over there," Charlie said as he pointed northeast.

"Yeah. Now I hear it."

"Well, c'mon. Lets go see if there's a boat or something we can use to get away from those crazy baboon things."

"That sounds like a great idea. Crazy baboons things, eh?" Troy and his sister Trixie dropped down from an overhanging tree limb—right in front of the boys, blocking their path to the rapids.

"Yeah. You heard me. Baboon things," Charlie said, as he tried not to show the fear he felt inside.

Troy snarled and lunged quickly toward the boys, to see if they'd flinch. Which they did.

"Ha! I knew you were scared," Troy snapped.

"What? You think we're scared of you and your baboon sister? Not a chance," Charlie snapped back, while trying to think of a way out of the situation they were in.

"Oh, yeah. I think you and your little brother are terrified. I mean, look at ya. You both look like a couple of scared little mice. Don't you agree, sis?"

"Yeah, I'd say they're both look'n a little wobbly in the knees."

Trixie's response made Troy start to laugh, which made her laugh as well. In fact, both started to laugh so hard they stopped paying attention to the boys, and more importantly, their surroundings. Caught totally off guard, the two baboonagins were blindsided by a stampeding heard of elephants, throwing them deep into the brush and knocking them silly. This allowed Charlie and Michael the perfect get-away.

"Hello, boys," a familiar voice shouted from above.

Charlie looked up to see who it was. "Ben! How'd you get here? And what are you doing riding that elephant?"

"Oh, you mean old Ellie here?" Ben said, while patting the elephant on the neck.

"Hey. Better watch who you're calling old, there, buddy," Ellie replied. "I wouldn't want to see ya fall, if you know what I mean."

"And she talks, too? Wow!" Michael threw in.

"Now-now, Ellie. You know I was only joking. No need to get upset or anything," Ben told the elephant. Then he addressed Michael. "Why, yes. Ellie here can talk just as well as you, me, or any other human. She isn't a real elephant. She's a high quality CGI animation, created specifically by Imagineers for the simulated Animal Kingdom you're standing in at this very moment. All the other animals in this park are CGI animations as well. So even though they look real, they're not. But don't be fooled. Just because the animals, or other things, in WONDER aren't real, doesn't mean they can't hurt you. As long as you're in their world, they are just as dangerous as anything that is real. So watch yourself, young lads. Understand?"

Charlie and Michael both nodded.

"But how did you know where we were, and how did you get here?" Charlie asked again.

"Let's just say the new friend you made at Zawani Traders told me. But no time to explain. You boys need to get to the Chakranadi River, find a raft, and head toward the Forbidden Mountain in the east. Oh. And pay attention to your ears along the way. You do still have them, don't you?"

"Yes. They're tucked behind my back," Charlie said as he pulled them out to show Ben. "It was really windy just a few minutes ago and I didn't want to lose them, so I tucked them into my pants while we were running from those baboon things. Hey! Speaking of wind, where did it go? It was blowing like crazy a minute ago."

"It was a spell front, created by Kunn, Dark Thorn Leader of the Animal Kingdom. But it's gone now, so I'd be putt'n 'em back on your head," Ben replied. "Your gonna be needing 'em. And make sure you pay close attention to what that ostrich stick tells ya. What's it going to tell ya, and when? I don't know. Just make sure you're ready when the time comes." Ben wasn't much help when it came to vital information, but he knew just enough that the boys respected his advice, especially since they knew he got his information from Frank.

"Spell front? Talking stick? I don't get it," Michael said.

Just then, the silence of their surroundings was broken. The sound of rustling trees and screeching monkeys rose up in the distance and continued to get louder and louder. It was quite obvious they were headed toward the boys.

"I'll explain later. You need to go. That way." Ben pointed toward the water, and the boys took off in a full sprint, scared and confused. "Don't worry, you have many friends here! We'll try and hold them off for as long as we can!" Ben yelled as Charlie and Michael disappeared into the jungle.

"There, straight ahead past the flowers. See it?" Charlie had spotted an inflatable raft docked along the river bank.

Next to the waterway was a little shack with an old beat-up sign hanging from one nail that read: Kali Rapids Expeditions. The boys went inside expecting to find someone to talk to, but instead, found nothing except an abandoned shed. The only thing that proved to be of any use were a couple of boat paddles sitting in the corner behind the desk.

"Here. We can use these," Charlie said, while grabbing the paddles and handing one to his brother. "Now let's get outta here before those monkeys or whatever show up," he said, as they walked out the door.

"Hey! Ouch! Get off of me, you stupid monkeys!" The hairy little creatures had caught up with the boys. Two of them jumped onto Michael's shoulders just as he stepped outside the shack. They immediately grabbed onto his paddle and were trying to pull it out of his hands. At the same time, four other monkeys were trying to steal Charlie's paddle. Two were battling to hold his legs steady, while the other two pulled on the paddle.

Their screeching was loud, their movements quick, and as small as they were, they had quite a bit of strength—enough so that Charlie and his brother were having a terrible time trying to hold onto their paddles. Eventually, Charlie was able to free up his legs and sling the two monkeys hanging onto his paddle into the water. When the two that had been around his legs came at him, he gave them a good swat with the paddle, knocking them right next to the other two—SPLASH! Michael had managed to out-battle his hairy opponents as well, with both ending up exactly where the others were. All wet.

However, that was just the beginning. Out of breath and scratched up from battle, the boys paused for a brief second, only to hear more rustling and screeching coming from the nearby trees. And then...an entire congress of red-eyed monkeys burst out of the brush. There were too many to fight off. It was time for the boys to retreat.

"C'mon, Michael! To the boat!" Charlie and his brother took off running toward the raft, staying just ahead of the crazed, red-eyed monkeys.

"I've never seen monkeys with red eyes before," Michael yelled as he was running.

"Remember what Ben told us? They're CGI animations. Not real!" Charlie said as he dove head-first into the raft.

"Yeah, but he also said they can still hurt us!" Michael hollered back as he dove into the raft right behind his brother. Two of the monkeys leaped toward Michael's legs to grab him, but Charlie's baseball experience paid off as he took a mighty swing with his paddle, knocking both monkeys back onto land.

"OK, Michael! You get up front and I'll take the back! Start paddling!" Within a matter of seconds, the boys were well off shore and on their way down the river. The congress of monkeys ran along the river bank, trying to keep pace with the raft, but it was too much to ask of them. They quickly became nothing more than a distant, annoying sound, no longer a threat to Charlie and his brother.

As they made their way down the river, the current became strong enough that paddling wasn't necessary. This gave them time to rest, after using so much energy to fight off the crazed monkeys. The boys lay lifeless, their energy spent. It was the perfect time to gather their thoughts as the boat peacefully meandered down the waterway.

"What do you think? Do you think Ben was telling the truth about the talking ostrich stick?" Charlie asked Michael.

"Really? Do you think a stick can talk?"

"After what we've seen so far, I wouldn't be surprised. I mean, think about it, Michael. Between the two of us, we've seen everything from talking animals to a talking tree. So why would you even doubt for a second that a walking stick could talk?"

"I don't know? Maybe because it's a stick. If you really think that silly stick can talk, why don't you ask it?"

"You know, he's right, Charlie. Why don't you ask me."

The boys both turned and looked at the stick in amazement.

"Gee whiz! That goofy stick really can talk." Michael said.

"I prefer to be addressed as Oteza, not stick, please. That is, if you don't mind," the stick said in a elegant female tone.

"See! What did I tell ya, Michael! The stick, I mean, Oteza can talk. Ha! Ha! Ha!"

"I'm thrilled you find my ability to speak entertaining. But we have more important matters to discuss."

"Yeah. Like how can a stick talk," Michael interrupted, which made the boys burst into laughter.

"Oh, dear. Please tell me when the two of you are finished. Or would you rather keep on laughing and miss your opportunity to rescue Frank? That is why the two of you are here, is it not?"

Oteza's statement grabbed Charlie's attention. "Michael, hush. Yes, sorry. We're here to help our friend Frank Wellington. So what are we looking for? I mean, we have no idea where to even begin."

"As was intended, to keep it a secret. Until now, that is. Frank didn't want vital information falling into the wrong hands, especially the hands of a Dark Thorn. Not even his loyal assistant, Ben, was told. Frank always takes great precautions when handling information as crucial as this."

"But how did he know ahead of time the Thorns would capture and hold him prisoner?" I mean, if he gave you information to help us rescue him from FOTO, then he had to be able to see into the future, right?" Charlie asked.

"True. Some Patrons of WONDER do possess great vision, with the ability to see into the future, though most of the time, their vision is very limited. So they can see some, but not all things."

"Oh. So he knew he was going to get captured by FOTO, and where they were going to hold him. But he didn't know exactly when they were going to capture him?"

"Precisely, Michael."

"That is so cool," Charlie said.

"And that is why he created me. To supply you with knowledge that will set him free. Would you like to hear what it is? We haven't much time."

"Yes. Yes, ma'am. I mean, sorry for interrupting. Go ahead. Please," Charlie said.

"Very well. Now listen carefully. Just beyond the white waters, you'll want to bear off course to stay on course. There will be three Vision Stones to seek out during your visit today in WONDER. Each stone will be different in color. One lies beyond the rising water, one beyond light, and one before our time. Together, the stones will reveal where FOTO is holding Frank captive and help to set him free."

"So, I'd assume those are the white waters," Charlie said, as he pointed toward the turbulent water that was only fifteen yards ahead. "Hang on, Michael, this is gonna get roooouugh!" Water crashed against their raft, flipping the boys from side to side, forwards, backwards, and upwards. It took all of Charlie's strength to hold the magic ears on his head with one hand, while using the other to hold on to Oteza and a hand strap, which kept him from being tossed out of the raft. Michael had full use of both hands and was able to maintain a secure position through the white waters, despite getting soaked like a wet mop. What had seemed to take forever, really only lasted for three minutes. But to Charlie and Michael, it was three very long minutes.

Just as things began to quiet down, Oteza hollered, "Right here! Right here! There's the split in the river!" Her shouts startled the boys, forcing them to sit up and get ready for more work.

"Which way do we go? They both look the same to me!" Charlie yelled.

"The sign. See the sign, Charlie?" Michael said. It says, RIGHT IS THE WAY."

"So that means we go left, right?

"Right. I mean, yeah, left, Charlie. Bear off course."

At the last possible second, each boy grabbed a paddle and did everything they could to make the raft veer left, fighting against the relentless current which wanted to take them right of the fork. But in the end, through sheer will and a lot of hard work, the boys overcame the way of the white waters, and their raft headed down the left side of the fork, toward the unknown.

Prior to Charlie and Michael's journey down the Chakranadi River, Ben and his elephant friends had done what they could to try and slow down the congress of wild jungle monkeys that were out to capture the boys. But the monkeys had been too great in numbers for them to stop. Though their valiant efforts to hold back the crazed monkeys failed, Ben proudly noted that they had two Thorn soldiers as captives—the baboonagins, Troy and Trixie.

"Well, Ellie dear, we did what we could to help our two young lads. Hopefully it gave them, at the very least, a good head start. Plus, you know, we still have those baboonigans to take back with us. So, not too bad, I'd say."

"You're right, Ben, we still have something to show for our efforts." Why don't you go over and check on our two captive soldiers, while I check the herd to make sure they're all OK."

"Right you are. Good idea." Ben walked toward the brush where the baboonagins had been thrown. As he approached the brush, he stretched his neck to see where they were. At first he thought little of it, as he enjoyed a little chuckle with himself. But as he searched deeper into the brush, slowly moving foliage out of his way, his stomach began to knot up. "Where? Where are they?" he mumbled to himself. His heart dropped to his stomach as he suddenly spotted an area of matted down brush where the two baboonagins had laid. "Ellie! Ellie! They're...I don't know how else to put it. Gone!

The river had calmed, the jungle was filled with sounds of the wild. The waterway opened up into a tranquil setting.

"Whooooa, check out those waterfalls, Charlie. Have you ever seen anything like that before?"

Charlie quietly stared as their raft passed through the mouth of the river and entered the tranquil waters. What stood before them was nothing short of breathtaking. A true wonder. In a word, inexplicable: a waterfall, nearly three hundred feet tall, with majestic stones that sparkled in the sun on each side. But what held the boys speechless was the water itself. Unlike ordinary waterfalls, the water flowed up, defying all laws of gravity and physics in the ordinary world. But this was no ordinary world. It was, of course, WONDER.

"Charlie, are you gonna answer me?"

"I must say, Charlie. It's quite rude to not reply, when asked a question," Oteza said. "Especially when someone asks twice."

Still, Charlie continued to stare in awe. Focused on the

waterfall, and even more so, on the glittering stones that flanked it. "Would you look at that," he said. "The sparkles in those stones. They look like...I think...yeah. I'm pretty sure those are diamonds."

Feeling rejected after being ignored by his brother, Michael replied sarcastically, "Yeah, right. I'm sure those are diamonds. Just sitting out here, wide open for anyone to take. That makes a lot of sense."

"Oh, Michael, why do you always have to be like that. It's not always about you, you know."

"Well, it's not always about you, either. Mom and Dad are always talking, Charlie did this, Charlie did that, oh, did you see what Charlie is doing. Charlie, Charlie, Charlie."

"No, they don't. They hardly ever talk about me. All I hear is stuff about you. Michael is so sweet. Michael's our little chicken. Look how cute Michael is."

For the next few minutes, the argument about who got more attention from Mom and Dad raged on—a typical sibling argument that, in the end, would go nowhere. That is, until it was Michael's turn to become distracted; as well as Oteza's.

"Charlie. Your ears. They're at it again."

As the boat drifted closer to the shoreline by the waterfall, Charlie's ears grew brighter and brighter, just like all the other times when something magical was about to happen.

"Yes, those ears on your head are quite a sight," Oteza said.

"What's at it again? My ears? Oh. My ears," Charlie said. "We must be getting close to something."

"Like a Vision Stone," Oteza replied.

"Yeah, like one of the three stones we need to find to help Frank. Exactly, Oteza. Let's pull up to shore over there to the right and see what we can find."

With the raft safely secured on shore, Charlie and Michael, with Oteza in hand, slowly made their way toward the giant waterfall over the rocky terrain. Every ten to twenty feet, they paused to looked up and admire the incredible view that towered over them until finally they reached their destination.

"See, I told you there were diamonds in the rocks, Michael. So do you believe me now?"

"Holy cow! Those really are diamonds. I guess I was wrong."

"And?"

"OK, you were right. I'm sorry."

"Thank you, Michael."

"Charlie, you need to cover up those glowing ears. They're so bright I can hardly see."

"Well, that means we must be really close. Keep your eyes peeled."

"More like I should keep my eyes covered, because it's so bright."

"Hey! Look over there. I see a ledge behind the waterfall. I have a feeling that's where we need to go next."

"I think you could also say that the ledge is beyond the waterfall," Oteza said.

Charlie and Michael looked at Oteza, about to criticize her remark, when it hit them.

"Right. Beyond the waterfall. So the ledge is beyond the water. That's brilliant, Oteza. You just figured out where we need to look for the first Vision Stone."

"Well, even an ostrich stick gets lucky every once in a while."

"Cmon, follow me, Michael. I think I see a safe path to the ledge through all these giant stones." The boys carefully made their way toward the giant ledge behind the waterfall.

"Hey, Charlie, looks like we're going to get really wet!" Michael shouted as they continued to climb over the awkward piles of stones that sat between them and the ledge.

Charlie paused and looked up at the waterfall, which was now almost straight above them. "No, I think we'll be just fine. You see, since the waterfall is flowing upward, there's no splashing at the bottom."

"Oh yeaaaah. No splash. I didn't think about that, Charlie. You're right. We should be fine," Michael said, laughing.

The boys continued to climb until they reached the ledge and managed to pull themselves to the top of its massive surface. From a distance, the ledge didn't look like much. But up close, it was quite a site to behold—dwarfing the boys with its incredible size. It was a natural surface, not perfectly flat in any way, with moss and vines growing up three enormous walls. Very little light made its way through the waterfall and back into the massive niche, carved in a three-hundred-foot cliff of diamonds and stones. The area behind the fall was roughly fifty feet deep by eighty feet wide, with a detailed animal mosaic carved into the first ten feet of the enormous back wall. In its center was the large face of a tiger with two giant diamonds for eyes, which sparkled brilliantly from the light of the magic ears. Entranced by the eyes, Charlie slowly walked up and placed his hands upon them, as if the ears were magically guiding him through his actions. While resting his hands on the large diamond eyes, the ears glowed brighter and brighter, illuminating the entire cavernous area where they stood. And still, the ears grew even brighter, to the point where Charlie disappeared into its brilliance. In a split second, the light condensed to its core, turned green, then shot through Charlie's body and into the tiger's eyes. The brilliant green light traveled quickly through the carvings in the giant wall, highlighting all its details and activating a small, hidden panel on the far right side that slowly opened.

"Michael, go... go see what's in there. I'm, I'm feeling a little dizzy and need to sit down for a second." The light that had shot through Charlie's body left him temporarily demobilized.

"Wow, Charlie. You gotta see this. I think it's one of the stones."

"Can you bring it over here?"

"Sure," Michael said, as he reached into the hidden panel to pick it up. But when he tried to move it, he couldn't. He tugged and tugged on the green stone, trying to remove it from the indentation where it sat. Some magical force appeared to be holding it in place. "I can't pick it up."

"Really? Is it too heavy?"

"No, it's small, like the size of an egg."

"Do you see anything around the panel, like a lever or button to push?"

Michael quickly looked. "No. Nothing like that around the panel."

"I think you may have to do it, Charlie," Oteza said.

"Perhaps you're right. I should be good enough to walk now. I'm coming, Michael." Charlie stood up and began to walk over. As he got closer, the ears began to glow softly. Charlie reached into the panel and put his fingers on the Vision Stone. His arm and hand became illuminated with a soft green light as he effortlessly removed the stone. "I guess you were right, Oteza."

Michael's description of the stone's size was dead on. It was the size of an egg, only flatter. And though it seemed to be a dark, opaque green sitting in the panel, in better lighting, the stone was actually transparent, with multiple transparent layers of green. In Charlie's hands, the stone emitted a subtle swirling glow, capturing the boy's attention.

"Yep, there's something special about that stone, Charlie."

"I'd say you're right, Michael. I guess we'll learn just how special it is after we find the other two."

"OK, gentlemen, you need to put that away. Like Charlie said, we have two more stones to find, and it would be wise if we do it before it gets dark out," Oteza replied. "You don't want to be wondering around this place in the dark. It can get pretty scary out here. Even if it isn't real."

"Oteza is right. We need to keep moving. Come on, let's go, Michael."

"You will travel by foot from here on out," Oteza said. There's a path just to the left of those trees near the shoreline. That's the way we must go."

The Dark Leader of the Animal Kingdom was losing his patience with Captain Wontdo's efforts to capture Charlie and Michael. Gazing into his magic waterfall, Kunn learned of the boys' success in finding the first of three Vision Stones. It was time to set a trap. "Guards, I need you to transport into WONDER and instruct Captain Wontdo to gather a few of his best men and head to the Forbidden Mountain. I will have a friend waiting there to greet them. On the route they're traveling, those little brats will have to go through the mountain to make it out of WONDER. It's time we put an end to this nonsense."

"How much farther do we have to go?"

"As far as it takes us to find the next Vision Stone, Michael."

"Hope it's not too much farther. My legs are tired."

"Mine too, Michael. But Frank is depending on us. Hey! Would you look at that! Just beyond the treetops. It's a mountain."

"There's no way I'll be able to climb that, Charlie. I'm way too tired."

"We'll see when we get closer. Maybe there's a way around it? Who knows." Charlie was trying to keep Michael's hopes up. The last thing he needed right now was an uncooperative little brother.

As they finished making their way through the jungle trail, the shadows of the enormous snow-capped mountain just ahead began to shade them from the sun. At its base there appeared to be an entrance, blocked by a large, irregularly shaped boulder. The magic ears lit up as Charlie approached the bolder. As the glow brightened, he started to recite a series of words, which Michael found to be rather strange. "Giant rock beneath the peak, listen well, whilst I speak. Awake from slumber to move your own, and let us enter to pathways unknown."

Slowly, the giant boulder started to shake, shimmer, and pop. First, a foot broke free, then the other. Both feet simultaneously planted themselves on the ground, then pushed against the earth, exposing two short, powerful legs. Next, two hands attached to stocky arms broke free from the giant rock. Last, two squinty eyes and a jagged mouth appeared on the face of the bolder. The giant face stood up, looked at the boys with a stern face, then stepped aside while gesturing with one of its extra-large hands for them to enter the mountain. The opening was large and irregular in shape, exposing a dark, curved staircase, lined with torches, which led upward into the darkness.

"Go ahead, Charlie. The mountain guard has given us permission to enter," Oteza said with confidence.

Charlie looked down at the ostrich stick and acknowledged her words. "OK, c'mon Michael, looks like we're going in."

The stairway seemed to go on forever as the boys went round and round, higher and deeper into the mountain. The farther they went, the darker it got. The torch-lit walls were no more. Only dark, cavernous areas now bordered each side of the stairway. Fortunately, the magic ears were once again glowing bright, which allowed them to see. Light from the sun did not exist here, which reminded Charlie of what Oteza had told him earlier about the location of the second Vision Stone."

"Oteza, are you awake?"

"Why, yes, dear, I never sleep. What is it? I sense you seek my help."

"I know we already found the stone beyond the rising water. But didn't you also tell us that one of them could be found beyond light, and another beyond our time?"

"Why, yes, Charlie. That is true. So what is the answer you seek?"

"So, I was thinking. It seems pretty dark here in the mountain. In fact, it's so dark that natural light does not exist here. Plus, the ears are glowing again. Do you think the stone that rests beyond light could be...well, hidden somewhere here in the mountain?"

"It certainly would seem so from the details you described, Charlie. I would suggest we keep a lookout for anything that may suggest a stone is nearby."

"Well, I suggest we get through this mountain as quickly as possible, Charlie. This place is giving me the heeby jeebies," Michael blurted out.

"Right. I agree, Michael. Let's keep moving. If we see something suggesting there's a stone nearby, we'll stop, but only long enough to get what we need."

The boys pressed onward, up the stairway, and eventually reached what appeared to be the top. The end of the stairway opened into a large, circular walkway with two sets of stairs (one set on each side) that led down thirty feet to the center of what felt like a very large and open space, possibly the core of the mountain. The area was dimly lit with torches along the walls and a large fire pit in the center of the recessed area below, giving Charlie and Michael just enough light to safely navigate their way around. Charlie's ears began to glow even brighter, signifying the second stone had to be near.

"Your ears, Charlie. They're so bright. I guess that means we're headed down there," Michael said, pointing to the fire pit below.

"I guess so, Michael. Let's go."

Once they reached the bottom of the stairs, the fire surging from the pit seemed much larger, with flames climbing upwards of ten to twelve feet. The pit was at least eight feet deep and ten feet in diameter, making the surface they were standing on about seventy feet in diameter—a very large space indeed. The towering, curved walls surrounding them were every bit of thirty feet in height, creating a sense of importance. As Charlie and Michael circled the parameter of the expansive area, Oteza, who was in Charlie's left hand and facing downward, began to notice glowing orange letters forming words on the stone ground as Charlie walked by. The first word was "Walk," the second, "over." Letters continued to take shape as Charlie and Michael walked by, unaware of what was going on behind them.

"Uh-hmm-hmm-hmmm. Charlie, dear, you need to stop and take a look behind you."

"What? Why is that, Oteza?" Charlie said as he kept walking slowly around the pit, looking at the walls for traces of the second Vision Stone.

"Well, how should I put this. Because what you seek is actually on the ground, right behind you."

"What, you're joking, right? We just walked past what's behind us, and there was nothing on the ground."

"I suggest you stop and look again, young man!" Oteza ordered.

"Alright, but I'm telling ya, there's..."

"Yes? What were you going to say, Charlie?"

"I...that I'm sorry for not listening to you sooner," Charlie said in an apologetic manner.

Michael turned to look as well, and was instantly amazed. "Cool. Fire letters. What does it say?"

"I don't know, but I'm going to keep walking around the fire pit until the letters stop forming. You stay here and let me know if they start to disappear or not." Charlie took off walking as fast as he could around the pit. New letters followed his every step.

"The letters are staying lit, Charlie. So I think we're OK."

"Alright, I'm almost back to where we started. See if you can find the beginning of the words. I'm assuming this is a message of at least one or two sentences."

"OK, Charlie," Michael said, as he started searching for a beginning.

"Charlie, I already know what the first word is. I saw it form, remember?"

"Oh, yeah. So what's the first word, Oteza?"

"Actually, the first few words are: 'Walk above the fire.'"

"Hey, Michael! Come over here! I think I see the beginning!" Charlie yelled to his brother, as he started to read the message:

> Walk above the fire, faith shall be your friend. The magic atop your head, will be there to defend. Through heat and flames there'll be, exactly what you need. To accomplish what you seek, to carry out the deed.

"Walk above the fire? Are you kidding me? How am I supposed to do that?"

"The ears, Charlie. They are the key," Oteza said. "You just have to believe. Listen to your heart. It will never lie to you."

Charlie looked at the fire, then paused for a second. "You know what, you're right. Here, Michael, hold Oteza."

"What? You don't actually believe you will be able to walk above that fire, do you?"

"Of course I do." Charlie handed the ostrich stick to his brother and walked toward the fire pit. He then paused for a brief second at the edge of the pit while gathering his thoughts. Charlie looked down at the fire before him, then looked up, exhaled slowly, and extended one leg outward as he took a large step forward. Expecting to fall into the fire and burn to a crisp, he was amazed at what happened next.

The ears burst into a bright blue sphere of radiant light that stretched and surrounded Charlie's body like a protective bubble that suspended him over the fire and protected him from the heat of the flames. The blue light grew brighter as trails of white light shot out of the ears and circled around Charlie's body. Faster and faster, the white lights traveled around the sphere, creating a loud series of swoosh-like sounds. The light emitted by the protective bubble had become almost too bright for Michael to look at. Slowly, it began descending into the fire pit, pushing back the flames of the fire. Down, down it went, until Michael's brother was no longer visible. Only the radiant light from the blue bubble was visible from above.

The blue light pushed outward, filling the entire pit. The fire which consumed the pit just minutes ago was now non-existent.

To Charlie's right, at eye level, was a small opening in the wall of the pit, barely large enough to fit a human hand into. He closed his eyes and searched for guidance. "Trust your heart," he heard from a whisper. Charlie reached in and felt a lever, which he pulled. To his left, one of the large wall stones moved backwards and another moved from the right to take its place, revealing a small inset shelf. And on that shelf, a three-prong stand held a brilliant blue marble-like sphere. The second of three Vision Stones!

"Charlie, I can't believe what just happened!"

"I can't either, Michael. But it did. Now let's get moving, we have one more stone to find."

"ROOOOOOAR! GRRRRRRRR! ROOOOAR!

"What was that, Charlie."

"Shh. Quiet. C'mon, we gotta get outta here. Fast!"

The boys quickly made their way out of the pit area and back to the upper ledge. They were now on the opposite side of the enormous space from where they first had entered. What they found was a jagged doorway, and through it, a narrow, descending pathway with a large drop off on the right side. Visibility was minimal, provided by a few scattered torches.

"Looks like this is the only way out, Michael."

"I don't know, Charlie, it looks pretty scary."

"Listen, whatever made that noise is headed toward us and it doesn't sound very friendly. Plus, it's coming from the only other way out of here. We have to go."

"Your brother's right, Michael. The Yeti really isn't something you want to come face to face with," Oteza said.

"Wait. You know what that thing is?"

"Why, of course, Charlie. The Yeti is the protector of the Forbidden Mountain. And just now, well, you stole something from the mountain. So he's probably not very happy."

"Really? How would he know I took the stone? He wasn't even there."

"The Yeti and the mountain are one in the same, connected in a spiritual sense. If the mountain suffers, he suffers. If someone steals from it? Well, then he feels like someone has stolen from him. And you just stole something. Oh, and there's one more thing I should tell you. He's also, well, controlled by Kunn, Dark Thorn Leader of the Animal Kingdom. So chances are, Kunn knows we're here and probably sent the Yeti to find us."

"I thought this mountain was a roller-coaster ride? I haven't even seen tracks yet, let alone a coaster."

"Ah, but you forget, Charlie. We're in WONDER, and the Dark Thorn has cast an evil spell over the entire Animal Kingdom simulation, which drastically altered its appearance, filling it with wild, overgrown jungle, a raging river with a waterfall that flows upward, and a dark cavernous mountain."

"I'm sorry. I forgot. So what do we do now?"

"ROOOOARR! GRRRR!"

"I'd say you need to run."

Thump. A giant hairy white foot with sharp claws stepped upon the ledge where the boys had first come up into the mountain core. Then a giant hand, with the same details, grabbed onto the corner of the wall. The Yeti emerged. Standing at least twelve feet tall, his large ape-like body and head were covered in long white hair which masked a set of electric blue eyes and a mouth that bared a set of large yellow teeth when he roared. His arms were long and muscular, with giant, powerful looking hands that hung well below his knees. And though his legs appeared to be short, due to the Yeti's large frame they were still every bit of five feet long, with thighs the diameter of large tree trunks and feet the size of bed pillows.

Fortunately, he hadn't seen the boys, who after taking a very brief look at the massive creature, quickly took off down the narrow pathway without hesitation.

"I'm not sure about this, Charlie. One wrong step off the path and, whoops, you're done for. I don't see a bottom."

"Just keep your eyes on the pathway and keep moving. And don't look over the edge, it'll help."

"Really, Charlie? Don't look over the edge? What? Do you want me to close my eyes. I may as well just jump off the ledge now."

"You know what I mean. Stop being so dramatic. It looks like the path widens just a little ways up, anyway."

"Oh, all right."

"Hey, it's either this, or we go and face that thing back there. Is that what you want?"

"ROOOOAR!" On queue, the Yeti burst through the jagged opening to the path the boys were on. His giant, powerful frame broke away much of the stone and created a larger opening in the process. "ROOOOAR! GRRRR!" He'd spotted the boys, now only a few hundred feet away.

"You must move faster, boys." Oteza said. "We have to stay out of reach."

"We're trying!" Charlie shouted back, as he looked to see where the Yeti was. "Oh c'mon! Are you kidding me. That's not right!" Charlie was shocked at what he saw next. The Yeti had leaped with its powerful legs from the narrow pathway to about thirty feet in the air, and started to swing from one giant stalactite to another, gripping each with his large, powerful hands while easily passing Charlie and Michael, who were moving as fast as they could along the pathway.

"Charlie! That big hairy thing is moving a lot faster than us! We're never going to get out of here!"

The Yeti was now at least a hundred yards ahead of the boys, and was fading into darkness.

"Where'd he go, Charlie? I don't see him anymore!"

"Maybe we should turn and go back the other way!" Charlie shouted out.

Just then, the noise of several unfriendly Thorns echoed from behind them on the pathway.

"Oh no, now what!" Charlie said, in a frantic voice.

"Keep moving forward, Charlie," Oteza replied firmly. "We've come too far to turn back. We're going to need a distraction to get the two of you out of this nightmare of a mountain. Just keep heading down the path. This has to be the way out."

Charlie looked back again. Whoever it was, was gaining on them.

"Look! Just ahead! I think I see daylight." Michael said.

"Yeah, I see it, Michael. We're almost out of this..." The light disappeared. "What? What was that? Did someone just close the exit door?" Charlie said. As he and his brother neared the end of the pathway, they were able to see what, or actually who, was blocking their way out of the mountain.

The Yeti had beaten them to the only way they had out of the mountain. His broad, burly frame blocked the entire opening as he stood squared up to the pathway, facing inward toward the boys, baring his ugly yellow teeth. Atop his broad, hairy shoulders stood two more unpleasant surprises. The baboonagins, Troy and Trixie.

"I have a feeling this isn't going to go well for us, Michael," Charlie said, as he stopped in his tracks.

"Well, at least you've got that right young man," a voice snarled from behind the boys. Three figures emerged from the darkness. It was Captain Wontdo and two of his Thorns. Wontdo was a rugged looking black man, with tattoos on one side of his face, both arms, and chest. He had a bald head and a large muscular body, which sported a floppy pair of Capri-styled burgundy pants and a pair of brown sandals. Worst of all, he was wearing a criss-crossed leather ammo strap that wrapped around his torso, over his shoulders, and across his back. And he had a large machete strapped to his left hip. Charlie and Michael found him quite intimidating to look at. The two Thorns he brought with him were more average in build, normally dressed, and not quite as scary.

"This is just getting better by the minute," Michael whispered, as he edged closer to his brother with fear running through his veins.

"Yeah, I don't see any way out of this," Charlie said, while looking forwards and backwards in rapid succession.

"Why don't you give me what you have in your pocket, young man! And those ears, too!" Wontdo shouted to Charlie. "Give us what we want, then you and your brother can go! That is what you desire, is it not?"

Oteza, thinking quickly, spoke quietly to the boys. "Listen to me. I still think there's a chance you and your brother can escape this mess. But you have to do exactly as I say."

Charlie and Michael both turned their attention to Oteza.

"Alright, then. You'll have to use me as a weapon against the immediate threat that stands before us. Front and back. But first, you'll need to tap me on the magic ears. Understood. Focus on the men behind us first, then we'll worry about what's ahead of us. Got it? Good. OK, time for action."

Charlie slowly raised the ostrich stick high, then used it to gently tap the ears. Instantly, he felt an invisible charge travel through his entire body and into the stick, which began to spark and hum.

"OK, Charlie! Attack Captain Wontdo and his Thorns!" Oteza shouted.

Something had taken over Charlie's body. He had become a warrior with mad skills and the ability to maneuver quickly and effectively, while twirling the stick around in such a way that it confused Wontdo and his men. Just as Charlie got within twenty feet of the men, he twirled the stick above his head, grabbed it with both hands, and slammed the ground with it. The pathway began to shake and shimmer. Rocks crumbled and the ledge area gave way, quickly tumbling off into darkness, leaving a giant gap between the boys and the three men.

"That's one problem solved, Charlie," Oteza said. "And now, time to take care of the other." Charlie turned and charged the giant Yeti and two baboonigans with fearless energy. He felt amazing, like nothing could harm him. The two baboon-like creatures leaped off the shoulders of the Yeti and rolled into attack positions. The Yeti crouched and braced himself for battle, letting out a horrendous roar. The baboonigans charged. Charlie spun around in mid air, with the stick extended in his left hand. He caught Trixie on the right shoulder, knocking her off the ledge and into darkness. Troy leaped high into the air, attacking from above. Charlie rolled onto his back, held the ostrich stick with both hands, and pushed upwards just as Troy was coming down on top of him, sending the creature off into the darkness. Only the Yeti remained. The brave young warrior charged. The Yeti stood tall and let out a giant roar. In one fluid motion, Charlie jumped off the Yeti's knee, onto his shoulder, then leaped far behind him. The Yeti, out of frustration in trying to grab the elusive young man, spun around, pounded the ground with both of his large fists, and roared again. Charlie had gotten by him. The way out was now open. But Michael was still trapped behind the Yeti, and the massive beast saw it as an opportunity to gain an advantage over Charlie. The hairy, white creature turned toward Michael and was ready to leap and grab him.

"Hey, you big white fur ball! Leave him alone! I'm the one who has the stones! Isn't that what you want?" Charlie shouted at the creature, in an attempt to distract him. It worked. "Go, Michael!" Michael took off running as fast as he could toward the great beast, whose upper torso was now facing Charlie again. In a fantastic athletic move, Michael slid low, right between the legs of the Yeti. And just as he did, the beast had turned back to look where Michael had previously stood. He was gone. The Yeti was confused and angry. By the time he spun around to face Charlie's again, Michael was standing next to his brother. In a fit of rage, the enormous creature mounted a charge toward the boys.

"Throw me!" Oteza shouted. "It's your only chance! Throw me at the beast!"

Charlie swung the stick around and around, over his head, then let it go toward the Yeti. The stick flew straight and true, striking the creature squarely in the chest and knocking it backwards, off the ledge, and into the darkness below. Charlie had done it. They were free to go. The boys turned and ran out of the mountain, into daylight, following the path deep into the jungle and far enough away until both felt safe. They had captured the second Vision Stone, but at a cost. Oteza was gone forever. She was a friend they had known for too short a time, and whose advice they could no longer seek in their attempt to find the third and final stone. At first, Charlie felt empty inside for their loss. But as the boys kept walking, he kept thinking. Searching deeper and deeper, until he remembered what the cast member had told him back at the Ziwani Traders. "Listen to your heart. It will never lie to you." That thought gave Charlie the confidence to carry on and finish their search for the third Vision Stone.

"Oh, I knew that blubbering Wontdo and his helpers weren't capable of carrying out such a simple task. Why did I even think they had a chance?" Dark Thorn Kunn was talking to his pet cat, Twizzles, back at his hidden lair outside of WONDER. It was the only living thing he truly cared for. Twizzles was a charcoal grey, short-hair cat with beaming yellow eyes, crooked whiskers, and a thin build who followed his master wherever he went. He was the only friend Kunn had. The dark magical abilities, creepy appearances, and loner personalities of all Dark Thorn leaders made them quite hard to befriend. In fact, it was pretty much impossible. All they really ever did was obsess over gaining control of what Walt had created in his lifetime and using it for FOTO's evil purposes. Besides, who would want to be friends with someone who wore a long, black cloak, was tall and bony, had light, pale blue, wrinkly skin, grey teeth, lifeless, solid black eyes, and a voice that would make fresh milk curdle.

"Well, my little friend, looks like we need to take matters into our own hands. As is usually the case. I tried to help, by letting them use the Yeti. It still wasn't enough. Time we use something a little more primitive, don't you think, Twizzles?"

"Meeeeow," the cat responded as it rubbed up along Kunn's leg.

"Ha-ha-ha-ha-ha. Yes, of course, Twizzles. It does sound rather unfair, doesn't it. Our little friends will be in for, how should I say it? A rather big treat."

Twizzles meowed in response while jumping up on a ledge near the magic waterfall, where Kunn gently stroked the purring cat with his long, bony fingers.

The boys continued marching down the jungle path, which eventually opened up into a surprisingly expansive area of barren land filled with large rock formations, canyons, and minimal plant life. Oddly enough, it was quite a drastic change from the jungle they had just left behind. As the boys continued on, they noticed that what they were walking in was actually a giant bone yard. Dinosaur bones! And that's when something beyond reasonable explanation occurred. Just a few hundred yards off to their left, a small sand tornado began to form upwards from the ground. Up, up it grew, snaking its way through the desert-like terrain, picking up more force along the way. It finally came to a stand-still and sucked up all the top layers of sand within a hundred-foot radius from where it stood, exposing all the dinosaur bones around it. Faster and faster the funnel cloud spun, creating such a force that Charlie had to hold on to his magical ears to keep them from being whisked away, even though they were still quite a distance from the tornado.

The boys found shelter behind a giant rock formation, which helped stabilize their position as they continued to observe the phenomenon. Large dinosaur bones surrounding the funnel began to break free from the ground and float around it, in a large circular pattern. Piece by piece, the bones joined together, forming three separate bodies. Larger and larger they grew, until it was clear what the storm had accomplished. Instantaneously, the funnel cloud dispersed, and three giant, bone formations hit the ground running. It was three tyrannosaurus skeletons, and they were headed straight for Charlie and Michael.

ROOOOOAR! ROOOOOAR! ROOOAR!

"What in the world? Did you see that? What now, Charlie?"

"Run! Run fast, Michael!" The boys turned and took off running toward a canyon-like area not far from where they had stood just seconds ago. "Quick! Over there, Michael! There's a narrow pathway on the left side of that canyon. If we can get in there, they won't be able to follow us." The boys ran as hard as they could, yet still the giant beasts continued to close on them with their enormous strides. Closer and closer, the giant bony creatures were nearly upon them. Just as the leader of the trio was about to pounce, the boys dove into the shadow of the narrow canyon trail. The large, skeletal creature, oblivious to its surroundings, quickly lunged forward, crashing into the sides of the canyon, which smashed the beast into hundreds of pieces. The other two instinctively changed course, with one going left, the other, right.

"I think we're safe now, Michael," Charlie said, as he tried to catch his breath.

"Yeah. I think you're right. So what is this place?"

"What?"

"Look behind you, Charlie."

Charlie turned and couldn't believe what he saw. It was a lush green forest, filled with towering trees, a flowing stream, and friendly wildlife. He couldn't have been any happier, though he was a little confused. And as if that weren't enough, an old friend flew down from a nearby tree to greet them. It was Alexios, the owl.

"Hey. What are you doing here?" Michael said, with a giant smile on his face.

"I was told you may be in need of my assistance. So, here I am."

"Was it Ben who told you?" Charlie asked.

"Yes. Yes, it was. Very good, young man. I see your way of thinking is growing every day."

"Thank you."

"So what exactly are you two young fellows trying to accomplish here?"

"We have to find the three Vision Stones so we can rescue Frank from the dark forces of FOTO. What is this place, anyway? It's quite different than..."

"Than what you expected in the middle of a desert?" Alexios asked.

"Yeah. A whole lot different," replied Charlie.

"A few of the Patrons sensed you were in need of assistance, so they injected this little slice of paradise into WONDER, to give you and Michael a chance to figure out two things. One, where the third stone is. And two, how you were going to transport out of WONDER and back to your parents, once you find it. They sent me in to help guide you along the way."

"Um, aren't you forgetting something? Like, how are we going to sneak past those giant dinosaur bone creatures," Charlie said.

"The answer to that question, you see, is actually simple."

"It is?" Michael said, with a confused look on his face.

"Why, yes. You see, the third stone rests in the chest of one of those giant skeleton beasts. If you were to look very closely, you would see it, suspended in mid-air, glowing magnificently in all its red brilliance. Right in the heart of the dinosaur."

"Of course. Oteza told us that one of the stones could be found before our time. And obviously, those dinosaurs existed, well, before our time," Charlie said enthusiastically.

"But I thought only Frank knew where the stones were hidden?" Michael asked.

"Right, Michael. So how could one of the stones be inside a dinosaur created by a Dark Thorn?" Charlie asked. "They would have had to get the answer..."

"From Frank," Alexios finished. "Yes, you're correct, Michael. At one time, Frank was the only one who knew where the stones were hidden. Unfortunately, the Dark Thorns must have figured out where the red stone was hidden by torturing Frank, removed it from its proper hiding spot, then placed it inside that monstrous arrangement of bones, knowing all too well that someone would eventually come looking for it. And that someone is you, Charlie."

"Torturing Frank?" Charlie said. "I don't like the sound of that. We need to get our hands on that third stone and go rescue Mr. Wellington."

"That's the spirit, young man!" Alexios said, explaining his brilliant plan, right down to the very last detail. Moments later, the boys stood in position, nervous but ready, to execute what the wise owl had thought up.

"OK, I see both of them, about two hundred yards off to the left. Just beyond those three tall rocks. Is everyone ready?" Alexios asked.

"Ready," replied Michael.

"Ready," Charlie said.

"Very well. Remember what I told you. Once you have the third stone, put it in your pocket with the other two. And make sure you and Michael are close together when doing so. Understood?"

"Yeah. But what about you?" Charlie asked the owl.

"No need to worry about me. I can take care of myself."

Charlie nodded to confirm.

"OK. Ready. Set. Go!" Alexios shouted.

The boys took off into the open, like two wild rabbits leaving behind their safe haven. Both were now clearly visible to the two large dinosaur-like creatures. The great beasts turned and shot off toward the boys, each roaring loudly as they opened up into full running strides, pounding the desert ground with their enormous feet along the way. The boys could hear every thunderous step the giant creatures took. The sounds of their heavy steps grew louder with each passing second. There was no time to look back. Fifty yards ahead lay a huge rock structure at least one hundred feet in diameter. Charlie ran to the left of it, and Michael to the right.

Charlie called out to his brother: "See you on the other side!"

"OK!" Michael shouted back.

The dinosaurs were closing quickly, now only a few seconds behind each boy. Their roars became deafening from such close quarters. The one with the stone in its chest pursued Michael on the right, while the other closed in on Charlie as he headed left. From the sky above, a mighty screech pierced the air as Alexios swooped in and circled the beast following Charlie, several times in rapid succession. The distraction confused the massive creature just enough that it lost a step or three on Charlie, giving him enough time to reach the back of the stone structure, where he planned to meet up with Michael. Alexios ascended high into the air again, repeating his actions with the dinosaur following Michael, giving him enough time to reach the backside of the stone structure as well.

Both giant beasts quickly regained their strides and were about to pounce, one coming from the left side, the other from the right. The boys locked eyes as they ran toward each other with fear in their hearts. Charlie's ears suddenly emitted a giant burst of light, blinding the dinosaurs, who were still running in full stride. There was a huge CRAAAAASH as the giant creatures collided with one another. The red stone broke free, flying through the air amongst hundreds of dinosaur bones, some forty feet above the boys. Alexios swept in and caught the brilliant red stone, then dropped it into Charlie's right hand. Charlie pulled his brother close with the other hand. Bones started tumbling toward the ground as Charlie stuck the third stone into his pocket with the other two. The trio was complete! Charlie's magic ears released a brilliant sphere of light, which engulfed the boys, then exploded into a cloudy whiff of dust and magic, twinkling particles. Charlie and Michael were gone.

As the light dimmed, Charlie came to the realization that something was wrong, strangely and terribly wrong. They had indeed transported out of the simulated world of the Animal Kingdom, as planned. But, instead of returning back to the One Man's Dream attraction in Hollywood Studios, where their parents were, the boys had been redirected to a dark, cold place, a place not even remotely close to One Man's Dream.

Chapter Ten

The air was chilly and damp. Not a sound could be heard, except for the dripping of water and the squeak of a rat that scurried about the low-lit hallway, just outside the cell holding Charlie and Michael captive. It felt as though they were a long way from Disney World. And yet, they weren't. In fact, they were still there, just in a different creative dimension. Instead of transporting out of WONDER as planned, the boys had been pulled deeper into it, ending up in Deep WONDER.

"What just happened, Charlie?"

"I'm not quite sure, but I feel kind of strange. Like, when we..."

"Were in Gepetto's workshop."

"Yeah. How did you know that?"

"Because, Charlie. We're cartoon characters again. Open your eyes and look around."

Charlie's eyes were closed. The transportation had made him very dizzy. He opened one eye at a time, looked at his brother and all that surrounded them, only to discover that what Michael had said was indeed true. "What in the world? We were supposed to transport back to One Man's Dream, where Mom and Dad are."

"Well, that sure didn't happen," Michael said in a sarcastic tone. "And what about your ears, Charlie?"

"What about 'em?"

"They're not on your head, genius."

"What? Sure they are!" Charlie reached for the ears atop his head. "Oh, no! Where'd they go. They were just there a minute ago."

"Thank you, Reginald," a familiar voice said from a dark corner, just outside their cell. A tall, gangly body emerged from the shadow. It was Captain Marty Shivers, fully animated and holding the magic ears brought to him by his sneaky pet rat, Reginald. "Oh, don't you be worrying about these ears, mate," he said while stroking the ears with his long, bony fingers.

Charlie and Michael couldn't believe their eyes.

"Yeah, heh-heh-heh. It's me all right. You're old friend Captain Shivers. And it looks like you're missing some ears, eh little chap?"

Charlie tried to reach through the bars and grab the ears from Shivers. "Give 'em back. Those don't belong to you."

"Oh, such a feisty young lad," Shivers said with a greasy smile that turned into a snarl. "Well, they don't belong to you, either."

"Yes, they do! Frank Wellington gave me those ears as a gift. And once he finds out you took them from me, you'll, you'll get what's coming to you!" Charlie said, with a look of frustration.

"Ha. Ha. Ha. You keep thinking that, boy. Maybe old Franky will show up and come to your rescue. Ha. Ha. Ha. Ha. Ha. Ha." Shiver's eerie laughter echoed through the darkness as he made his way around the corner and down the blue-tinged hallway. His long, outstretched shadow trailed behind.

Feeling helpless, yet trying to comfort his younger brother, Charlie sat on the cold, hard bench next to him, with his head down.

Michael, who was completely exhausted, curled up into a ball next to his brother and fell fast asleep.

Charlie closed his eyes and cupped his weary face with his hands. "I need to figure this out. There has to be something we can do," he said to himself quietly. He leaned back, sighed, and rested his head against the stone wall, joining his brother for a long night's sleep. It had been a strenuous day for both.

Clankity, clank, clank. Clankity, clank, clank. "Hey! Wake up, you pathetic little buggers!" an unpleasant voice called out.

Day five of Charlie and Michael's vacation had begun, and not in a way they had hoped for. Had the day before just been a long, terrible dream? Charlie's eyes were closed, his mind still not fully awake.

"C'mon, ya two little gillywags! It's time to get mov'n! The captain wants to see ya down the hall for breakfast. He's got important business to discuss with ya. Wrrrrrrrrep! Get up, let's go. Wrrrrrrep!"

"Charlie. Wake up, Charlie." Michael said, while elbowing his lifeless brother in the side.

"OK. OK. I'm awake. What are you yelling for?" he said, while slowly sitting up and rubbing the sleep from his eyes.

"Check these guys out, Charlie."

Charlie opened his eyes and looked toward the cell door. "What the..." He shook his head, then looked again. "Toads. Giant talking toads." What Charlie saw, his mind could not comprehend, but his eyes were telling the truth. There were indeed two human-sized brown toads standing on their hind legs. Both were fully dressed in guard uniforms and carrying large spear-like weapons. And they continued to bang on the cell bars with metal cups, trying to stir up the boys so they could take them to see Captain Shivers.

"C'mon, c'mon! Quit loafing around. Wherrrp!"

"Yeah. We ain't got all day. Wherrp! Let's go!"

Feeling glum, Charlie and his brother stood up and walked through the cell doorway opened by the guards. One of the toads led the way to the breakfast hall, while the other brought up the rear to assure the boys did not try to escape. The dark, stone hallway was in no way perfect. Its floor was uneven, the walls crooked as can be, and the torches, which provided an inadequate amount of light, burned cool blue—highlighting the dampness on the stone block walls.

"Well, there they are. Feeling a li'l down in the dumps today, are we, boys?" Shivers spat out in an unfriendly manner. "C'mon over here and have a seat with the old Captain, aye. We have a lot to talk about."

"We do?" Michael questioned.

"Why, yes, of course. There's gonna be lots of changes going on around here, now that we have those magic ears of yours."

"And why is that?" Charlie asked. Do you really think the Patrons need the ears to keep you and your evil friends from destroying all that is good in the kingdom?"

"Heh, heh, heh, heh, heh. Yes. Yes, I do, mate. And here's why. You see, those ears is what people around here like to call an Object of Magic. Now these objects possess special powers of sorts, which can be used to access certain kinds of things around here that can change a person's life forever."

"Oh, yeah, like what?" Charlie snapped back.

"Well, uh. Uh, well...you see, I'm not really sure. That there's secret information the Dark Thorns keep amongst themselves. They don't trust anyone when it comes to those sorts of things. All they told us is that there are five of 'em."

"If there are five, then what are they?" Michael blurted out.

"Nice try there, little fella. But ya see, I don't know. They won't tell us that, either. And even if they did, I wouldn't be telling youse two kids anyhow. Ha. Ha. Ha. Oh, that really cracks me up. You think I'd really let you in on a secret like that, do ya? Oh. Ha. Ha. Ha. Ha. Ha. You should see the looks on your faces. Ooooh, boy. Yeah, mates, that ain't ever gonna happen. Never," Shivers said, as he slammed his cup of coffee down on the table and stared at the boys with an awful, scowling look that would make most young kids start to cry.

"You hear that, Michael? Captain Shivers here thinks he's beaten us."

Charlie's comment made the captain tilt his head like a curious dog, trying to figure out what kind of angle the young boy was playing. Then he straightened up and spat out, "Yeah, that's right. Youse two boys might as well give up now, cause without those ears, you've got nothin', your Patron friends got nothin', why, the whole jolly Disney community's got nothin'. Ahhhh ha. Ha. Ha. Ha. Ha."

The captain's comments were intended to get a rise out of Charlie, but it didn't work. "You did say there were five Objects of Magic, did you not?"

"Yeah, and what if I did?" Shivers snapped back.

"Well, it looks like we've got four more chances, Michael."

"What? No! I just told ya, you bratty kid. Youse got nothin'."

"But if there are four objects left, then we still have something."

"No! No ya don't!"

"And why's that?"

"Ohhhhhh! Because ya needs all five. Each object has the power to find one crystal."

"Really? What crystals?" Charlie asked.

"Oh? What! You, you tricked me, ya litter bugger." In a furious rage, Shivers fell backwards in his chair, and onto the floor.

Charlie and his brother broke into laughter at the expense of Shiver's clumsiness. "See that, Michael, the captain knows more than he thinks. Ha. Ha. Ha. Ha. Ha."

Unfortunately, their laughter didn't last too long. The captain quickly got back on his two big feet and slammed both bony palms on the table. His face was red and his breathing heavy as he leaned in toward the boys with a crazed look in his two different-colored eyes. "That's the last time you'll ever get the best of the old Cap'n! You hear me! Those ears of yours. They've been locked away, deep in a secret hiding place that only the Dark Thorns know about. You're never going to find them. You're never going to find the crystals. And you're never going to make it out of here."

The boys instantly went silent.

"Now I have your attention, don't I. That's right. Youse two heard what I said. You are never getting outta this place. To make sure of that, I had me boys bring a little surprise for ya."

Charlie and Michael looked at each other, not knowing how to react.

"Alright, get up youse two. I've got something to show you down the hall. Guards! Help 'em up, will ya."

The toad guards hustled over and forcefully pulled the boys to their feet, then gave them a shove toward the open cell door.

"Get your slimy hands off me, wart face!" Michael said to one of the guards.

"Now, now. No need to get all feisty, chap. The guards are only trying to be helpful."

"If that's trying to be helpful, I'd hate to see how they act when they're angry," Charlie whispered to Michael.

"Come along youse two, we ain't got all day," Shivers snipped. And on cue, the guards prodded the boys with the blunt end of their weapons to keep them moving along down the hallway.

"Ah, here we are," the Captain said, as he looked back at the boys with a big sinister smile. He had stopped in front of a large wooden door with a small barred window too high for the boys to look through. "Willie, the keys, please." One of the guards removed a bundle of keys from his belt hook and handed them to Shivers. As the captain inserted the key and began to unlock the door, he turned to the boys and said with an evil grin, "I think you chaps are gonna like what we've brought for ya."

As Shivers slowly pushed the door open, Charlie and his brother peeked in to try and get a glimpse of what waited beyond the door. Straight to the back was a cozy fireplace, with two logs burning and popping. The orange glow from the fire provided just enough light to see the details of the room. In the center sat a round area rug. On the left was a small dresser and a simple bed. Leaning against the wall in the back left corner was a broom for keeping the floor swept and a small pile of wood for burning. To the right of the fireplace were shelves for cups, plates, and eating utensils. A little farther toward the doorway was a small wooden table with two chairs. And in one of the chairs sat an elderly man who was facing the fireplace.

"We brought ya some company. Would ya like to meet 'em?" Shivers asked the man.

He turned his head, revealing a blank stare and kind smile, the details of his animated face highlighted by the soft glow of the fire.

"Frank! What? Is it really you?" Charlie stuttered, hardly able to speak.

"What did you do to him?" Michael exploded. His short temper got the best of him as he tried to charge Shivers. The guards pushed him away from the captain, who laughed uncontrollably at the boy's ferocity.

"Old Frank here was thirsty, so one of the Dark Thorns made him up a special potion to quench his thirst. You might say Frank won't be thinking too much from here on out. About the only thing that'll concern him from now on is what time his meals come and putting logs on the fire. Ha. Ha. Ha. Ha. Ha. Ha."

"How? How could you do this to such a brilliant man," Charlie said. "You mean he can't remember anything?"

"Oh no, he can remember, all right. He just don't care. Even for youse two. Guards!"

The two guards grabbed the boys and took them out of Frank's room and down the dark corridor, returning them back to the breakfast hall where Shivers intended to get more information out of them, one way or another.

As they were pushed down the dimly lit hallway, Charlie began to worry. He was worried about Frank. He was worried about his parents and what they must be going through, knowing their children were missing. And he was worried there might be no way to escape without the magic ears.

"Wherrrp! Alright, boys. Grab a seat at the table, just like last time," one of the guards said, as the other pushed the boys in that direction. Shivers was following right behind them and came barging into the room, led by his big floppy feet. He made his way to the end of the long wooden table and plopped down, throwing his boat-like feet up on the table. He leaned back in the chair, flipped the front bill of his old wrinkly newsboy hat up, then stared the boys down with his two different-colored eyes. It was quite intimidating.

"Now, where were we?" the captain growled in a low tone of voice. "Ah, yes, before I took ya to see your old friend Frank, we was discussing how the two of you wasn't ever gonna get out of here. Which brings me to my next point. To guarantee nobody comes and tries to do something foolish, like rescue you and Frankie, I needs to tie up a few loose ends. And I can think of only one loose end that knows both you and the old fella. That li'l red headed chap, Ben. So, tell me. Where...is...he?"

"Ben? I don't know," Charlie replied.

"Oh, sure ya do. You just saw him yesterday. I'm bet'n he told ya where he'd be if ya needed any help."

"No. Actually, he never told us anything like that."

"Grrrrrrr. Of course he did. Don't ya be trying ta lie ta me now, boy. Ask the guards over there. They'll tell ya. Guards! Tell these two young fellas what'll happen if ya lie to the captain!"

"Oh, wherrrrp! You don't want to be lying to the cap'n, mates. I mean, look at us. We was once two strap'n lads."

"That's right," the other guard said. "Once, me and my mate here were two of the best look'n chaps in the whole outfit."

"That is," the first guard continued, "until one day we made up a lie to tell the captain so weez wouldn't get in any trouble for miss'n his birthday party. You see, the old captain here, he's a hard one to fool. Anyhow, he eventually found out we was goofing off instead of attending his party. One day later, he took us to a Dark Thorn and had us turned into animated toads."

"And now, here we are. Stuck as toads, wherrrrrrrp, forever."

"You mean you can't ever be changed back into humans?" Michael asked.

"No, chap, we're toads and toads is all we'll ever be. So if I was youse two, I'd be tell'n the cap'n what he wants to hear. Wherrrrrp!"

"There. You see, mates. Now, what do ya have to tell the old captain?"

Charlie couldn't stop thinking about the toads. "You mean, even if you transport out of WONDER? Uh, I mean Deep WONDER, and back to reality, you would still be toads."

"That's right. Still toads," Shivers replied.

"But, how can an animation exist in the real world?"

The captain was losing his patients. "Oh, they wouldn't be animated, they'd be real toads."

"Really?" Michael said. "I've never seen real toads that big before, have you, Charlie?"

"They wouldn't be giant toads! They'd be the size of normal old toads! There! Does that answer your question?" Shiver's shouted at the top of his lungs. His face, now bright red.

"Would they still be able to talk?" Michael asked.

"Yes! Yes! Yes! They can still talk. Talk'n toads. There! Is that it?" Shivers hollered while frantically looking back and forth at Charlie and his brother, his mind unable to tolerate any more off-topic questions.

"Yeah. I think that's it for now," Charlie said, while gesturing to Michael to be quiet.

"Good!" the captain said, as he slowly regained his normal breathing pattern. "Now, as I was saying. what do ya have to tell the captain?"

"Honestly, we don't know where Ben is. Really," Charlie said, trying as best he could to plead their case. But Shivers was a heartless man with no room for pity.

"Grrrrrr! Oh, guaaaards! Take them and lock 'em back up in their cell until I can figure out what to do with these two little brats."

"I'm telling you it's hopeless, Michael. You heard what Captain Shivers said. Without Frank or the magic ears, we have no chance of escaping and finding the first Kingdom Crystal," Charlie said, as he and his brother sat hopelessly in their cell, trying to think of a way out.

"Didn't Oteza say the Patrons of WONDER possess the ability to see into the future?"

"Yes, why do you ask?"

"Well, you still have the stones, right?"

"Yeah, Oteza said that Frank created those to help us find and rescue him from the Thorn Order. But we've already found him, so what good are the stones now?"

"I know we found him, but Oteza also said the information she gave us would help to set him free. And what if "setting him free" wasn't necessarily a physical thing?"

"You mean..."

"Yeah. Maybe the stones will give us the insight needed to free Frank from the spell he's under."

"That's brilliant, Michael! And Shivers forgot we had them," Charlie said, as he pulled them out of his pocket. "Oteza said the stones need to be together, so let's see what happens if..."

"Wait a minute, Charlie, can I see the green and blue stones a second? I think I noticed something." Michael took the two stones and turned them over. "See, look, Charlie. There are recessed shapes carved in the backs of both stones." He proceeded to fit the two stones together. "When you put them together, the notches form another shape."

Charlie held up the red stone and compared its shape to the recessed shape formed by the other two. "Would you look at that," he said, while placing the red stone into the setting. "It's a perfect fit."

No sooner had Charlie set the third stone into place when all three lit up. A purple light shot four feet up from the stones and formed a three-dimensional mask-like face resembling Frank. The Vision Stones hummed softly as Frank spoke.

"If you are receiving this message, then I would presume your hunt for the three Vision Stones was a success. Congratulations! You boys have done a swell job. But now, we must discuss the next task at hand. As you already may know, one of the Dark Thorns has put me under a spell using an evil potion. The good thing about potions is, there is always a remedy to counteract its effects. Having the ability to see into the future allowed me to know what potion they would give me ahead of time, and thus, provide a remedy in this message. But first, you'll need to escape the cell you're in."

"Wow, that's impressive," Michael said.

Frank continued. "Yes, you're trapped in a cell. And yes, those bars are made of steel. But keep in mind, you are animated figures. So the normal laws of physics that exist in reality do not apply here, in Deep WONDER. Anything you can imagine is possible. So getting out of this cell should be no trouble at all for two young minds such as yours."

Charlie and Michael looked at each other with excitement.

"Now, once you've escaped the cell, head down to the potions chamber. It'll be at the bottom of the spiral staircase, which is located all the way down at the end of the corridor to the right of your cell. Once you get there, re-assemble the stones and I'll tell you how to make the potion."

Shoooop! Floating Frank disappeared.

Charlie grabbed the stones and put them back in his pocket. "OK, Michael, you heard what Frank said. Let's try and get out of this cell. I'll go first." Searching through his memories from years of cartoon watching, Charlie imagined his entire body turning into a rubber-like substance. With little effort at all, he stuck his leg between two of the bars. Then his head, shoulders, and torso. And finally, his other leg. With each segment, his body parts conformed to the tight space between the bars by squishing together, then expanding back to normal size on the other side, until Charlie was entirely outside the cell. "OK, Michael, now you try."

Michael, being the way he was, took a slightly more comical approach. He ran as fast as he could, face first, into the stone wall, which turned him into a giant human pancake. When he turned sideways, his body was barely visible. Slowly but surely, he sidestepped his way between the bars, then expanded back to normal by blowing on his thumb several times, like a balloon. "Piece of cake!" Michael said. Charlie chuckled a little, as he always enjoyed his brother's strange sense of humor.

"This way," Charlie said, while pointing to the right of the cell they had just escaped from. The corridor was just as they'd expected: dark, wet, and creepy. There were several wooden doors they passed on the way to the end of the hall, each a mystery as to what lay beyond them. With every cautious step they took, Charlie's heart pounded faster and faster—expecting any second for one of the doors to swing open with the captain right there to grab them by their shirts, or an unexpected Thorn to come walking around one of the adjacent hallway corners and take them by surprise. The silence was nerve-wracking. The end of the hallway seemed so far away. Would it ever end? There's no way we're going to make it, Charlie thought to himself. And then, there it was, the top of the spiral staircase, eerily marked with two raven —statues sitting atop vine-wrapped pillars. The pillars flanked the stairway, which was dimly lit with blue flame torches that descended into darkness, down and around the curved walls.

"This must be the staircase," Michael said, with a nervous rattle in his voice.

The boys made their way down the staircase, spiraling deeper and deeper with large looming shadows trailing along the cold stone walls. Finally, they reached the bottom, and in front of them stood a wooden door with a dusty, bronze skull knocker and an intricately designed door knob, which had an open eye as its center. Above the door was an elaborately crafted wooden sign that read: POTIONS.

"Looks like we found it, Michael."

"I'd say so."

Charlie slowly placed his hand on the door knob and turned. There was a click as Charlie felt the door release and start to open. The hinges were very loud, creaking badly, as if the door had not been opened in quite some time. As he pushed the door open, cobwebs broke free from the entryway and floated into their faces, which they feverishly swatted away. The large candle holders mounted on each side of the doorway magically ignited, startling the boys. The walls were covered with dusty old wooden shelves. And on those shelves were hundreds of well worn books—potion books, they assumed. Below the shelves was a sturdy, U-shaped table, which supported dozens of cob-webbed vials, beakers, and things used to mix and conjure up the darkest potions imaginable. The boys stepped into the room. The door quickly closed and locked behind them, catching them completely off guard.

"Not to worry, Michael. If Frank told us to come here, then I trust we'll be safe." Charlie removed the three stones from his pocket and assembled them like before, on the table. Frank's purple floating face re-appeared. Directions to create a remedy potion were given, and the boys got to work whipping up the magical brew in no time. Though it smelled and looked something terrible, Frank assured them it was supposed to be that way, and no matter what the boys thought, the potion would work. Charlie corked the vial, opened the door, and quietly headed up the stairs, with Michael following closely behind.

Charlie slowly opened up the door to Frank's room and found him sitting at the table, just like before. "Hello, Frank. It's me, your friend, Charlie. I brought my brother, Michael, as well. We're here to help you."

The man slowly turned and stared at the boys with a kind smile.

"We brought you something to drink. It's kind of smelly and looks like muddy water, but it's supposed to be good for you," Charlie said, while handing the uncorked vial to Frank.

Without hesitation, the old man began to drink the disgusting potion. But then he stopped, making a funny face of displeasure.

"I know. It's really bad, isn't it. But it will help you get better. I promise," Charlie said.

Believing what Charlie had told him, Frank squeezed his nose with two fingers to kill the taste, then quickly downed the rest of the potion. Thirty seconds passed. Then forty-five, as he sat back in his chair, waiting for something to happen. Suddenly, Frank's eyes began to sparkle, his nose twitched, his mouth puckered, and the long grey hair on his head began to dance.He began to bounce uncontrollably in his chair until it tipped over. Before the boys knew it, he was dancing around the room as if it were a grand ball. Then…he stopped, quickly turned around, and looked at Charlie. "You did it, young man! You and Michael have set me freeeeee!"

"We did?" Michael said.

"Yes, Michael. My mind has been freed from that evil potion. I'm free to think, free to do, and free to create. Now, I need…your…help. Yes, I need your help. Right now."

"Sure, what can we do?" Charlie asked.

"Simple. Just take your brother, go back to your cell, and act like none of this ever happened."

"What? I'm afraid I don't understand."

"Hmmm. Right. I don't expect that you would at the moment. But there's no time to explain. Just go back to your cell and wait for a signal."

"A signal?"

"A signal that it's time to take action. And trust me, you'll know it when you see it. Understand? Good. Very well then, tally-ho my friends!" Swirling into a human tornado-like spin, thanks to his animated abilities, the eccentric old Patron morphed into a sparkling display of glittering dust—then poof. He was gone.

A short walk down the dimly lit hallway from where Frank Wellington had just disappeared, Captain Shivers was hashing out his plans with a room full of Thorns under his command.

"So, what is it you're think'n Cap'n?" one of his men asked.

"I'll tell ya what. I was think'n I'd take you and feed ya to the crocodiles if you don't shut your trap, that's what." The entire room of undesirables burst into laughter. "Quiet! Now listen up, all of youse. We've got two little rodents caged up down the hall who just might be key to the Patrons undoing. That is, if we plays our cards right. And it's very important that we do. Otherwise, some us might end up on the short end of a Dark Thorn spell. Understand me?" Everyone in the room agreed wholeheartedly, out of fear for what might happen if they didn't. "Now, like I was saying, we's got two little rodents locked up down the hall in a cell, and our old pal Frank under a potion spell in another room." Shivers pointed toward everyone in the room and said. "Your job is to make sure them little buggers don't escape, while I figure out a way to catch Frank's old buddy, Ben Glimmer. Got it?"

"Sure, Cap'n, you can count on us. But what about the old fella, Frank? Don't we needs to keep an eye on him as well?"

"I'm glad you asked, Caldwell. No, you won't need to be worry'n about old Frankie. He's what you might call incapacitated, thanks to Dark Thorn Oltar's potion. You see, after drink'n the magic juice, lucky ol' Frank don't have a care in the world, not for his Patron mates, not for those two little kids down the hall. Why, if he has any pets, not even for them."

"So you're saying the old man ain't even in the game anymore, eh?"

"That's right, chap. He's out. You just keeps a watchful eye on those two snot sniffers," Shivers said, as he opened the door and exited the room.

"What kind of scream was that."

"Sounds like Captain Shivers just found out that Frank escaped," Charlie said with a smile. "But seriously, remember what he told us, Michael. Act as if nothing has happened."

"Right. Got it."

Clunk. Clunk. Clunk. Clunk. The sound of Shivers' giant floppy shoes pounding the pavement echoed through the hallway, followed by the heavy footsteps and ranting of a dozen angry Thorns. Charlie stared toward the bend in the hall, highlighted by a single torch that was hidden just around the corner. First came the obscure shadows on the wall of Shivers and his hostile Thorns, quickly followed by the angry looking captain and then his men, stomping right behind him. It looked like the boys had their work cut out for them.

"Stay calm, Michael, and let me handle this."

Shivers and his crew reached the cell. The captain grabbed two of the cell bars and squeezed so tightly, his knuckles turned white. His face was tomato red, his breathing heavy, and his eyes blood-shot and burning yellow. "Soooooooo! What do ya boys have to say for yourselves? Thought you could pull one over on the ol' captain, eh?"

Charlie gave Shivers a look of curiosity. "What's that? Is something the matter?"

"Oh, pleeeeease! Don't pretend you don't know what I'm talking about."

"I'm sorry, but...I don't know what you're talking about."

"Are you trying to tell me you know nothing about what happened down that hallway?" Shivers said, pointing towards Frank's room.

"Oh, is there something wrong with Frank?"

"Grrrrrrrr! Yes, there's something wrong, you blasted little toad. Your pal Frank has escaped. And I think you and your li'l brother here had something to do with it."

"I don't know what to tell you, captain. Michael and I have been doing nothing but sitting in this cell since you put us back here. How could we have helped Frank escape when we're locked up in this cell?"

"Hmmm. Well, maybe you're right. But that still don't mean I believe ya."

"Well, maybe it's time you start."

"Oh. Ha. Ha. Ha. Ha. Not in this lifetime, mate. Youse can bet on that. I've never trusted anyone who's friends with those do-gooder Patrons, and I'm not about to start with the likes of you. C'mon, men. Time to start search'n. We've got a rat to catch. And his name is Frankie," Shivers said in a mean tone, as he slowly turned and began to walk away from the boys' cell. But then he stopped, turning once more to face the boys with a diabolical look on his face. "Jimmy, while I'm think'n about it, go grabs me track'n lizards. And don't forget to bring some of me torturing devices as well. We're gonna teach old Frank what happens when you try and escape from Captain Shivers."

"Oh, boy! Torturing devices! We haven't used those on anyone in quite some time, have we, cap'n?" one of the Thorns said.

"No, you block head, we haven't."

"Which ones do ya want us to bring, Cap'n?"

Feeling distracted by the incompetence of his crew member, Shivers turned his eyes away from Charlie and Michael, and focused on the unfortunate soul who dared to ask such a silly question. "It doesn't really matter, now does it?"

"Uh, I guess not, Cap'n."

"Right. So just pick a few, and hurry up about it."

Without hesitation, three of the men scurried off down the hallway to fulfill his requests.

The captain turned back to the boys, pointing at them with his long, bony finger. "As for you two, don't youse be get'n any ideas of escaping from here. Otherwise, we'll have to throw ya into the pit with ol' Snip and Snap."

"Who?" Charlie asked.

"Why they'd be me two pet crocodiles. And I'm sure they'd love to eat... I mean, meet ya. Ha. Ha. Ha. Ha." Shivers turned and walked away. His laughter echoed through the hallway as he and his crew slowly faded into darkness.

"Did you hear that Charlie? He's gonna feed us to his crocodiles. We gotta get outta here!"

"No. We can't do that. You heard what Frank said. We have to stay here and wait for a signal."

"But we're gonna end up as croc crackers before that happens!"

"Get ahold of yourself for just one second, and think, will ya. Frank told us to trust him. And that's exactly what we're going to do. We need to have faith in what he said, and stick to the plan. It's the best chance we have to get out of here, and back to Mom and Dad. So, are you going to trust me, or not?"

"Yes," Michael replied.

"Good. So we sit and wait for a signal, just as Frank intended."

Chapter Eleven

Somewhere well beyond all that is real, and even the common dream, a 2D-animated Frank Wellington was searching for something rather extraordinary, a powerful source of magical energy known only by those considered honorable enough to be called Patrons, or despicable enough to be labeled Thorns.

Sitting in an upside-down umbrella, wearing Bermuda shorts, a flowered luau shirt, and white sneakers, the only thing standing between the wise old man's vision and the misty spray of salty sea water created by the dolphins pulling him along using two stands of rope was a pair of goofy-looking goggles. Fortunately, the dolphins were swimming at such a high speed, the water from the wake of the umbrella carried well over Frank's head, leaving him remarkably dry. But of course, something like this could only happen in a place such as Deep WONDER.

The sea Frank was traveling across did not exist on a map. The water filling the sea was not in the least bit real. And the dolphins pulling him along were nothing but a small creation of Frank's imagination. It was a perfectly fun way to travel across a giant animated body of water that didn't exist. On the horizon, just minutes away, Frank spotted his destination: a large tropical island covered with palm trees, sandy beaches, and an enormous, snow-capped volcano toward the center which towered well above everything else on the island. In fact, it was so tall that its peak disappeared into the clouds above.

"Aha! There it is! Eruption Island!" Frank shouted to the dolphins. "Full steam ahead, ladies! We're almost there!"

Hearing the excitement in Frank's voice, the dolphins increased their efforts and reached the shallow waters of the shoreline even faster than expected. One dolphin turned left, the other right, while both simultaneously let go of the ropes fastened to the umbrella. Sheer momentum carried the old man sitting on his umbrella all the way to shore, out of the water, and onto dry sand, before stopping abruptly. The sudden stop threw Frank forward, out of the umbrella, and tumbling head over heels into the sand, until he came to rest in a sitting position. His hair was filled with sand and his head was, spinning like a top.

"Well, that wasn't the prettiest of landings, but nonetheless, I made it!" he shouted to the island in celebration. Frank turned and waved to the dolphins for their help, who both did a flip in the air and landed with a big splash to acknowledge their friend. The spunky old man stood up, threw his goggles into the sand, and brushed himself off before eagerly reaching into his pocket and pulling out a small sketch of a map he had drawn just before hitching a ride with the dolphins. As he curiously stared at the drawing, Frank scratched his head, scanned the island, then looked back at the map. "If my drawing is right, there should be a hidden cave entrance at the base of Seagull Rock, just beyond the sandy shore," he said to himself. The map showed Seagull Rock on the west side of the island, where the sun would set. While looking toward the sky, he could see the sun starting to favor the left side of the island as it continued its slow descent to the horizon. Frank folded the map, put it in his pocket, and headed down the shore toward the sun.

The only sounds to be heard were the gentle waves washing up along the sandy beach, and the seagulls circling above the shore waters. Frank could not be more relaxed than he was at that moment. But as he made his way around a sharp bend in the island, his mood drastically changed. The white sandy shore was replaced by rocky boulders and jagged cliffs which the water smashed itself against with endless waves of forceful energy. What had seemed like a peaceful, relaxing stroll just minutes ago had turned into a dangerous challenge for a man of Frank's age. With courage in his heart and the will to succeed, he pressed on, carefully watching every step he took so as not to slip and fall into the rough waters below.

The wind was gradually picking up strength as an unfriendly storm front rolled in fron the south side of the horizon. It wouldn't be long before it reached the shore. Could it be? Frank thought. Is it possible the Dark Thorns know I'm here and have conjured up this wicked storm to force me away from what I seek? With no time to waste, Frank pushed on, searching for the rock formation that marked the way.

On his very next step, the cluster of loose stones beneath his left foot broke loose. His body quickly slid down the side of the giant rock on which he had just stood. Frank reached up with his right hand, barely able to grab the top edge. With all his strength, he hoisted his left shoulder around and secured his position with his left hand. Slowly, he pulled himself up, swinging his right leg atop the rocky surface, then the other leg. He rolled onto his back, out of breath, tired, yet grateful to still be alive. And there it was. Like a giant silhouette holding steady through the stormy weather, its majestic stone beak protruded outwards from the shoreline over the rough sea waters below. Its jagged figure, a couple hundred feet high, rose upward out of the rocky cliff banks. Naturally carved into the shoreline by the forces of nature, as only an Imagineer from years past could have dreamed up, it was Seagull Rock.

Meanwhile, far away, in another realm of Deep WONDER, Captain Shivers and his crew continued to pester Charlie and Michael for answers about Frank and Ben's whereabouts.

"Alright boys, now that I've got me track'n lizards, your old pal Frankie's not gonna have a chance to get too far before we catch him. And youse two still need to tell me where that little red-headed fella is hiding, as well. Cause I know you know where he is."

"Really, we have no idea where Ben is. We already told you that. You think those funny-looking things are going to help you track down Frank? They look like a mix between an iguana and a fat alligator on a leash. And their eyes? How can they possibly see anything with eyes like that," Charlie said in an effort to get Shivers worked up.

"Go ahead, make fun of 'em. Say what you will. These two fellas are the best trackers in all of WONDER. They don't need to see well. Its their tongues that do the work. They can smell what they're looking for from miles away. Even pick'n up scents a few days old is easy for them. What? Are ya scared there, boy? Afraid of what we're gonna do when we catch your pal?"

"You mean, *if* you catch him."

"What? Your pal Wellington's got no chance against me and my track'n lizards. And don't go thinking he does. Cause he don't."

Charlie's plan was working. The captain's blood was starting to boil, causing him to completely forget his true intention—to find out where Frank and Ben were, so they could go catch them. Charlie's plan was also allowing Frank more time to achieve what he needed to do, and Ben as well—an added bonus in Charlie's mind.

"What are ya grinning about, mate? If I was you, I'd be shaking in my boots about now."

"No. I actually feel quite comfortable at the moment, thank you," Charlie calmly replied, in an attempt to hide his fear from the captain.

"Why you little... Huh? You don't say. Ha. Ha. Ha. Ha. Ha," Shivers replied, after a guard had interrupted by mumbling something into his left ear. "Well, well. It looks like we've solved half the problem," the captain said with an evil smirk. A few of my best spies just located that crazy old friend of yours. So, we're done here. C'mon men, we've got work to do."

"But what about the red-headed fella, captain?" one of the men asked.

"First we catch the old man, then we'll worry about little Ben Glimmer," Shivers answered back, as he and his crew marched off down the dark corridor. Unfortunately, this made Charlie and Michael start to think about the well-being of their dear friend, Frank Wellington, and to contemplate if staying in their cell, as he had told them, was the right thing to do.

On his way down the hall, Shivers turned and hollered, "You two toadies stay behind and keep an eye on them young fellas! Got it?"

"Aye aye, Cap'n!" they replied.

Frank Wellington had managed to find the secret cave entrance beneath Seagull Rock, but he knew it had to be more complicated than simply walking into a cave and grabbing something as powerful as the magic light charm. And indeed, he was right. The cave was completely cloaked in darkness. The old man was able to feel around and find an unlit torch just inside the entrance, which he was able to light using a match he found in his shirt pocket. As he cautiously scanned the dimly lit area, Frank was able to make out a short walkway of flat surface stones, and just past it, two sets of shattered skeleton bones. Hanging ominously above the pile of bones was a large rectangular boulder, suspended by a thick vine. Obviously, the other two visitors had been unsuccessful in their attempts to obtain the light charm. Studying the walkway stones, he noticed three of them were slightly different from the others. They were a shade darker and about a half-inch taller, and scattered randomly across the walkway, making it nearly impossible not to step on at least one of them while passing through. Frank was quite positive these three stones had to be the triggers which cause the giant boulder to drop and crush any unsuspecting passerby. Step by cautious step, Frank slowly made his way across the stone pathway, while also keeping an eye on the giant boulder suspended above. After just a few nerve-shattering seconds, the wise old Patron had made it across the walkway and past the intimidating bolder. His body and mind exhaled in relief. "That's one trap avoided," he mumbled to himself, though Frank knew too well there had to be more.

Slowly, he made his way through the cave, batting cobwebs from his face, as he moved down the sandy pathway. It was clear that no one had been through here in quite some time. The sand eventually gave way to yet another stone walkway, blocked off by a large set of wooden posts which ran vertically into the top and bottom surfaces of the door-like passage. But the wise old imagineer had foreseen this obstacle in his dreams, and knew how to remove it. Closing his eyes, Frank searched his mind for an answer. His eyes opened wide. Turning backwards and looking to his left, he spotted a group of small stones embedded in the wall. Each had a symbol chiseled into it. He walked up and pushed three of the stones farther into the wall in a sequential order: swirl, triangle, sun. Quickly turning back, he saw the large posts had drawn back. The path was now clear.

While continuing to ascend farther through the cave, the sound of repetitive screeches welled up through the jagged corridor. As Frank turned to the right, the narrow pathway opened into a large area which towered endlessly upward and fell deeply downward, into a sea of darkness. The pathway he had been carefully following had come to an end. And below it, flying in erratic patterns, were thousands of screeching bats.

Frank searched around for a way to move on, but there was no obvious solution. Inching closer to the edge of the walkway, he blindly stared downward toward the sound of the bats, but it was too dark to see them. Gradually, his eyes began to adjust, the torch in his hand providing what little light there was to see. At that moment, a hint of something caught his eye. It was a subtle detail of vine growing down the rocky wall, highlighted ever so slightly by the torch he possessed. And though the walls seemed impossible to navigate, the vine offered an opportunity to keep moving forward. Frank held the torch in his mouth and carefully lowered himself over the ledge of the walkway, grabbing the vine tightly with both hands. Slowly, he repelled downward toward the swarm of bats, not knowing whether what he was doing was actually going to work. Regardless, it was too late to turn back.

Down and farther down he went, passing through the thick swarm of erratic bats, until eventually darkness turned to light. At the bottom of the vine was a large circular floor where Frank gained his footing, grabbed the torch from his mouth, and walked toward the middle. It was there he discovered an ornately bordered ten-foot circle with an embossed image of a star over a volcano in its center. Around the outer perimeter of the circular floor were three smaller, but still large circles. Engraved in each was a series of living things. As Frank carefully looked over each one, his mind processed what his eyes took in.

There was a snake, penguin, octopus, and tiger in one circle; a tortoise, hen, and elephant in the second; and a lion, eagle, vulture, eel, and rhino in the third. All of them were connected to the center image by ornately detailed lines. What did all three have in common with the center? Were they answers of some sort? Parts of a whole? Frank's mind searched for answers, yet nothing came to him. He focused on the animals that were grouped together, but could not find a connection. Then he thought about the circle of life, from *The Lion King*. But that led nowhere. Searching deeper, Frank began focusing less on the animal names and more on individual letters. He thought about mixing the letters up within each animal name, which quickly became far too complicated. Then, unexpectedly, it all clicked. Like a spark in the night, Frank's mind flushed out all the excess, and the answer became clear.

It was so obvious, he wondered why he hadn't thought of it from the start. By taking the first letter of each animal and putting them together, one word was spelled out within each circle, together forming the answer he had been searching for. So, snake, penguin, octopus, tiger spelled "spot." Tortoise, hen, elephant spelled "the." And lion, eagle, vulture, eel, rhino spelled "lever." "Spot the lever." Frank had solved the riddle, and began to search the area for a lever. Assuming it would be located on or in the wall, he slowly walked along the perimeter, feeling the wall along the way for traces of a lever or a compartment containing a lever. He scanned everything within his reach. About half-way around, a small rectangular stone caught his attention. It was roughly three inches wide by five inches tall—an unusual size compared to the other stones that made up the wall. So he pushed on the top edge. Nothing. He pushed on the bottom edge. The top moved outward. Excited by his discovery, he worked his fingers behind the the top of the stone and pulled down until he heard multiple gear-like noises under the floor. On the last loud clunk, the circular floor began to turn. Not knowing how to react, Frank froze in place.. The floor continued to turn slowly, until he was standing on the other side of the room. Again, the gears under the floor made a loud noise as the floor locked into place. Slowly, a hidden door opened, revealing a rugged pathway leading upward.

Cautiously, Frank entered through the doorway and glanced up the path as he began to venture forward. The lighting was dim, yet good enough to see in. As he continued upward, Frank's confidence grew to a point that he knew the light charm had to be waiting for him at the end of the path. And when he arrived at the top, Frank saw exactly what he had envisioned in his dream. Highlighted by glowing energy, and suspended in mid-air, was the light charm, radiant and pure. Thrilled beyond his greatest expectations, he searched for a way reach it. Underneath it was a small rock formation, oval-like in shape and fairly flat. But to get to it, he'd have to walk across a narrow rock bridge. However, there were dire consequences awaiting those who failed to make it across the bridge. As Frank peered downward, he saw a large pool of red-hot lava, and upward wasn't any more promising, as he carefully studied what appeared to have once been an opening for the lava below. It was then that Frank realized where he was: the volcano, the one he had seen as he approached the island, the one shown in the center of the room he had just come from. If it were to erupt, that would be it. No more Frank Wellington.

Steadying his nerves and focusing on balance, Frank carefully made his way across the bridge as he felt the sweltering heat from the hot lava below. "Steady there, fella," he said to himself, attempting to stay calm. "Almost there. Ah! Made it." As he stood directly under the charm, it became apparent the object was levitating higher above the ground than he had anticipated, making it impossible to reach. But Frank wasn't about to give up. Envisioning his hand grasping hold of the charm necklace, he went into a crouched position, ready for the task at hand. Focusing his energy, the valiant Patron pushed off the ground and leaped high into the air, as only a man his age could do while in WONDER. As he reached maximum height, Frank stretched out and grabbed for the charm necklace, but his hand went right through it, as if it were air. Instantaneously, everything changed.

"Get him, boys!" a familiar voice shouted out.

Frank had fallen into a Thorn trap!

"I don't know, Charlie. We've been waiting for quite awhile and no sign of anything," Michael pleaded to his brother, as they continued to sit and wait patiently in their cell. "You know we can easily get out of this cell, right? I mean, we're cartoons, so we can pretty much do anything."

"Yes, Michael, I know. But it's important that we follow Frank's orders. I'm sure he has a really good reason. We just have to trust him."

"Yeah Charlie, but..."

CRASH.

"What in the world!" Charlie shouted.

A large ball-like object had smashed through the rear wall of their cell, creating a huge mess of stone fragments and dust, with an opening large enough for them to easily walk through. But what was it? Or who was it? As the boys looked more carefully, the ball-like figure unfolded into a short portly man with red curly hair.

"Ben? Is that you?" asked Charlie.

Brushing himself off, the man turned and said, "Why of course it's me, lad. Wowee! That was fun. I'll have to remember that trick for another time. How was that for a signal, eh? Ha. Ha. Ha. Ha. C'mon, old fella, flap those wings and get in here," Ben called out, toward the hole in the wall.

Alexios came flying into the cell and perched himself on the pile of broken stones, coughing from all the dust. "Do you think you could have made any more noise with that ridiculous entrance? You probably alerted the entire Thorn army," he snipped at Ben. "We should have done it my way."

Ben just looked at the old owl and rolled his eyes.

"Hey, Alexios. It's good to see you again," Charlie said.

"It's good to see you too, young man. Now, Ben and I are here to lead you out of this ghastly place, before the Thorns discover our intentions."

"But what about Frank?" Charlie asked.

"Frank is busy doing other things at the moment. That's why he sent us," Ben said.

"This way, boys," Alexios said, as he flew through the opening in the back wall of the cell.

As Charlie and Michael passed through the wall and started heading downhill, they took on a view overlooking a small underground town. All the buildings were rather shabby and run-down, with jagged chimneys, broken windows, busted railings, and crooked stairs. Since everything was animated, all the imperfections were over-exaggerated and out of proportion. The entire view was dark, dreary, and void of bright colors, except for the tiny bits of glowing yellows and oranges coming from some of the windows. Instead of a sky to look at, there were thousands of stalactites hanging down from above. There were no vehicles of sorts, since it was underground. All of the Thorns who resided there traveled by foot or by wagons that were pulled by old, worn-out horses. The lumpy brick roads paved the way for the wagons, while the old sidewalks were cracked in various ways.

Looking back and upwards from where they had just escaped, Charlie could now tell they had been held in a large, castle-like structure which sat above the city. All the windows were barred and guard towers marked each corner. There was an elevated walkway connecting the towers, allowing guards to cover the perimeter of the building from a higher point of view. Just as Charlie turned his attention back toward the town, trouble found them. One of the Thorn guards up in the rear left tower had spotted them escaping the castle. "We've got a breakout on the south wall! It's the boys, and they've got help!"

Sirens began to wail. Floodlights combed the area. The giant front gate opened as a hundred Thorn soldiers came boiling out to hunt down the escapees.

The hilly, rock-covered terrain the boys and Ben were on was difficult to walk on, making it hard for them to quickly get to the roadway which led out of town. The boys and Ben had quite a ways to go, and were moving half the speed of the Thorn guards, who had been created up for situations such as this. Being faun-like creatures from Greek mythology, their half-man, half-goat qualities allowed them to quickly navigate the jagged terrain and make easy prey of those who tried to escape. And in this case, it was Charlie, Michael and Ben. Alexios, on the other hand, had a substantial advantage over the others, including the guards, as he could fly. Unfortunately, though, his three friends could not.

"This way, Ben!" Alexios called out from above. "The terrain over here should be easier for the three of you to walk on."

"Right-right," Ben replied. "This way boys, we're almost there!"

Michael looked back to check the guards, who were now only about a hundred feet away and gaining. "Charlie! We gotta move faster! Or else those goat men are going to catch us!"

"We're moving as fast as we can, Michael! I don't know what else we can do. Well, maybe? Hey Alexios, can we get a little air support?"

"Already on it, young squire," the mighty owl screeched, as he turned from high above and dove toward the guards closest to them in an attempt to knock them off balance. His first few dives were successful, buying his friends more time. But soon the agile Thorn guards caught on to his tactics and began their own counter-attack. Some carried with them small nets with weighted stone ends that were used to capture escapees. Several guards began throwing the nets at the owl as he dove to attack. Because he had to avoid the nets, his aerial assault grew less effective, giving the guards a chance to close in on Ben and the boys.

There were simply too many Thorns. Ben and Alexios' plan to rescue Charlie and Michael was beginning to crumble, as their pursuers closed in from all directions. Not even Alexios could help them anymore, circling high above to avoid the nets. The sounds of grunting guards, the smell of musty air, and the look of defeat on Ben's face were almost too much for Charlie and his brother to bare. All hope was fading away as Ben held the boys close, trying to shield them from their inevitable defeat. Looking up toward Alexios, Ben began to quietly ask for help. "Please, please, Patrons of WONDER. We desperately need your assistance. Hear me now and show us the way."

"Alright, fun time is over for youse three. We're taking you back to the holding cells, until the captain shows up!" One of the guards yelled, as three others took each of the captives by the arm to lead them back to Thorn Castle. The fight was over. The plan had failed. All Alexios could do was watch from above as the guards started walking Ben and the boys back to the castle through the rugged hillside.

Scratched, bruised, and tired from their attempt to escape, Charlie, Michael, and Ben reluctantly walked alongside their guard escorts without saying a word. The guards decided it was best to go back in through the castle's front gate, which was around the corner and a bit farther than the hole in the wall Ben had created for the boys' escape. As they rounded the front corner of the castle wall, Ben thought he'd liven things up with a little conversation to brighten the boy's spirits. "So, big fella, when do we get to talk to your captain?"

"I told ya already. When he gets back," the guard snipped back.

"Yes, of course. But when exactly is he getting back?"

Angered by Ben's questions, the guard yelled! "Halt!" to the other guards. Then he turned and looked down at Ben with an evil stare. The goat man was easily a foot-and-a-half taller and three times as strong as the little red-headed fellow. But intimidation wasn't a part of Ben's belief system, so he just smiled and looked the guard right back in his dark, soulless eyes.

"He's getting back when he gets back, and that's all you need to know. Ask me that question again and it'll be the dark box for you, little Benny."

Terrified by the guardsman's words, Charlie and Michael waited for Ben's response.

"Well, can you at least tell me where he went?" Ben asked.

The boys held their breath.

"If you really want to know, I'll tell ya. But ya ain't gonna like it."

Ben continued on with the conversation, still hoping some sort of miracle would soon find him and his friends. "Why sure, you can tell me anything you want. I can take it," he said with doubtful heart.

"Fine. Have it your way. The captain and some of his best trackers are out capturing your old buddy Frank. They found out where he was headed, so they took off quick-like to beat him there, and set a trap for him. He was chasing after some kind of light charm; thought it would give the Patrons an advantage over us Thorns. But it's hard to outsmart Cap'n Shivers. I'm think'n by now they probably sacked the old guy and are headed back. So your plan, whatever it was, well, it ain't gonna work now. Ha. Ha. Ha. Ha. Ha." In response, all the other guards burst into laughter as well, breaking Ben's spirit.

The little red-headed man lowered his head and began to sniffle as he turned toward the boys without making eye contact, and quietly said. "Sorry. I...I'm so sorry, boys. I should have tried harder. I...I don't...don't know where things went wrong. I must apologize. It's all my fault."

Charlie and Michael stood speechless. Tears began to run down their dirty cheeks. The thought of Shivers and his crew capturing Frank, plus never seeing their parents again, left them emotionally drained, scared, and at the same time, extremely angry.

"No! No! It can't end like this!" Charlie shouted." In a fit of frustration, he freed himself from the guards grip and pulled Michael free as well. "We need to go. Now!" The boys tried to push through the circle of guards, only to be easily stopped. Ben could hardly bear to watch.

"Ben! We have to help Frank and get back to our parents!" Charlie yelled.

The guards began to laugh again, which fueled the boys' fire.

Michael snapped. With all his might, he kicked one of the guards in his goat shin, causing him to fall and set off a chain reaction of awkward events. The falling guard knocked over several other goat men. Charlie broke free and shoved another guard, who lost his balance and started tumbling down the hill into even more guards. Ben, sparked by the boys' determination, bowled over three other guards who fell into six more goat men. It was like a giant domino effect that was picking up steam as it traveled down the unforgiving terrain of the jagged castle hillside. Alexios, seeing this as an opportunity, instantly perked up and began dive bombing the discombobulated guardsmen, causing even more to fall as they tried to protect their heads from the mighty owl's air attacks.

Amid the chaos, Ben and the boys ran, hopped, and bounced over and around all the fallen or outreaching guardsmen as they made their way toward the bottom of the hill. It was there, at the base of the hill, where trouble arose. Just as they were approaching the road, an unlikely and terrible thing happened. Captain Shivers and his tracking crew came walking out of the dark roadway tunnel that led out of town. The boys and Ben stopped in their tracks. Alexios came to rest on a nearby chimney, continuing to observe from a safe distance.

"Well, well. Look what we got here, boys. A couple of kids and a little red-headed fella who are up to no good," Shivers growled. "I thought I told you boys not to try and escape while we was gone?"

Charlie noticed immediately that Frank was not with Shivers, which explained why the captain was extra cranky at the moment. It also gave Charlie hope. If Frank was still out there, then they might still have a chance, he thought to himself, while trying to hide his emotions.

By now the guardsmen had regathered themselves and had formed a solid barrier to the rear of where Ben and the boys stood. Again they were surrounded.

"So you thought youse were gonna make it outta here, besting my guardsman and all." Shivers gave the goat fellas a scowling stare, then turned his attention back to Ben and the boys. "But, ya didn't expect the old captain and his crew to come walking through the tunnel, now did ya? Well, to show my appreciation for youse guys trying to escape, I think I'm gonna have ya all thrown in the dungeon. At least, that is, until I can figure out what I'm gonna do with ya."

"Oh, no! Not the dungeon!" Ben replied. "These boys are too young for that!"

"Hush up. I don't want to hear another word outta you," Shivers snapped back. "Or else I'll be feeding you to Snip and Snap. Got it?"

"Snip and Snap, sir?" cne of the men questioned.

"Yes, you blithering idiot! Me crocodiles!" Shivers yelled.

"Oh, right, the crocodiles. Sure, that'll fix 'em.

The captain rolled his eyes, then turned back to the boys and Ben. "Guards! Take these three and put them in the dungeon. They'll make good bait for old man Wellington. And when he tries to save them..."

BOOM. There was a sudden burst of wind and blinding light atop the hillside. The wind gust so hard, it took everything the guards had to keep from being blown farther down the hill. Shivers held onto his hat with both hands as his cheeks flopped loosely in the wind. Ben, Charlie, and Michael leaned toward the ground to avoid the wind as best they could, while Alexios used the chimney to shield himself from the mighty gust. As the wind died down and the beacon of light dimmed to a peaceful glow, a figure arose from its core. There, standing before them, with the light charm necklace gleaming brightly and floating around his neck, was Frank.

"Why, you old coot!" Shivers hollered. "How did you ever get your hands on that necklace?"

"Oh, that's my little secret. And something a man like you will ever know," Frank replied with a smirk. The crafty Patron began to move his arms and hands around in a sphere-like motion. Within its center, a radiant orb of brilliant light began to grow, until it was nearly the size of a bowling ball, at which point Frank threw his arms wide open, and said, "With this light, I empower you!" The words echoed down the hillside and through the town. With a clap of his hands, the bright orb simultaneously broke into several small, meteor-like pieces, which shot off toward Ben and Alexios, striking each squarely in the heart. With their bodies aglow and eyes crystal blue, the three assumed attack positions as they squared up for battle.

"Well, don't just stand there, you idiots! Get them!" the Captain commanded his guards, who immediately broke into three groups and mounted a charge toward each of the three threatening subjects. The first group of goat men headed straight up the hill toward Frank, who swirled his right hand above his head, creating a large tornado-like funnel of light which sucked up all the charging guards and carried them over the giant castle wall. Near the bottom of the hillside, another group of guards charged toward Alexios, who was sitting atop the roof of a nearby building. Quickly, he shot high into the air, then came screeching downward with talons out. The aggressive owl skirted the heads of his enemies, leaving a trail of illuminated dust which shrunk every guard it touched to the size of a mouse. And right in the middle of it all, Ben curled up into a ball-like position as his body began to spin rapidly like a top, sending every attacker he made contact with hundreds of yards through the air, into buildings, garbage cans, and other objects, rendering them unconscious.

Captain Shivers spun into a fit of rage, kicking dirt and spitting words unsuitable for even the oldest of ears. His face turned bright red as he grabbed the frazzled hair sticking out of his hat and shouted. "This can't be happening! Where are my best soldiers? Can't anybody stop these fools!"

In response to the captain's words, Frank raised his right arm, palm forward. A ray of light shot from his hand and encompassed the foul captain. As the gifted Patron lifted his extended arm, Shivers' entire body came off the ground and was suspended twenty feet in the air. Frank moved his hand to the left, and Shivers' body followed. Slowly and effortlessly, Wellington guided the captain's defenseless body toward a nearby building, which had a flagpole extended outward from its rooftop. Shivers began kicking and waving his arms in frustration, but there was nothing he could do. Frank dropped his arm quickly to the side, releasing the captain from the air and onto the top of the flagpole where he hung, suspended by his worn-out old britches, screaming and hollering for someone to get him down.

Ben, Alexios, and the boys all began to laugh as they gathered around Frank. The humble Patron looked at each of them and said, "I think it's time I get you boys back to your parents, don't you agree?"

Charlie smiled and replied, "Yes. Yes, I do."

"Alright, then. Until next time, my honorable Patrons," Frank said, while looking at Ben and Alexios to show his gratitude.

"Very well, sir," Ben replied.

"Here-here, my good fellow," added Alexios.

Frank extended a hand to each of the boys and said, "Charlie, Michael, take a hand, please". The light charm grew brighter and brighter as the three joined hands. "OK. Let's go find your parents," the wise old Patron said with a smile. And in a flash of light, they were gone.

Chapter Twelve

Charlie and Michael had been missing for more than a day, including almost the entire fifth day of their vacation. Charlie was almost certain their parents would have had nervous breakdowns and contacted park security by now, and that park security would have contacted the state police, who would have contacted the FBI and CIA, in a desperate attempt to find their children, resulting in him and his brother being in deep, deep trouble. Fortunately, Frank had foreseen all that recently happened, and made sure their parents were placed in a memory knot, to assure they would never notice the boys were missing. As Frank had explained to them previously, "A memory knot is a powerful, yet harmless, mind spell the Patrons of WONDER use quite often on park guests to protect their secrecy of operations. It basically creates a knot in one's memory, blocking anything within a certain time period from being remembered." And sure enough, when Charlie and Michael returned to see their parents in Epcot that late afternoon, they acted as if the boys had been with them all along.

"Hey, boys, this has been an amazing vacation so far, don't ya think?" their father said.

"Uh. I guess so? I mean, yeah, Dad. It's been amazing, alright," Charlie replied in a perplexed manner.

"Oh, honey, your father likes to tease. Isn't that right, Ed?"

Charlie and Michael looked at each other in astonishment, realizing what Frank had told them really was true. After a couple quick hours of hanging out in the east side of World Showcase, the boys began to finally feel normal again. But just when they were beginning to enjoy a peaceful family evening of eating, browsing, and laughing, normal went away. Frank came walking by, disguised as a zany cast member, and introduced himself to their parents as the senior advisor of

Magical Experiences. The boys gave him an odd stare as he shot them a quick wink and a smile. And before Charlie could even speak, the eccentric Patron waved his left hand and their parents immediately took off toward the Germany Pavilion shops, oblivious to their children's presence.

"What, what was that?" Michael blurted out.

"That, young man, was a memory knot," Frank replied.

"You mean, they're not going to miss us if we leave right now?" Charlie said.

"Precisely."

"But we just got back. This doesn't seem fair," Michael squawked.

"Michael, let Mr. Wellington finish," Charlie calmly replied.

"Charlie, please call me Frank. Yes, I know, Michael. That's why I wanted you to see your parents so you could be assured that they were alright, and that they hadn't missed you. We still have a little work to do before your trip is over. If all goes according to plan, we should be able to finish tonight, which will still give you a few wonderful days to enjoy the parks with your parents."

"And of course, by helping you, we're going to accomplish something very important, right?"

"Yes, Charlie., more so than you can ever imagine."

"There, you see Michael. Mr. Wellington, I mean Frank, needs our help and it is our duty to help him. Besides, if it weren't for him, we'd be stuck in a dark castle dungeon somewhere far away from Mom and Dad."

Michael looked at both of them and conceded, "Yeah, I guess you're right."

"Very well, then. Follow me, boys. I need to explain a few things to you before we move on." Frank led the boys into the Germany Pavilion where they headed toward the back, through the archways, and just past the Sommerfest walk-up eatery.

"Looks like a dead end to me," Charlie said, while looking at the mural on the wall.

"To most, yes," said Frank. "But, to someone who dares to look deeper, there is more." The old man walked over to the right of the mural, checked to make sure nobody was watching, then pushed in one of the corner stones, setting off a slide puzzle reaction in the mural, which created a magic portal. "Quick! Follow me, boys!"

As they passed through the portal, it was easy to see they were no longer in the real world. "Whoa! I didn't know this attraction was here," Charlie said in amazement. "Is it on the park map? If it is, I missed it. I mean, I didn't see it."

"No, Charlie, you won't find it on any map."

"You mean we're back in WONDER?"

"Exactly, my boy."

"But where did all these people come from?"

"Just like all other simulated parks in WONDER, this is an Imagineer's vision of what this attraction would have looked like on a perfect day in Epcot, including guests."

"I thought we needed the magic ears to transport into WONDER?"

"You do, Charlie. You do. But you see, I don't," Frank said with a smile. "OK, pick a line, boys. I suggest we sit near the back of the boat. So the line to the right would be best."

"What exactly is this attraction?" asked Michael.

"This is the Rhine River Cruise, a colorful journey down Germany's famous rivers, highlighting key landmarks of the country along the way."

"Sounds pretty cool," Charlie said.

"It is. I mean, it would have been, if it had actually been built. Anyway, climb aboard, boys. I have lots to tell you." The three of them climbed aboard the ride vehicle, which began moving forward toward a dark archway immediately after they sat down.

As they passed through the archway and took in their surroundings, Frank began to enlighten the boys with a story. "Many, many years ago, as Ben has already explained to you, a select group of Imagineers secretly developed a magical world, a world created by their dreams and ideas. They called it the World of Natural Dream Enhanced Realities, or WONDER, as you already know; a place where both reality and dream-like fantasy coexist. More important, it was created, and has been expanded through the years, to preserve all the positive energy Disney instills upon us. Now, the first generation of Imagineers knew that something so perfect, so pure, so magically powerful as this, would some day attract evil intentions. And it turned out they were right. A jealous artist, whose identity is unknown to this day, assembled what would eventually be known as the Forest of Thorns Order with one intention in mind: to undo all the good that Disney has spread around the world. You and your brother have already experienced first hand, the capabilities of this evil organization, and those who work within it, including Captain Shivers and his despicable Thorn soldiers."

"Yeah, I hope we never see them again," Michael said.

"That makes two of us," replied Charlie.

After pausing and smiling at the boys, the wise old man continued on with his story. "Once the Imagineers caught wind that FOTO had formed, they immediately began developing safeguards to protect WONDER, five of which Walt proclaimed the Kingdom Crystals. When placed together, the five crystals possess the power to unlock a key element used to penetrate the Dream Core—a place, I know, Ben also briefly mentioned to you.

"So, what is the key element?"

"I think it best at this time that you did not know, Charlie. What you do not know will help protect you from the evil forces of the Dark Thorns."

"Are they as bad as Captain Shivers and his Thorn crew?"

"Much worse, Charlie. Let's hope we can keep you and Michael out of their grasp for as long as possible. But for now, you need not worry. I have more relevant information to tell you."

"Sure, I understand. Go ahead, we're listening," Charlie said.

"The first generation of Imagineers developed the Kingdom Crystals to help protect WONDER from evil-doers—and in particular, FOTO. But that wasn't enough. Living up to Walt's expectations has taught Imagineers through the years to always go one step beyond their goals. To think up the unthinkable. So, with that mindset, the second generation of Imagineers decided to hide the five Kingdom Crystals in random places. The hiding places magically change from time to time, and each place is so unimaginable, that to find them, one would need a bit of, what we like to call, magical guidance—which is provided by five special objects."

"Are those five objects the Objects of Magic?"

"Right you are, Charlie. Five Objects of Magic were chosen by a select group of Imagineers and infused with special powers which enable those who possess them to travel back and forth between reality and the first two layers of WONDER, by transporting from one Dream Dot to another."

"Dream Dot?"

"Yes, Michael. Dream Dots are magic portals located throughout all Walt Disney World properties, Disneyland properties, and a multitude of locations within the layers of WONDER. The snowman you and Charlie used in Hollywood Studios is an example. At first, most Dream Dots were set up and used by Imagineers, such as myself. Unfortunately, the Dark Thorns have learned how to create and transport between Dream Dots as well. They transport between them using some sort of wrist-band device powered by dark magic."

"Oh, that doesn't sound good," Charlie said.

"Yes, it's quite challenging, even dangerous at times, I must say. But, there's more. And this is something you need to remember. Not only do the Objects of Magic provide the ability to seek out the Kingdom Crystals by way of Dream Dots, they provide the power to acquire the crystals as well."

"So it sounds like the Objects of Magic are extremely important."

"Yes, Charlie. They play a very important role in protecting the Dream Core. And that's why we need to retrieve the Ears of Virtue as soon as we are done with this attraction. Its power will be needed later this evening."

"But Frank, you were able to get us out of Deep WONDER and back to our parents today without using the magic ears."

"True, Charlie, but my powers can only take us so far. We'll need the ears, or I should say, you'll need the ears for what lies ahead this evening."

"So an Imagineer cannot use an Object of Magic, like the ears?"

"That's right, Charlie. Only a chosen outsider can wield the power of an Object of Magic."

"But Frank, why would the Thorns want the Objects, if only an outsider can use their power?"

"Because Charlie, they have outsiders, too," Frank said quietly.

"Oh, now I understand."

"I hope what we're doing tonight isn't too scary," Michael said. "I've seen enough scary stuff for this vacation."

"Now don't you worry, Michael. Where we're going tonight, and what we have to do, should prove to be quite an enlightening experience for you, your brother, and even me. And in no way will it be scary. I promise you that, young man."

Frank and the boys had transported from Epcot to a hidden corner of the Muppets 3D queue in Hollywood Studios by way of Dream Dots and were waiting for the theatre doors to open.

"So why are we here, Frank?" Charlie asked.

"Did I tell you that Captain Shivers has a huge admiration for the Muppets?"

"No, I don't believe so.

"Well, as you know all too well, Marty Shivers has a cranky personality. And who better a role model for such a man than Waldorf and Statler, the two grumpy old fellas up in the balcony of this show?"

"OK. But what does that have to do with finding the ears?"

"If there's one thing I've learned through all my years of dealing with Thorns, Charlie, it's that you can always count on them to tell lies. So, if you take what they say and think the opposite, there's a good chance you'll know exactly what they're thinking."

"OK?" Charlie replied, in a doubtful tone.

"And in this case, just after I managed to escape Shivers' light charm trap, the captain became so angry that he basically told me where he had hidden the Ears of Virtue."

"He did? So how did you find the light charm, anyway?"

"That's easy. Everyone familiar with WONDER, good or bad, knows the light charm is hidden somewhere on Eruption Island. Or at least they did know. Ha. Ha. Ha. Anyway, Shivers had set a trap in the volcano, using a holographic projection of the light charm to lure me in. And when I found it, and tried to jump up to grab it, my hand went right through the image and Shivers men tried to sack me."

"But Frank, how did they know where to set the trap?"

"Well, that part's not so easy to explain, Charlie. All I can tell you is that I'm pretty sure the Dark Thorns were able to gain vision into where I would end up, then directed the captain to have spies follow me to the volcano and set the trap."

"Yeah. That make sense. I remember now. When we were still locked up in the Thorn castle, Captain Shivers did mention he had spies following you."

"There, you see, Charlie. You know more than you think. Now, as I was saying. Shivers' men tried to sack me as I leaped for the holographic image of the charm. But somehow, amid all the mad scrambling, I managed to slip away. And as I looked down to watch my steps while escaping, there it was, the real light charm, hanging graciously about thirty feet below me in a recessed nook of the volcanos' inner wall. But to get to it was quite challenging. With a bit of courage and a pinch of faith, I ran and jumped off the rock bridge, landing safely on the small ledge of the nook where the charm was located."

"But what about the captain and his men? Didn't they try to come after you?"

"Oh, heavens no. With me on the ledge, they had no place to land. And if they missed? Well, they'd of fallen right into the hot molten lava below. And that's when the captain lost his temper and basically told me where he hid the Ears of Virtue. He said they were locked away in a secret hiding place where I would never find them."

"He told us the same thing!" Michael shouted out.

"So there you are, boys. The perfect example. Shivers told all of us the ears were locked away in a secret hiding place. Now, if you take what he said and think the opposite, there's a real good chance he hid the ears right out in the open. And knowing Shivers is a fan of the Muppets, I would say they are either on the head of Waldorf or Statler in this very show."

Just then, the queue doors opened and Frank and the boys headed for the back-row seats of the theatre in order to get a good look around. As the show began, all three turned toward the balcony to look at the two cranky old men, and true to Frank's words, Statler was wearing the ears. Charlie and his brother both looked at the old man with mouths agape.

"Wait one moment, boys. I'll be right back," Frank said with a smirk. He touched the light charm necklace, and like that, vanished. Seconds later, he reappeared. It was dark and the show was in full stride, so no one sitting on either side of them noticed what had just happened. "Hey, look at that, will ya," Frank whispered as he pointed toward the old men in the balcony. The boys looked over and noticed the ears were no longer on Statler's head. Frank slowly revealed what he was hiding in his lap. The Ears of Virtue.

"What? But how did you..."

"Shh, Michael. We don't want to spoil the show for others, now do we," Frank said. "Here, Charlie. Put these on. After all, they belong to you, right?" Charlie took the ears and placed them on his head while they all sat back an enjoyed the rest of the show.

Amongst the guests exiting the Muppets 3D theatre were Frank, Charlie, and Michael. As they dropped their 3D glasses into the return bins, Frank began to slowly describe their next destination: the secret location of the first of five Kingdom Crystals. "OK, gentlemen, now that Charlie has his ears back, we can move on to our next stop. Everybody grab a hand, we have a crystal to find." The three joined hands as they continued to walk past Mama Melrose's Restaurant. As they rounded the corner, Frank reached up with his free hand and touched the light charm. They were gone. Seconds later, the three crystal seekers found themselves standing next to the Aztec calendar in the Mexico Pavilion, and Charlie's ears were glowing. "Charlie, I need you to repeat what I say, while touching the stone," Frank said quietly.

"OK," Charlie said as he placed his right hand on the stone.

"Big round calendar made of stone, open a path so we may roam."

Charlie repeated the old man's words, and the ears grew bright, sending an electric blue stream of light through Charlie's body and into the stone. But, nothing happened. All three stepped away from the large stone calendar, waiting for something to occur. Just as Michael began to speak, the stone tablet started to open from its center, creating a circular entryway large enough for them to climb through. The three looked at each and smiled, then quickly climbed through the magic portal. Within seconds, the opening closed behind them.

Oddly enough, what they saw was exactly where they had just came from, only everything was on a much grander scale. The village was the size of a real village and the streets were crowded with happy guests dressed in colorful clothes. The Aztec pyramid beyond the village was much farther away and almost two-hundred feet high. And the jungle surrounding the pyramid was very much real, including the volcano. It was easy to see they were once again in WONDER.

"It's something, isn't it, boys? I mean, look at the colors of the evening sky and how they compliment the volcano, the village, and the pyramid. The people here really know how to dream, don't they? Speaking of pyramids, there's an Imagineering rumor that claims one of five Kingdom Crystals is currently hidden within that very pyramid. But, the only way we're going to find out is if we go and explore it."

"Really? So how do we get there, Frank, swim across the river?"

"Oh no, Charlie. We take a ride on the Gran Fiesta Tour. The boat dock is just to the left of the village over there," the old man said while pointing. As they approached the dock, the boys admired how quickly and efficiently the boats stopped, were loaded up with guests by the cast members, then took off on their festive way.

"Climb aboard and enjoy the Gran Fiesta Tour," the cast member said with a smile, as Charlie, Frank, and Michael boarded one of the water-ride vehicles and sat down. It was a smooth and effortless departure, as their fiesta adventure began.

Up until they approached the pyramid, everything had been pretty normal, with their boat following another boat just ahead. But that's when something out of the realm of normal grabbed their attention. A large statue that looked like the head of an Aztec warrior, positioned just right of the pyramid, spoke to them. "You go left. You go left," the statue chanted. And on command, their boat veered left, off the main path, and headed toward the pyramid.

Frank let out a quiet chuckle as he smiled at the boys and said, "Looks like we're headed in the right direction."

Shortly after, the boat docked near the pyramid and the three adventures climbed out, with Frank anxiously leading the way toward, and up, the two-hundred-foot-high pyramid stairway. Halfway through their ascent, Frank and the boys stopped to catch their breath. "Only half way to go," Frank said as he shook his head, then continued upward.

Several minutes later. after a very strenuous climb to the top of the pyramid stairs, the three paused and turned to look back at their achievement. "Well, I guess we got our exercise for the day," the old man said, as he bent over and tried to regain his breath. The boys, doing the same thing, looked at Frank and smiled, feeling happily exhausted.

"Yeah, that was...quite a climb, but the view...is incredible," Charlie said as they all took in the beautiful sight from atop the pyramid, overlooking the enormous interior of the colorful pavilion and all that it had to offer.

"This is amazing," Michael said in awe.

"Yep, quite a site. I can only imagine what we're going to find inside. What do ya say we go take a look," Frank said, with excitement in his voice as he led Charlie and Michael into the small room atop the pyramid. Dimly lit with torches and no more than ten by fifteen feet, the walls were completely covered with Aztec patterns, symbols, and figures. Frank took a wall and instructed the boys to do the same, each one of them closely studying everything their eyes took in.

"Charlie, does any of this make sense to you?"

"Uh, no, Michael. I've never had a class where we learned about this stuff."

"And that's quite all right, Charlie," Frank said. "The Ears of Virtue will help us find the way. Just put your hand on the wall. If my instincts are right, we should see something rather amazing."

Following the wise old Patron's suggestion, Charlie placed his hand on the wall, and instantly, the ears lit up. Two blue sparks of radiant light shot outward from where he touched the wall, weaving their way through the intricate Aztec artwork in both directions of the room and leaving behind two neon blue light trails until they met at a small circular symbol of a sun on the opposite side from where Charlie stood. Both trails began to travel around the circle, over and over again, until the symbol glowed bright orange. Frank and the boys all walked over to take a closer look.

"I think this is it, Charlie," Frank said as he stared at the glowing sun.

"This is what?"

"What we've been looking for."

"Oh. The Kingdom Crystal. But, I don't understand. This is just a symbol of a sun on the wall. It's not a crystal."

"The sun is just a marker, Charlie. It's what lies beyond the sun that we came for."

"Beyond the sun?" Michael said, in a confused tone.

"Yes, Michael. Wait just a minute and you'll see. Charlie, repeat these words, then touch the center of the sun: ever more, ever lasting, a gift, not to be told."

As Charlie began to repeat the old man's words, the ears started to glow brilliantly, filling with mini firework-like patterns that repeated over and over again.

Frank continued: "sworn by those who shall protect, its past, its present, its future to behold."

As he finished repeating Frank's words, the light from the ears became so intense, Charlie's entire body was now engulfed with sparkling dazzlement, forcing Michael and Frank to turn away and shield their eyes.

"Now, Charlie! Touch the center of the sun now!"

Charlie reached out beyond the light that consumed his body and touched the center of the sun icon. There was a sudden burst of wind, and all the energy from the light surrounding Charlie shot into the sun. The icon opened from its center into two curved halves that receded into the sides of the wall, revealing a bright purple, metallic enclosure. At its center, glowing brilliantly and suspended in mid-air, was a large tear-drop-shaped crystal, roughly the size of a child's hand.

"That, boys, is a Kingdom Crystal, a key to everlasting happiness," Frank said softly, as they all stared at its beauty.

Translucent in appearance, its core was pure light, which radiated out in all directions. As Charlie reached in and removed it from its hiding place, the crystal's bright core slowly dimmed, making it appear rather ordinary. Simultaneously, the small opening in the wall closed, leaving no trace of what had just taken place.

"Charlie, please place it in here," Frank said, as he opened a small black box lined with a magical material. "It'll be safe now."

"Safe from the Dark Thorns?" Charlie asked.

"Precisely, Charlie. The Dark Thorns won't be able to detect its positive energy as long as we keep it hidden in here," he said while closing the box and putting it in his pocket. "Now then. I need to get you two back to your parents, and the crystal somewhere safe. Come-come. Everyone grab a hand. The three joined hands and Frank touched the light charm. Just like that, the room was empty.

Chapter Thirteen

The last two days of their vacation, Charlie and his family enjoyed a multitude of attractions, parades, tasty meals, and other fun family activities. They even managed to get Michael on Big Thunder Mountain, as his dad had promised. It was hard to believe that seven days could go by so fast. For the boys, it felt like they had just started their vacation yesterday. Yet now, here they were, enjoying the final few hours of their trip at the Magic Kingdom. The biggest challenge was trying to decide what to do before they had to leave. With only seven short hours to go, every choice was a big decision. Where do we want to eat our last meal? Do we have enough time to go on Pirates, the Haunted Mansion, Peter Pan, and the PeopleMover? Where do we use our last snack credits? The choices for fun were virtually limitless.

As noon quickly approached, the Zastawits family was just wrapping up their perfect morning, thanks to a masterful plan involving the creative use of FastPasses. Having just left the Haunted Mansion, with plans to go on Peter Pan next, Charlie and his family decided it was the perfect time to grab lunch. A counter-service meal at Columbia Harbour House sounded like the best place for a mid-day meal. As their parents placed the order, and the boys went to gather napkins, forks, and things, a familiar voice came up behind them.

"Hello there, boys. Looks like you're pretty hungry, eh?" It was Frank, and he had come for one last visit before the boys left for home. "I have something important I need to discuss with you, and I figured what better way to do it than over a meal. Here come your parents. Just follow my lead and everything will work out. OK?"

Charlie and Michael confirmed Frank's request, though both were a little confused at the moment.

As their parents approached, Frank jumped right into his role. Disguised as a cast member, he began to spin his web of trickery. "Well, hello there, Mr. and Mrs. Zastawits. We've been tracking your stay and were hoping to have a brief conversation with you regarding your experiences. And of course, in return, we would like to offer your family a twenty-five percent discount off your next visit to Walt Disney World. Good for one calendar year. And, as a bonus, unlimited FastPasses for the rest of today."

"Well, with an offer like that, how can we say anything but yes," Mr. Z replied enthusiastically. "By the way, you look very familiar. Have we met before?"

Thinking quickly, Frank rolled his eyes and said. "Hmmmm. No. I don't believe we have. In fact, I'm sure of it." Immediately, he jumped back into his fake pitch. "Anyway, we think it's wonderful that you agree to talk with us. If you and your family would please follow me upstairs, we have a secret little nook overlooking the park where we can discuss all the magical experiences you've had during your stay with us." The wise old Imagineer shot Charlie and Michael a wink as they all headed up the stairs. The nook Frank had described was indeed the perfect place for a private meal, a special meal, a meal where no other guests could witness what was about to happen. After everyone was seated, Frank spoke again, waving his hands and arms in the process to better illustrate his point. "First of all, I want to tell you how much we appreciate you doing this. This conversation will help us tremendously to better serve our guests." As he finished his sentence, it became apparent why such a private area had been chosen for their discussion. Charlie and Michael's parents had just been placed in another memory knot.

"What? Again?" Charlie said with frustration. "But we leave today. How much time is this going to take?"

"Don't worry, Charlie. It'll only last long enough for me to explain a few more things before you go. When it wears off, your parents will think that we just had a wonderful discussion over lunch, and you'll be on your way to enjoy the rest of your afternoon. Oh. And please remind me to start including face recognition blocks when using memory knots. That was a close one."

"What was a close one, Frank?"

"Your dad, Charlie. He almost remembered who I was from our previous meetings this week. I gotta remember to work on that for next time."

"Oh, yeah. He almost had you, didn't he," Charlie replied, with a chuckle.

Frank just scratched his head, then continued. "So, as I told you downstairs, there are a few things I still need to talk to you about before you leave. But first we need to go somewhere a little safer than this. Lots of shady characters wandering around this place, if you know what I mean. So, everyone grab a hand."

"But what about our parents?" Michael asked.

Not to worry, Michael. They'll just sit here while continuing to eat and talk with each other, as if they were alone on a date. And we'll be back very shortly. I promise."

The boys conceded, and the three joined hands. Frank pulled the light charm out from underneath his shirt, and within a fraction of a second, all three disappeared, leaving behind the boys' parents, who were eating and chatting as if nothing had happened.

"Well, here we are," Frank said. "My little corner of the kingdom, as I like to call it. It's really quite small, but I got a great view."

"So, where are we?" Charlie asked as he looked around.

Frank did not hear young Charlie's question, as his mind was occupied making room for the boys to sit.

It was a small studio apartment, dimly lit, with walls completely covered in Disney memorabilia, photos, paintings, and such. A large oriental rug covered much of the hardwood floor. The kitchen area was barely large enough to cook in, but you could tell it was used quite frequently. Just to the left of it, a small wooden table sat with two chairs. In the back right corner was a twin-size bed with night stand, which looked very much lived in, as did the rest of the apartment. Up near the left side of the front door was a small brown love seat and burgundy cushioned chair with foot rest. A tiny end table sat in the corner, separating the chair and love seat, with a Tiffany-style lamp atop its surface. And just to the right of the front door was an old drawing table with wooden shelves above it, filled with hundreds of drawings, renderings, notes, and things that Frank had created through the years. Between the sofa and eating area was a small cat bed, with a red, broken-in cushion and a tiny basket of pet toys.

"Do you have a cat?" Charlie asked. "We have two. Cocoa and Skatz."

"Yes, actually I do have a cat. He must be sleeping under the bed. That seems to be his favorite place to sleep during the day. Let me see if I can get him to come out and meet you. Trust me, this is one cat you're gonna want to meet. Midnight. Here kitty. kitty. Midnight. I have some friends here for you to meet. Here kitty. kitty."

As they waited for Frank's cat to come out from hiding, Charlie repeated his first question as he walked over to look out one of two windows. "So, where are we?"

"Right above the Plaza Ice Cream Parlor. Isn't it great?"

"Yeah. I can see the castle from here!" Michael shouted as he continued to stare out the window. "This must be the greatest place to live in the whole world."

"You bet it is, Michael. Anyway, boys, please have a seat, won't you? Oh. Here comes my kitty. Hey, Midnight. Come meet my new friends."

"That's quite a cat, Frank." Charlie said.

"Yeah, he's the biggest cat I've ever seen," Michael added.

As Midnight crawled out from under the bed and slowly made his way toward the boys, it was clearly obvious this was no ordinary cat. He was easily twenty pounds, well-rounded in the mid section, with a head almost twice the size of any cat they had seen before. His calm eyes sparkled electric green, and his long, grey-striped tail swayed slowly back and forth on his walk across the room. Charlie and Michael's legs became targets of affection, as Midnight rubbed against them with a sustained purr and handsome meow that resonated through the room.

"OK, Midnight. That's enough bonding," Frank said. "You can go lay back down.

"Oh, he's OK," Charlie replied, while he continued to pet the purring cat.

"See, Frank, they don't mind," Midnight replied.

"Holy smokes! A talking cat!" Michael shouted.

Frank let out a great big laugh. "See, I told you you'd want to meet him. Midnight is quite special. He's my WONDER cat."

"What exactly is that, Frank?" Charlie asked.

"He's something I dreamt up long ago, during my early years as an Imagineer. And as I got older, and eventually became a Patron of WONDER, it became apparent to me that I could use a friend to keep me company. So when I created this apartment, using my imagination, I brought Midnight along. We have lived here together for quite some time now."

"So let me ask one more time. Where are we?" Charlie said, knowing well there was more to Frank's previous answer to the same question.

"Right above the Plaza Ice Cream Parlor, just as I had said earlier. Oh. I did leave something out, didn't I," Frank said with a chuckle. I guess you could say this is the WONDER version of the Magic Kingdom."

"Aha! I knew it," Charlie replied. "So you actually live in WONDER?"

"Yes. You could say it's a good place for me to hide from the Dark Thorns—which brings me back to why we're here. I brought you here because I couldn't risk any Thorn ears hearing what I'm about to tell you."

"Oh, right, Frank. I was a little distracted by your cat."

"Please, Charlie. You can call me Midnight. 'Cat' sounds so pet-like."

Charlie let out a giggle, which also made his brother laugh. "Right, Midnight. I'm so sorry. Please, Frank, continue."

"Now where was I?" Frank asked. "Oh, yes." Do you recall, Charlie, the crazy dream you had about Ben, Alexios, and Captain Shivers?"

"Yeah. I do. Captain Shivers was chasing Ben, and then Alexios showed up to help him escape with some sort of old red box. But how did you know about that?"

"You could say the Patrons of WONDER may have had a little something to do with it."

"Really? How is that possible? I mean, you didn't even know me when that happened."

"Yes. Yes, I can see that may seem a bit confusing. So let me try to explain it to you. Almost a year ago, the dark shadow that lingers over this land, which you've come to know as FOTO, had grown so powerful that it was beginning to have a neutralizing effect on the positive energy Disney instills upon the world. That's when we, the Patrons of WONDER, decided the time had come to choose an outsider and begin the search for the five Kingdom Crystals. And as you are already aware, when placed together the five crystals possess the power to unlock a key element used to penetrate the Dream Core. This in turn would give us the ability to overcome the dark forces of FOTO, and restore balance between good and evil in all that we create within the Disney universe."

"And I was the outsider you chose?"

"Very good, Charlie. Yes. The Patrons of WONDER chose you through a world-wide, voluntary essay contest that we secretly developed and released on the Walt Disney World website, to avoid any unwanted attention from the Thorns. And it just so happens, this was the contest you participated in, and obviously won. You see, Charlie, your essay showed us what was in your heart, how deep your passion runs for all things Disney, and that you, my young friend, are worthy of the cause for which we are fighting. Not to mention, the mighty little sidekick you brought with you."

"Hey! I'm not little," Michael snipped back.

"There, you see. Tougher than nails, and sharp as a tack," Frank said with a warm chuckle.

"Oh, don't worry, Michael, Frank means well. Don't you, Frank?"

"Indeed I do, Charlie. Why, without your brother's help, I'm quite sure that what we accomplished here this week would not have been possible."

Michael grinned, then went back to looking out the window.

"Anyway, Charlie, once we had chosen you as our outsider, our next step was to educate your mind with what lay ahead. That's where the dream comes in. The chocolates you ate the night before your dream were carefully Imagineered using our new micro-dream particles. We injected over a hundred thousand of these tiny little things into the chocolates you had to eat. Once digested, the micro dream particles worked their way into your bloodstream, and then your brain, where they attached themselves, allowing us to access your dreams. And once we could see into your dreams, we were able to insert elements into them, and extract things out of them. It's really quite amazing. It took us decades to Imagineer this technology. Decades."

"So you're telling me you were able to look into my dreams, even alter my dreams, by using little, what did you call them?"

"Micro-dream particles," Frank replied.

"Right. Micro dream particles that were hidden inside the chocolates I ate?"

"Precisely, Charlie."

"That is so cool. But it's kind of scary, too. I mean, what if something had gone wrong? Those particles could have messed up my brain."

"Ha. Ha. Ha. Ha. Ha. Oh, no, Charlie, it's all perfectly safe. No need to worry about that. We never release any new technology before thoroughly testing it. In fact, that's why it took us so long to Imagineer the micro-dream particles."

"Well, that's a relief," Charlie replied, exhaling.

"And not only can we see into, or alter, someone's dreams, Charlie. We can also save dreams using what we call, the Magic Dream Expander."

"The Magic Dream Expander? That sounds...well, like nothing I've ever heard of before. So what does it do, Frank?"

"It serves two purposes. First, it accesses Imagineers' dreams and uses them to develop new, or alter existing, realms of WONDER. Second, and in rare instances such as your case, it can be used to access a chosen outsider's dreams if the need arises. You see, Charlie, the dark forces of FOTO have recently uncovered our secret, and are now aware of the Magic Dream Expander and what it's capable of doing. They will stop at nothing to take it from us."

"I hate to ask, but what happens if they gain control of it?"

"Imagine, if you will, all that is good about Disney being overtaken by evil forces. The villains would win in all the movies, so there would be no more happy endings. The parks would be overrun with dark and dreadful things. WONDER would become a place of nightmares instead of dreams. Basically, the most terrible things imaginable would happen. All that Walt strived to build for the good of humanity would be destroyed by the dark forces of FOTO, and the villains would rule it all."

"Oh, no. That's so wrong, I don't even want to think about it."

"And that is why we need you. That's why we chose you, Charlie. You are...the chosen outsider. The one person, with the assistance of your brother, who can help the Patrons of WONDER protect the power of Disney, and the infinite happiness it instills upon the world, from the evil forces of FOTO."

Charlie stared at Frank in silent thought, then looked out the window at the castle. "I understand, Frank."

"Thank you, young man. Oh, and I'm sorry, but I need to ask a great favor of you. I need the ears back."

Caught off guard, Charlie instinctively covered the Ears of Virtue atop his head, not wanting to let them go. "But I thought the ears were a gift from you to me?"

"I know it's not an easy thing to do, Charlie. Or easy to understand, for that matter. But it's the right thing to do. The ears need to be kept somewhere safe, hidden away from the evil clutches of the Dark Thorns. However, I do have some good news as well." Frank reached behind his back and pulled out another set of ears, which looked almost identical to the magic ears. "They even have your name on the back, just like the others."

Charlie gave his friend a humble smile as he slowly pulled the magic ears off his head and exchanged them for the others. "That's OK, Frank. If it will help the Patrons of WONDER, then it's the right choice for me."

"I'm very proud of you, young lad," Frank said, as he patted the boy on his back. Don't forget, Charlie, we still have more crystals to seek out. And to find each one, a new Object of Magic will be required. Besides, you still have Merlin's magic looking glass to take with you as well, do you not? It's a very magical object in its own right."

Charlie responded to Frank's words with a grateful smile.

Slowly, Frank carried the Ears of Virtue over to his desk, where he pulled out a red box—the same red box Charlie had seen in his dream.

"Is that..." Charlie paused in shock, pointing at the box.

"Yes, it is, Charlie," Frank replied, putting the ears into the box. As he placed the lid on top, Charlie's name, which had been stitched on the back of the ears in magical gold thread, disappeared. "There we go, all ready to be safely stored away. Now, we need to get you and Michael back to your parents, don't we? I mean, you still have several hours left in the park to enjoy, right?" Frank said, with a grin.

"Yeah...yeah. I mean, yes, sir, right," Charlie replied, while trying to get his thoughts off the red box.

"Very well then, everybody touch the lamp. That means you, too, Michael," Frank said, as he called the young boy away from the window.

"I do have one more question before we go. Something I've wanted to ask you ever since we first met, if you don't mind?"

"Sure, Charlie, fire away."

"How did you ever get my father to book a trip to Walt Disney World so we could come down here in the first place?"

"Very simple, Charlie. We sent him such an incredible offer, we knew there was no way he would ever be able to refuse it. Where do you think those tasty chocolates you ate came from, anyway?" Frank said, with a smirk and a chuckle. OK, boys, come-come. It's time to take you back."

Charlie smiled back at Frank, while Michael said goodbye to Midnight. Then all three touched the lamp and vanished.

Late afternoon came too quickly, and Charlie's family had just finished gathering last-minute goodies at the Main Street Confectionery to use up the rest of their snack credits. And since he had already received a very special set of ears from Frank, Charlie decided to use the gift card his friend back home had given him for Christmas, to surprise Johnny with his very own set of personalized ears. A kind gesture, indeed.

As they made their way around Town Square, Charlie took one last look down Main Street. To his pleasant surprise, sitting next to Roy and Minnie on the bench near the flagpole, was Frank. Charlie stopped and waved, then gave him a big smile, which Frank gladly returned as he hollered over the joyful sounds of Main Street and the train whistle, "I'll see you soon!"

With happiness in his heart, Charlie nodded, then ran to catch up with his family. As they exited under the train station, he spun around for one final wave goodbye to his new-found friend. Only Roy and Minnie remained.

The Watchmaker's Gift

A sneak peek at chapter one of the sequel to *Ears of Virtue*...

It was 1959. *Sleeping Beauty* was showing in theaters across the country. In one such theatre, near Anaheim, California, sat an artist, slouched low in his seat near the back—a shadow amongst others. Maddened. Furious. Enraged. The jealous artist sat, staring at the big screen before him with fists clenched, teeth grinding, and legs twisted up like a pretzel—critiquing each and every creative element, in each and every scene. The more the audience applauded, the more furious he became. *I was the chosen one. Full-length animated movies were my idea. I was the one who should have succeeded. This should have been me, not him. No, no, no. Not him*, he thought to himself.

This was not just any artist, not by any means. This was a man who had once worked side by side with a young artist named Walt Disney. This was an artist who had worked just as hard and just as long as Walt. A young confident man who had grown as a budding artist alongside Walt. Had had meaningful and creative conversations with Walt. He'd brainstormed with Walt about the future of art, animation, its impact on society and the power of imagination. He had worked with Walt at the Disney Animation Studios as a lead character animator. And at one point, had even been considered for the position of creative director over all Disney films. But the position was eliminated. Walt thought it best to spread the creative responsibility amongst many, as in the Nine Old Men, in order to develop the best product possible. But this decision did not sit well with the talented artist whose name never made it onto a Disney movie credits list. He felt slighted. Passed over. Humiliated. And now, here he sat, alone, a failure, a nobody—his mind filled with hateful, vengeful, and evil thoughts as he watched a movie that could very easily have been his creation.

Then, she appeared; green skinned, piercing eyes, cloaked in black with staff in hand and armed with a personality which commanded attention. The dark fairy. Maleficent. She fit his mood—strong, dark, intimidating. She was a true leader of undesirables. She made sense. This was to be his motivation. All the years of anger, all the years of jealousy—the built-up hatred inside him finally had a purpose, a goal—a dark and devious goal. Take Disney's very own villainous creation, or better yet, creations, and use them to bring Walt's creative empire to its knees.

Marching down the rainy sidewalks of Burbank—head down and mumbling mad gibberish to himself, the shell of a man made his way back to an old dilapidated hotel complex with a red neon no-vacancy sign that read: NO V AN. He barged through the front door, striding into the lobby in wet shoes that squished with every step. He turned right, then made his way to the elevator doors, completely ignoring the front-desk staff in the process, as he left a trail of water behind.

"Quite the odd fella, don't you think, Elsie," one of the desk clerks said to the other.

"Oh, yes. That man hasn't spoken a word to me since I started working here. And that was over a month ago," she replied.

"Yeah, well, I've been here almost two years and the only time I ever recall him speaking to anyone, including me, was the day he checked in. And even then, he didn't make eye contact with me. He's a real piece of work, that's for sure. I mean, what kind of person wants to make an old run-down hotel like this their permanent residence anyway?"

"I agree, Ed. I agree," the woman said, while staring over the rim of the reading glasses resting upon her nose, as she continued to study the eccentric artist in drenched clothes who stood by the elevator doors.

Feeling unwanted eyes upon his back, he eagerly tapped the up button with his bony right index finger. Slowly, the arrow above the door started to move counter-clockwise toward the first floor. The rickety old elevator clanked and thunked its way down to its caller, louder and louder, until it came to rest with a sudden THUNK. The doors opened and he stepped inside. With fifteen buttons to choose from the brooding artist hit number nine, then nine again, and one more time. If this were a properly functioning elevator, the button would illuminate, but not in this case. Money for repairs did not exist in hotels such as this. Soap, shampoo, and even towels were considered luxury items. The doors awkwardly closed and the elevator ascended, floor two, three, four...and finally, nine. The doors clanked open, exposing a dimly lit hallway. Only two lights out of eight were working, one of which flickered on and off. The floor was covered with a thin coat of what used to be blue carpeting; it was flanked by water-stained walls—covered with sixty-year-old floral-patterned wallpaper that once may have been white, but now was dirty yellow with streaks of brown and peeling everywhere. The first door to the left, facing the elevator, was his destination. Apartment 913. With a shaky wet hand he reached deep into the front right pocket of his rain-drenched trousers, the water from his long dark bangs dripping down his forehead, over his crooked nose, across his lips, and off the end of his chin, before finally hitting the junky old carpeting which sat between his oversaturated shoes and the door to his room. Pulling out a single key, his shaky hand repeatedly aimed for the key hole—once, twice, a third time—a difficult thing to do for anyone in such dark accommodations. Finally, the key and lock became one, his hand turned, the lock clicked, and he bumped open the old battered door with his right forearm. Anxiously rushing inside, he slammed and locked the door behind him, taking off his coat and casting it to the floor. He immediately headed for the drawing table in the back corner of the room near the window and turned on the dusty old table lamp. Instantly flooded with a fluorescent yellow-cast light, the table revealed layers of sketches, notes, and diagrams—and more sketches notes and diagrams, piled high in an unorganized fashion. Alongside the table was a trash receptacle, overflowing onto the floor with countless crumbled balls of paper containing hopes, dreams, and ideas—all of which had been crushed by the realities of the harsh world. But that was all in the past now. *No more*, he thought to himself, *no more*. The drenched artist mounted his stool, and in one fell swoop, pushed all the spent piles of paper covering the table to the floor. Grabbing a pencil and a clean sheet of paper, he began to plot his scheme.

"Name, hmmm," he mumbled to himself while scratching his head. Evil. Evil is to be key, he thought. Villains Against Walt? No. United Villains of Evil? No. The Evil Doers? Nope, not scary enough. For nearly two hours, the crazed artist obsessed over the perfect name for his diabolical organization—writing and scratching out names, again and again. It had to carry purpose. It had to be dark. It had to strike fear in the hearts of ALL Disney lovers who heard it. Something memorable, something simple...something undoubtedly sinister.

He stared out the window at the rain, massaging his temples, thinking...thinking. The soft glow of the lonely street light on the corner whispered for his attention. And then, it went dark. Wait, that's it. He had it. Yes! It's perfect. Frightfully perfect. It shall be called...The Dark Order.

Deep into the night, the dejected artist scribbled down his thoughts, filling sheet upon sheet of paper, until all the thoughts in his head had been emptied out. His plan of attack; to build a secret army, a dark collective group that will possess the ability to destroy, crush, and abolish all the joy, all the happiness, all the goodwill Walt and his company had worked so hard to build and spread throughout the world. Indeed, this was to be the beginning of the end for all things Disney!

About the Author

Raised along the sandy shores of southwestern Michigan, Charles was always one sunset away from his dreams. A child of the 70s, his passion for Disney began in the summer of 1973 when he visited Disneyland for the first time with his mother, grandmother, and aunt.

Charles holds a B.A. in graphic design from Western Michigan University, and currently works as a brand Manager/ art director for Round 2 Corporation in South Bend, Indiana.

ABOUT THEME PARK PRESS

Theme Park Press publishes books primarily about the Disney company, its history, culture, films, animation, and theme parks, as well as theme parks in general.

Our authors include noted historians, animators, Imagineers, and experts in the theme park industry.

We also publish many books by first-time authors, with topics ranging from fiction to theme park guides.

And we're always looking for new talent. If you'd like to write for us, or if you're interested in the many other titles in our catalog, please visit:

www.ThemeParkPress.com

Theme Park Press Newsletter

Subscribe to our free email newsletter and enjoy:

- Free book downloads and giveaways
- Access to excerpts from our many books
- Announcements of forthcoming releases
- Exclusive additional content and chapters
- And more good stuff available nowhere else

To subscribe, visit www.ThemeParkPress.com, or send email to newsletter@themeparkpress.com.

The
CATS of the
CASTLE
BART SCOTT

MURDER
IN THE MAGIC KINGDOM
Annie Salisbury

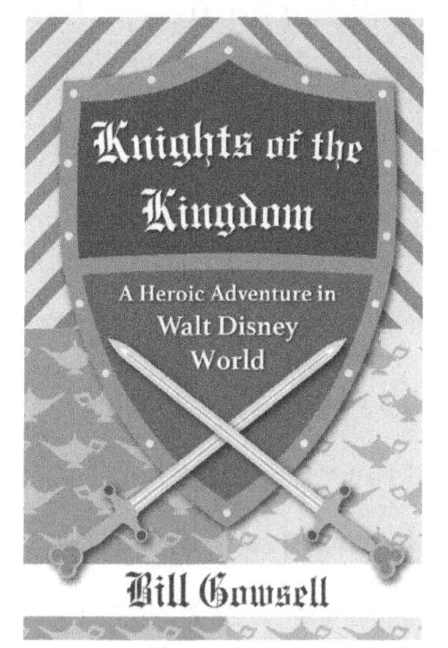
Knights of the
Kingdom
A Heroic Adventure in
Walt Disney
World
Bill Gowsell

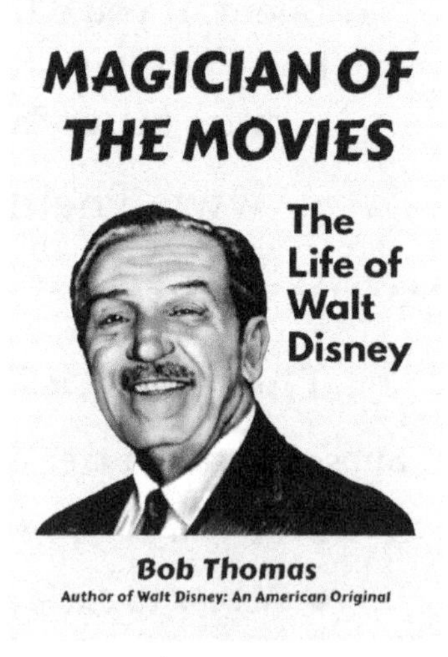
MAGICIAN OF
THE MOVIES
The
Life of
Walt
Disney
Bob Thomas
Author of Walt Disney: An American Original

Made in the USA
Middletown, DE
29 May 2020